Second Chance Cowboy

COWBOY WANTED
BOOK TWO

BA TORTUGA

The Second Chance Cowboy

Copyright © 2024 BA Tortuga

Cover Art Illustration by Alexandria Corza. Used with permission.

Editing by Sue Meadows

This is a work of fiction. Any resemblance to any person, living or dead, is purely coincidental.

Printed in the United States of America.

ISBN: 979-8-8693-1996-8

1st Edition Turtlehat Creatives 2024

BA's Cozy Cowboys

If y'all are interested in warm, joyous novels where the cowboys have kids and love saves the day, please check these BA Tortuga books out:

Back in the Saddle

Cowboy Haven

Cowboy in the Crosshairs

Cowboy Logic

Cowboy's Law

In the Morning Light

Ranch Manny

Security Detail: an AusTex novel

The Cowboy Contract

The Cowboy Guardian

The Meaning of Life

Trial by Fire: an AusTex novel

Two Cowboys and a Baby

Two of a Kind

For Michelle, Steve, Jay, and Mike. They know why.
As always, to my wife.
I'd love to thank my editor, Sue; my alpha readers, Jaymi, Kim,
Michael, and NolaKim; and my Ream supporters: Aliana,
Ann Alaskan, Debbie, Dyan, Energymomma, KayMTee,
LisaG, RhondaN, Sue Brown, and Xaneria Ann.
Y'all make me better.

Prologue

"So, this is a weird one, babe." Tom walked into Koby Foster's home office, a sheaf of papers in his hand.

Koby glanced up from his computer where he'd been studying a ranch in Rangely that was selling their beef themselves, cutting out the middleman. "A weird what?" His lover, Tom, did all his spreadsheets and websites and answered his phone and emails. So it could be anything.

"The Cowboy Wanted request I just got."

"Yeah?" He sat back in his chair, grinning even as his spine popped and crackled. Oh, that part was fun as hell. "Tell." He did love his side business, Cowboy Wanted LLC. It gave him something to think about besides ranch work, and it never failed to make Tom smile.

"Cowboy needed for escort to Cattleman's Ball. Must be between twenty-five and thirty-five, handsome, well-dressed, intelligent enough to fool my ex into thinking I'd date him, and not well-known in the area." Tom was damned near bouncing and the diamond stud in his nose caught the light, the heavy man-bun barely hanging on.

That gave him absolutely non-work-y ideas in his littlest brain.

Instead of opening his mouth and asking for quickie over the desk, he blinked. "Well, that's specific."

"Yep. I sent a quote to kind of stall him, and he said to send him an invoice." Tom propped himself on the edge of the desk, one leg swinging like a pendulum.

"Him? Like a him-date. Huh." Oh, damn. That was interesting. They were gay-friendly as a rule in Aspen, but that was damn clear for a cowboy.

"Yes, love. A cowboy-boy date. At the ball. We shattered that rainbow ceiling." Tom winked at him, and he remembered that night, six years ago, walking in with Tom on his arm and proposing to the fine son of a bitch on the stage. No one would ever say Koby was ashamed of his wild, amazing, techy geek of man.

"Well, you got a point. That makes it even more important to get this right. We got anyone on tap?"

"A few guys who haven't done a job for us yet." Tom leaned over, and he got a whiff of pure heaven—black pepper, Dove soap, and a hint of the sandalwood chips he kept in his underwear drawer. Perfect. "But check out the name."

He took another glance, trying to focus. "Liam McMartin. Why do I know that name?"

Tom pursed his lips, and Koby was so tempted to steal a kiss. "Babe, he was Sawyer's husband. You only have lunch with Sawyer Canton once a week."

He sat back in his chair, eyebrows rising. "So I do. I never met the ex, though." His buddy Sawyer had been divorced for about a year. They'd met nine months ago at some rodeo cowboy tribute they'd both attended, their formal cowboy wear chafing. The cowboy community in the Roaring Fork Valley was pretty small. "Well, let me call him."

Tom tilted his head. "Is that not a confidentiality breach?"

"I haven't read the paperwork, love." He wouldn't spill any beans, but he wasn't going to step in a huge cow flop on purpose either.

Tom rolled his bright blue eyes, shaking his head. "You're awful. Okay, but I need to know who to tap for this soon."

"Sure. I have someone in mind, but I want to make sure it works."

Tom shrugged, but then nodded, gaze dragging over Koby's belly, landing solidly on his crotch. "You about ready for lunch?"

Fuck yes. More than.

Still, work was work, right? Dammit. "I'll be there in ten. Let me just check in on Sawyer."

"Don't keep me waiting, lover."

"I won't." In fact, he thought he might take the afternoon off and lock the front door.

He grabbed his phone and searched his contact list.

He happened to know that Sawyer Canton was still dead silly over his ex. So, this could really get interesting.

Chapter One

Sawyer pulled into the parking lot at the City Market and parked before blowing out a hard breath. Okay. So, he had to get through this exchange without making an ass out of himself. That was it.

Anyone would think he knew how to do this now after a year of going to get the kids three days on and three days off. But he was still just— He didn't know how to do this.

He was never going to know how to do this.

Seeing Liam twice a week was like scraping open a wound every time it had just started to heal better, keeping it fresh and bleeding all the goddamn time.

The fancy-assed silver Escalade was waiting there already, and he knew Liam would be on his phone, the front seat filled with blueprints and his iPad and the rolling office that followed him everywhere.

Liam was an architect. He had a paper or a tablet or a blue-print for everything. His jeans were neat, his boots polished, and no one ever saw him sweat.

Him? Hell, he wouldn't know what to do if his fucking boots weren't covered in shit. Sawyer ran a sizeable ranch that raised bucking horses, and it had been in his family so long he had sunshine, horsehair, and dirt dug so deep into his skin it would never wash. He could barely remember a grocery list. Which his momma had written, and he had tucked into the front pocket of his snap-front shirt, because they would need to run into the store and get food for the girls while they were with him.

His cupboards were pretty bare. They'd had a bit of a mouse problem, and he'd had Harriet clean them out completely so the exterminator could do his thing.

Good thing his housekeeper wasn't scared of anything. They'd found the nest in the far back of the pantry underneath a case of Mac and Cheese boxes. That cheese packet seemed to be quite the mousey draw, for sure.

A knock on the window made him jump, and he grinned at Emily, his impatient eight-year-old in her gymnastics tracksuit, hair pulled back so tight it squeaked, who wasn't about to let him have a little nap in his truck.

He motioned for her to step back before opening the door. "Hey, kiddo. How's it going?"

"Well—"

Oh, fuck.

"—It's going. Rosie got hit in the face with a toy in daycare. Da had to take her to the doctor and cancel a big meeting. She hid under a chair when they went to sew up her face."

"Wait. Sew up her—"

"She's fine. Don't worry. It won't scar."

"But—"

"Daddy! Listen!"

He was fixin' to have a stroke.

"So, when he pulled her out, she sprayed blood on his good white shirt, and when she saw the blood? She puked all over him! Can you imagine?"

As a matter of fact, yes, but how come Liam hadn't called him?

"Anyway, they're both mad, and I am *so* over this." She sighed dramatically. "She's a baby and he's a worrywart. Can we leave her with Da? Please?"

Jesus save him from this brilliant, talented girl who had wanted to eat her sister from the day Rosie was born.

"Hey, no. I know you get frustrated sometimes, but she can hang out with Gran and we'll go to the barns, okay?" Poor Em was at that age where eight and four was a huge gulf, and her sister made her nuts. "Let's get her, and we'll grab something to snack on for the drive home when we get groceries, okay?" Hangry was a thing. He put her backpack in the truck, then took her hand to hurry to Liam's Escalade and get his Rosie.

Liam unfolded himself from the car wearing a skin-tight white undershirt, his face a thundercloud. "Sawyer."

"Why didn't you call?"

"I did. Your mother answered."

Fuck his life. Seriously? Unless Rose had been dying, Liam wasn't going to say shit to his momma, and he knew it.

"Is she okay?" Sawyer could hear Rosie screaming, "No! No! No!" over and over.

"I hope you have a good weekend," Liam spoke directly to Em, who rolled her eyes.

"It's started out like a dream."

"Tell me about it. This isn't Rosie's fault."

"Nothing is ever her fault."

"Guys!" This wasn't Liam and Em. Those two were thick as thieves.

"You're right. I'm not up for a fight. I have to get back to the office." His ex arched an eyebrow at Emily, and Jesus, Liam seemed wore to the bone. "You going to kiss me goodbye?"

"Nope. I'm not feeling it right now."

Oh, ouch.

Liam shrugged, those blue eyes going like chips of ice, and God help him, didn't he know how fast Liam's hurt feelings could slice a person out with surgical precision. "Fair enough. Have a good weekend. I'll pick you up Tuesday after school."

She frowned at him, her baby sister still screaming bloody murder. Thank God for car seats, because this fight out here was way bigger than the tantrum in the car. "You're not coming to my gymnastics meet tomorrow?"

Emily was pushing her da, hard, and Sawyer opened his mouth to intervene when Liam pursed his lips and inhaled deep. "I guess I could tell you it depended on whether or not I was feeling it, Em, but that would be hurtful and nasty to say to someone I loved, so yes. I'll be there." Then Liam turned to him. "It appears Rose is in a bit of a mood, Saw, and there's a list of instructions from the emergency room. Do you want me to keep her?"

"No. I got it. But I can call if I need to?" Liam was never a dick to him about the kids, and they worked hard to still present a united front to them.

"Of course." Once upon a time, Liam would have teased him, waggled his eyebrows and winked and said, *"Nope, not answering the phone."*

Those days were gone.

Both girls had Liam's blue eyes, and Rosie had the black curls where her big sister had a coppery red mane that was as uncontrollable as could be. Rosie had Sawyer's temper, though, loud and furious and snapping, and she glared at him when he opened the car door.

"NOT GOING!"

"No? Why not, baby girl? I have a comfy couch, and you can hang with Gran."

"Hurts, Daddy!"

"She's got three stitches above her eyebrow. It shouldn't

scar. She's got a headache, and the hospital scared the fire out of her."

"I bet. Come on, sweetie. We'll be done here in just a few, and we can go home." He needed to get moving.

Liam went to get Rose's backpack, plus the sheaf of papers from the hospital. "The prescription for her headache was called in."

"Okay, cool. I'll grab it here." He resisted the urge to touch Liam's hand as they made the exchange. It wouldn't be welcome. He'd just screwed up too much, and they'd never recovered.

Em went and hugged Liam hard, whispering. "Sorry for being mean. I hate this part, and Rosie scared me."

"Me too," Liam whispered back. "I'll be there tomorrow with my pompoms and signs."

"Okay, Da." She beamed, and Sawyer got Rosie in his arms, where she clung to him, crying. Poor baby.

"I know, but we'll get your medicine and some snacks, okay? Come on. If you're good, I'll buy you a color book."

"Colors?" She sniffled. "My head."

"I know, baby girl. Remember that time little Gremlin kicked me right in the face." That mini horse was evil incarnate.

"Bad horsey. So bad." She leaned into him. "Da holded me for the shot. I cried."

"It's hard to be brave when your head hurts so bad. You can ride in the cart, huh? We'll get some good stuff at the store." He hated it when his kids hurt. "Tell Da goodbye."

"Love you, sugarbutt." Liam winked at her. "Call me if you need me."

"Okay, Da. Love you."

Like Rosie would need to call. Em? Yes.

She would have forgotten her hair spray, her shoes, the leotard she liked, and bobby pins. He didn't do her hair so it stayed; she'd want Liam to bring her the 'special' water bottle, and she'd need to make sure Liam was right in front to watch her floor routine.

"I love you both. Be good. I'll see you tomorrow."

"Okay, Da. Bye."

They all watched Liam get into the Escalade and leave, and he bit back a sigh.

"All right, hooligans. We're in need of food. We had mice in the pantry. Can you believe it? We need to get a couple of totes for your mac and cheese, too. That's what they went after." He put Rosie's bag away, locked up the truck, and took them to the store, carrying Rosie and holding Em's hand.

"There are no mice in the condo," Em pointed out. "And it's next to the coffee shop too."

"Uh-huh. But there are no horses or goats or dogs, either." The girls loved all the animals at the ranch. And the swimming pool in the summer.

"Yeah, I guess." Em grinned at him, though, even as she rolled her eyes. "I sort of like Peaches..."

She loved that old mare, and he knew it.

"And you like the practice gym I set up for you in the tack barn." No condo had that. So there.

"Yeah, that's cool. Marnie is dying from jealousy. Just dying."

"Is Marnie still a frenemy or are you back to being friends?" He felt Rosie giggle when he asked.

"We're mostly friends, even though she's kinda mean..."

"Well, watch your back, huh? Kinda mean can turn snake-mean if you're not paying attention."

"I know." She flipped her hair dramatically. "But I have Kylie."

"If I say I like her will you stop being friends? Because I don't want to ruin it."

"Daaaaddy. I'm too big for that kind of drama."

"Oh, sorry. Of course." Eight was damn near ancient. Completely grown.

She sniffed, and he shook his head at Rosie. "Sounds like she'll go to college next week, huh? You're on your own."

"Ha," Em shot back. "I'm going to Oxford. I've already told Da, and he said okay. You'll miss me when I'm gone."

"Oxford. Wow. That's a long way. What do they have that CU doesn't, honey?" He knew better than to just flat-out say WTF. She had huge dreams, like all kids her age, and who was he to squash them?

"Daddy! It's in England. It's fancy and important." She shrugged, shot him a look, but there was uncertainty lurking there. "Shouldn't I want to do important things?"

"Absolutely. And fun things too. England sounds like a hoot, baby." They got inside, and Rosie was asleep in no time, her little bruised head drooping. "What kind of cereal do you want, Em?"

"Can I have Lucky Charms?"

"Sure." Liam was fussy about artificial this and processed that, but the girl wanted marshmallow unicorn cereal.

"Yep. And we'll get Rosie her Froot Loops." And he would get him some Chex for when he had less time. Mac and cheese. Some canned soup. He got a bunch of fruit and veg too, so Liam couldn't bitch about what he fed them too much.

Not that Liam would tell him. He would tell Em, who would then call him and tell him he'd gotten her in trouble. Wash, rinse, repeat.

God, he hated this.

He hated that it had been him, being suspicious, being jealous, being accusatory that had led Liam to stare him down and walk out.

Fuck. The memory still burned to the bone.

Oh, there had been other things. Liam had been working

like a dog at his architecture firm, his partner dropping the ball left and right. He'd been crazy busy getting started in the reining horse business, which paid a hell of a lot more than bucking horses, though he loved his mustang mixes.

But it had been his damn fault that it had all finally broke.

"Daddy, can we have noodles and sauce for supper?" Em asked as they wandered the pasta aisle.

"Sure, baby girl." He added several packs of spaghetti and a couple jars of that Classico flavor Em and Rosie agreed on. That would be easy-peasy with some cheesy toast.

"We need Gatorade and grapes for the meet tomorrow, don't forget."

"For just you, or am I doing the team snacks?" He chuckled. Last-minute Em. That was his girl. At least with the kids around he had way less time to dwell.

"The team! It's our turn."

"All right." Lord have mercy.

By the time he'd picked up Rosie's prescription and everything else in the entire store, Em had seen three kids from her class, and two guys had stopped to talk brood mares, it was late, everyone was grumpy, and he stopped to grab burgers, fries, and milkshakes on the way home.

He'd make spaghetti tomorrow after gymnastics.

Dinner, baths, bed. Once the kids were settled, Emma reading in her room and Rosie out like a light, he headed to his mancave and poured a whiskey.

He might even work up the energy to drink it.

Chapter Two

"Liam McMartin, you cannot spend your entire waking hours working."

Liam chuckled at his best friend, Darin, who was the househusband for a lovely couple with five kids and six German shepherds and still managed to find time to call him. "You spend your entire life with Lisa and Alan and the kids. That's work."

"That's love," Darren shot back.

Yeah, well, he'd given that shit up.

"I just do what I do, Dare. You know that asshole Erik left me with a real mess." His business partner had carried a different work ethic, which was the biggest understatement in the history of understatements, and when they'd split up the business it had taken him ages to rebuild the firm. "And that doesn't include the kids."

Who he was missing bad today. Yesterday was the final gymnastics meet of the year, Em had managed to place, and little Rose had been there, her tiny scar barely pink now, so excited that she could do it next year too. He'd wanted to be the one to go out to celebrate with them, but it was the asshole's day with the kids, so he'd missed it.

It was the luck of the draw. They were three days on, three days off, so Liam got an equal number of days. It sucked anyway.

"—listening to me?"

Oh shit. "Totally," he lied.

"Baloney. What was I saying?"

He took a shot in the dark. "You were threatening to muzzle one of the dogs."

That earned him a sigh. "Lucky guess!"

"With that many dogs, it's not much of a guess." He missed the border collies on the ranch, but they'd been working dogs, really. Not house dogs. He and Saw had talked about something more kid-friendly for the girls, but there had never been time, and now there was no room at his condo.

He checked the clock. He got his reasons back at four.

Soon he would get in the car, drive to the parking lot, and it would all be closer to okay. There would be homework and bedtime stories, cartoons and "Da, look at this YouTube video" to fill up every second of his time.

Unless, of course, Em wanted to yell at him about not being at *her* celebration supper. She didn't get why he and Sawyer the ex of doom couldn't simply get back together for her. Why they couldn't just be grown-ups and deal.

It wasn't as if he could just tell her that if Saw didn't trust him, he couldn't fix it. He had never cheated, he'd never considered it, and he'd still been accused of it.

Complete with screaming and slamming down sheafs of printed-out emails and a private investigator hired to find what? Nothing, because he was in love with Sawyer, even if he was a raging asshat.

And then he'd been swamped with work, because he had

been trying to start this damn business, hadn't he? He had been drowning, and they hadn't talked, and...

It had been easier to go. And to serve Saw with divorce papers. And now they had nothing to talk about but the kids.

So no. He could not have been at that supper.

Because the simple fact was, they had been adults, and sometimes adult problems weren't fixed by being in love.

"Anyway," Dare said, "You need to get out more. Maybe you should try a dating service."

"I'm not interested." He didn't have enough energy to try. He didn't want to try.

"Well, someone might be interested in you. Then your life would be better."

He didn't even bother to try to not roll his eyes. "Sure. I did so well at being in a relationship."

"It wasn't your fault!" Dare's denial was instant and dear, because Dare was his oldest friend, and this was their job.

"We both know it was partly my fault. He knew very well I wasn't a cheater, but he obviously felt neglected." Liam sighed, shook his head. He'd gone over this—again and again. If he'd been a better person—smarter, quicker on the ball—he might have seen that Saw doubted him, but he'd been so shocked. Utterly taken aback.

I can't believe you'd fuck around on me. Go behind my back. We have babies.

The fury had been like a hammer slamming him in the center of his chest, cracking him. And he couldn't take it. He'd walked.

"Well, he was an ass."

"He was." Liam shook his head, even if Dare couldn't see. "Hey, you, this is all pretty depressing. Can't you tell me something good?"

"I love you, and Lisa's pregnant again."

"Again? Wow!" That was a lot of babies. Surely they knew what caused them. "Congratulations!"

"Yeah. Thanks. We're excited, but we wish you were here. Closer."

No, he wouldn't take the girls away from Sawyer. He was a better man than that. "I can't. You know that."

"I know. I just wish...I mean, damn. I miss you guys."

Oh, good lord and butter. "Dare. She's supposed to be hormonal, not you."

"I know. I know. Tell me you'll come to Denver soon, hang with me?"

That he could promise. "I will do my best. I swear."

"Thanks, Liam. I just want to put eyes on you."

"Maybe on my holiday with the girls."

"Are you each going two weeks at a time over the summer then?"

He winced at the thought of two weeks without them, but he loved the idea of two weeks away with them. "I don't know. I have to talk to the ex."

"Ah. Well, you should do it sooner rather than later. Send an email."

"Are you kidding? Saw usually has his phone in his hand, but emails? No." The mother-in-law of doom saw those.

"Cowboys," Dare teased. "That's what you get for hooking up with one."

"Yep. I should have run like the wind, but he just kept sitting in my section." Liam had waited tables to get through his undergrad, and Saw had been in Denver on business. He hadn't fought the attraction for long at all.

Like not even a whole two days. When Sawyer had given him a phone number, he'd called it. And he'd ended up at the Grizzly Rose, two-stepping the night away.

There may have been a fistfight in the parking lot, which

had led to the hottest blowjob he'd ever given, right in the cab of Saw's truck.

Lord, he hadn't done anything that spontaneous in...well, possibly forever. He wasn't living the spontaneous kind of existence.

Everything in his life now revolved around work and his kids.

He groaned, rolling his head on his neck. "I need to go meet the girls at the City Market, man. I love you. I'll talk to you later, huh?"

"Absolutely. Tell the girls Uncle Darin says hi."

"Will do." He put his phone in his pocket and forced himself not to sigh.

It was becoming a bad habit, and his girls were coming home.

He knew three days wasn't long, but it was three days with no reason to stop and eat and smile.

Now he had a good reason, someone to talk to. Two someones.

No one ever told you how hard it was, to work alone, to go upstairs to an empty condo just to go back down and work.

Maybe he needed a dog.

A purse dog. Something he could bond with and talk to in the office.

That wasn't unreasonable, right?

He thought Rosie and Em would be over the moon.

They could stop at the shelter after he picked the girls up.

Chapter Three

"Hey, boss. I got the mail on the way in from town." One of the hands, Jae, handed him a sheaf of paper bullshit.

"Ugh. Thanks." At least he'd been on his way into the house. He had some calls to make, and he needed to spend time going over accounts and paying some bills.

He'd much rather be out playing cowboy.

"Hey, sweetie," his mom said when he walked in.

He winced, hoping she didn't have some weird thing she wanted him to do for her or some wild idea about how to redecorate the house, which was at least a quarterly argument.

She wanted to eradicate any remnant of Liam, even though she liked his ex a lot. Said it would make things easier for him.

Sawyer liked the house the way it was.

"Hey, Mom. What's up?"

"I just wanted to tell you I'm making King Ranch casserole for supper. Unless you'd rather have chicken broccoli."

You could take the girl out of Texas, but no one could ever take the Texas out of his mom. "King Ranch is fine."

"Good deal. I was making chicken anyway, and I know you have the girls tonight, so I thought I'd just make us both supper, you know?"

"Yeah. That sounds great." Em loved King Ranch. He was sure his mom would leave some chicken out for Rosie, who was still deeply suspicious of casseroles.

"Are you okay? You seem down?"

Seemed down. Shit. He was never up unless he was riding or with his girls. "I'm fine, Momma. Just working."

"Did you want me to pick the girls up from school? I can. I'll be in town."

He thought about it, then nodded. "Sure. They shouldn't need anything from Liam's."

"I still don't see why you didn't just try for full custody..." she muttered, and he knew she missed them almost as much as he did. Hell, she lived three minutes away and walked over to see him and make coffee almost every morning.

"Because Liam deserves time with them." He knew it was a hard arrangement for all of them.

"Still, it's supposed to be about what's good for them, not Liam."

"I know, but they love him, Mom. And they love staying in town half the week, being close to school and their friends." He shrugged. What could he say? He sat at the kitchen table, sorting mail.

One of the envelopes was heavy paper, fancy, and he put it aside.

"Of course they love him, but that condo above the office isn't good for them."

"Momma, please." His head was starting to pound. Now, a packet of checks from Hiram, who was on the road with the reining team, helped. That would pay a lot of bills.

Not that they were hurting, but he liked to put money back into things he'd paid out for so they broke even.

He intended to prove that his horse concept was going to pay out big enough that he wasn't going to be leaning on old family money. Cowboys were stubborn to the bone, he reckoned. Some things never changed.

"I'm just trying to take care of you, son."

Yeah, he knew. He really knew, but it didn't matter. "Well, thank you, Momma, but I need to take care of that stuff for myself."

His fingers fell on a heavy envelope, the paper stiff, the embossing super formal. He frowned. What the heck? No one he knew had a kid graduating, and no one was getting married, he didn't think.

He opened it, pulling out the card, and then grinning at it in disbelief.

"What is that, son?"

"I got an invite to the fancy Cattleman's Ball. Not the Central Colorado Association one, but the ritzy Aspen club thing."

"Well, you have come into your own, haven't you? Congratulations, son!"

"Thanks, Momma." He put the envelope aside. He didn't have anyone to go with, so there wasn't any sense in it.

"Well, I think it's amazing. You'll be able to have fun. You'll have a ball." Momma smiled at him. "You deserve to go out and about."

"Uh-huh." He wasn't gonna argue with her.

"We'll have to take you shopping."

Oh, Lord. "Now, Momma."

"Seriously. It's a formal event. You need new boots." She nodded as if it were all settled. "Emily and Rosie will be so excited for you."

"My dress boots are just fine."

She gave him an arch glare. "Your dress boots are eight years old."

"That doesn't mean they're not fine. I got them resoled." They were comfortable, and he liked the way they made him feel.

Liam had liked them too and had always let him know.

"But—"

He held up a hand. "Momma. I have a vicious headache, okay? Can we talk about all this later?"

She gave him a knowing glance. "Sure we can. Maybe over lunch out on Friday."

"Lunch on Friday. You got it."

She gave him a warm smile. "We'll go have burgers at that little diner. Maybe share a milkshake, hmm?"

He reminded himself that she worried about him, that she'd lost his dad, his brother, and she was trying to fill her time with him. She was lonely.

"That sounds great, Momma. Really fine." He found a smile for her. "And I'm holding you to the King Ranch casserole."

"It's done, with a little bit of chicken and cheese left on the side for our Rosie-Posie."

Sawyer rolled his eyes. "Yes. Because she's at the casseroles-are-scary phase."

"She'll get over it."

"I sure hope so. I want chicken spaghetti. And lasagna. And—"

She laughed. "You're doing that just to mess with her."

"I am?" He chuckled. "Maybe. But casseroles are important. Lord knows she eats enough mac and cheese."

"That baby is going to turn orange, I swear to God." They laughed together, and she put a bottle of Excedrin on the table for him, along with a fresh cup of coffee without him even asking.

"Thanks, Momma." He knew it had always been a bone of contention with Liam that his mom was around so much, but he couldn't up and ask her to not be. She was a momma. It was what she did.

His eyes fell on the invitation. The Aspen Cowboy Ball. He'd be damned.

He must be going up in the world.

"LORD HAVE MERCY, HOW MUCH LAUNDRY CAN TWO girls make?"

Liam had on his favorite pair of ancient jeans, the Eagles blaring, and his feather duster hooked in his waistband. This condo was a mess.

Work had been eating him alive, and for the first time in he couldn't remember when he had nothing to do down in the office, and his girls home without plans.

"Da! I putted my blocks away!" Rosie crowed. "What next?"

"Pick up all Daisy's toys and put them in the basket, angel baby."

"Okay!"

That would take at least an hour. How one tiny rescue shih tzu could have so many toys was a mystery. And Rosie would start playing with her rather than getting them all put away.

"Yes, sir!"

He started another load of tiny clothes before he went to check on Emily, who was the neatnik child of his heart. "How goes it, my dancing queen?"

"It goes like a going thing!" She laughed for him, and he loved to see it. She was so much more relaxed now that gymnastics was over for the year, spending hours decorating her room and playing with their wee rescue dog. "Can I have the duster?"

"Yeppers." He unclipped it to hand it to her. "I'll get you the dust mop for the floor."

"Ooh…Daisy loves that. Can I pick the next playlist?"

He nodded. It would be something from one of the Disney channel girls, possibly Taylor Swift. He reckoned he learned a lot about where his girl's mind was through the music.

And it kept him up on stuff. He guessed that was good. He and Sawyer had always joked that their taste in music was a good twenty to thirty years older than them.

His folks had been older, so at least he had an excuse. Saw's was most likely that he was a cowboy, and he could like what he liked.

"Thanks, Da." She blew him a kiss and danced away.

He did love the times when Em allowed herself to be a little girl, when life was cartoons and Barbies and stuffies and not stressing about friends and tumbling and whether she was ever going to get breasts.

They grew up so damn fast, and the girls in this area were precocious, to say the least.

"Da! I did the Daisy toys! What's next?" Rosie did the cutest butt wiggle.

"Put all the pillows and blankets up on the sofa for me to fold?" He was running out of easy, fun cleaning chores.

"Pillows!" She went running. He was going to owe both of these girls lunch.

Maybe he'd take them for a long walk, get lunch, maybe pick up a book and a cup of coffee. They loved the bookstore, and he needed to grab the mail.

Before long, the cleaning was done, they were all dressed in fresh clothes, and they were headed out into the late spring sunshine. It felt great to be outside, and while Daisy had been sad to be left behind, come summer she would be trained enough to go with them to the open "petios".

Rosie danced along, her hand in his, while Em fluttered more like a bird, wandering off, then coming back to check-in.

"Da?"

"Yes, my love."

"Do you love me so much?"

He chuckled and glanced down at her. "More than that. I love you and Em more than anyone on earth."

"Even Daddy?"

God, what a question. "More than anything."

"Okay." Rosie swung his hand, but Em gave him a side-long glance. Or maybe even a side-eye.

"Do you still love Daddy?"

"Em."

She shrugged. "It's a fair question."

"It may be, but it's an adult answer, and I don't know how to explain it."

"You married him. You had kids. Do. You. Still. Love. Him."

"Yes, but we couldn't stay married, and I'm sorry, but that is the truth." Liam would always love the son of a bitch, but that didn't make a marriage work.

"He still loves you too."

He sucked in a breath. "Baby girl, this hurts to talk about, okay?"

She frowned at him, but she nodded. "I'm sorry. That stinks. I love you."

Oh, thank God. He couldn't handle this right now. "Thank you. I love you too. Do you know what book you're going to get?"

"Nope. Maybe something about gymnasts. Or horses. Or maybe the book for that TV series."

"Oh, that one seemed cool. I'd like to read it too."

"You could read it to us, Da!" Rosie bounced. "It would be momatic?"

"Mom…"

"Romantic, Da." Em blushed dark. "We were watching soap operas with Granny."

"Ah. Well, I can see that." God help him. Barb was a good woman, but pushy and nosy and involved in every fucking thing known to man. And she was encouraging his girls to watch soaps…

Rosie smacked her lips and made kissing noises.

"Like you know what that means," Em muttered.

"It means having bubble drinks and wearing jewelry and reading by the fire to be happy!"

He snorted. "Uh-huh. Oh. Look at the window, huh?" He distracted them with a mystery game window at a game store.

"Oh…we should do a jigsaw puzzle." Em nodded to him. "Let's get one."

"That sounds fun." They loved to spread a puzzle out now that Rosie was old enough not to lose pieces. They would just keep Daisy out of it by leaving it up.

"Da, those are hard." Rosie frowned at him. "Can I have one like at school?"

"Of course. We'll do two at once."

"Yay!" Rosie twirled. "Oh, look Da, a puppy." Rosie loved seeing dogs out on the street.

"No running, and ask first, please." Sawyer had taught the girls to respect an animal's boundaries.

Stop thinking about him! God, why did every fucking thing lead back to Sawyer.

The puppy turned out to be a giant Great Dane mix, who sat very pretty and let the girls offer hands to sniff and pet its ears. Then they headed in to buy puzzles before finally making it to the bookstore.

"No wandering off too far, Miss Em. And you have half an hour." Em had a kid's smart watch, since she was too young for a phone, so she could keep track of her own time.

"I promise I won't leave the store."

"I'll keep an eye on the door, Liam." Maggie, who owned Bent Corners, was a good friend. Hell, he'd designed her house.

"Thanks, Mags." He grinned at her. "I need a coffee." And maybe a cronut.

"Sheri's got goodies next door at the coffee shop, or I can pour you a cup of regular here."

"Oh, I'll wait." Rosie was still young enough that drinks and books were a challenge, at best.

"Cool. Just let me know if you change your mind."

"Will do." Rosie held out a hand, and he grabbed it, letting her drag him to the kids' section.

"Da! Can I have a book about a dog?"

"Of course you can. There are totally dog books." He'd been very into Dr. Seuss at Rosie's age. Oh! "There's a dog in the *Grinch* book."

"Uh-huh. We have that, Da. I want something about a ranch dog. Or a Great Dane."

"Okay, let's ask Miss Maggie. She'll know what to do." He figured that was easy, right?

They found books—a boxed set for him to read to them, two chapter books for Em, two dog books for Rosie, and two new fantasy novels for him—before they grabbed the mail from the kiosk he rented and popped in to have a coffee.

Lord have mercy.

He sat with his cronut and a muffin, because he was suddenly starving, watching the girls suck whipped cream off their drinks, and taking a breath. Then he flipped through the mail, sorting junk from bills. He needed to go paperless on more of them.

One of the envelopes was heavy paper, so a wedding or a business event that was going to cost him a fortune. Yay.

When he opened it, the invitation was for a fancy cowboy

ball event the city put on every year to rival the Cattleman's Association. He'd never been invited before.

He wasn't sure why he'd been invited now.

"What's that, Da?" Rosie asked, slurping her drink.

"Don't slurp, sweetie. It's an invitation to a grown-up party."

Emily leaned to see. "Really? When is it? Are you going? Are you going to wear a tux?"

"Da never goes to parties," Rosie stated. "He's boring."

"Hey!" He wasn't boring. He was busy.

"You don't. You work and work and work. That's all. Daddy rides horses and goes to the movies."

"And the roping pen," Em added.

"And for a beers."

"It's just a beer." Em frowned, head tilting. "But a couple of beers, right?"

"Yes. One beer. Two beers." Wait, why was he having this conversation? Why was Sawyer going out for beers? Who was he going with? Why did he care?

No. No, he didn't.

"I think Daddy is going to that party." Em waved a hand. "Gran said he had to buy new boots for some fancy 'do'."

"Oh?" He wasn't interested, dammit.

"Uh-huh. Granny says he has to find a date, and soon, because this is important for him." Em took another sip, then licked her lips. "Everybody's excited."

A date? Sawyer was ready to go on dates? And go for beers? He was just at the fantasizing about Henry Cavill without guilt part.

God, he was pathetic.

Liam firmed his lips. "I think I'll go."

"Da! Yay!" Em bounced, almost spilling her drink. "We can help you pick out clothes."

"Daddy will be so excited!" Rosie crowed. "Are you finding a date too?"

"Yes." He wasn't sure how or where, but he knew the girls would be telling Sawyer he was going, so he needed a goddamn date too. Someone amazing. Someone to make Sawyer regret ever accuse him of cheating.

"Cool." Em grinned. "Make it a cowboy, Da."

"Mmm." Where was he going to dig up another cowboy? He'd already had one, and it had gone poorly.

Kind of spectacularly so.

Dammit.

Liam took a sip of coffee, forcing himself to relax. He was a smart dog. He could figure this out.

If he had to, he'd hire a date.

Chapter Four

"Hey, man!" Sawyer grinned, grabbing Morgan's hand to shake it. They were at the roping pen, and he hadn't seen Morgan around in a couple of months, so it was good to see the guy. "New horse?"

"She is. She's a quick little girl, loves her job, turns on a dime." Morgan stroked the dapple gray's neck, the heavy gold nugget ring on his finger shining in the light and highlighting the way that middle finger had been snapped off at the second knuckle.

It would go on a chain before Morgan started roping, but it had been Morgan's dad's, and he always had it on him.

Always.

"Nice. Harley is still doing pretty well, so we're a pair." His bay gelding was a good buy, solid, and he didn't spook at all.

"Fair enough. Ranch keeping you busy?" Morgan had a spread of his own—little, but he bred high-dollar horses for rich townies who needed something for their kids to do.

"Hell, yes. Between the reining horses, the bucking horses, the damn cattle I keep for the taxes, and my mother? I'm swamped." And lonely. And bored.

"Good lord. I thought I was busy. Of course, you have those babies..." Morgan shook his head, grinned. "They're something else."

"They are." He lived for those girls. And he missed them fierce when they weren't with him. "Momma wants me to try for full custody, but I just can't do that to Liam." And who knew if it would work?

"Are they unhappy with him?"

"No. No, they love being with him." *So did I.* He missed Liam like a sore tooth. And he kept poking at the wound by asking the kids how Liam was doing, and Em was always happy to tell him how cool her da's condo was, and how he took them downtown to shop, and how it was so much cleaner than the ranch.

No mice.

But it wasn't as big. And there was only Daisy the Purse Dog.

Seriously.

A purse dog.

What was Liam thinking?

If he'd wanted a dog, Sawyer could have gotten him one who would work. Literally.

Not a fluff ball with no use but to wag and snuggle, for fuck's sake.

He shook his head, and Morgan raised an eyebrow. "Thinking about the ex?"

"Only two-thirds of the day. The other third I do things like work."

"Well then, you're getting better and better every day." Morgan winked at him as if he knew.

"I am." Only not. He wanted to see Liam. Touch him. Beg forgiveness like he hadn't before.

He just needed to figure out how to make it happen, how

to make it work. He hadn't been able to get Liam in the same room with him at all. The same parking lot, yes.

"You know, you could kidnap him."

Sawyer hooted. "I guess I could." In fact, that could be fun. Not a scary kidnapping, but a—did they have a nice kidnapping?

A romance kidnapping, as Rosie would say.

"There you go. Just, you know. Grab him."

"Shove him in the back of the truck and drive." Maybe they could talk like adults then. "I like it." He wouldn't do it, of course. "So, I got invited to the cattleman's thing."

"We all get invited."

"No, man. Not the central Colorado one. The swanky thing in town. You know. Two hundred dollar steak."

"Oh, no shit? Spiffy! You going?"

"I have no idea. I mean, it seems like a waste."

"Yeah, but it means you're moving up in the world." Morgan chuckled and shook his head. "You got to rub elbows with the big dogs, man."

"I guess." He pondered that. "Want to go with me? You can pimp your horses."

Morgan tilted his head, dark eyes laughing at him. "I might could, yeah. I mean, you could just invite the ex?"

"Right. Like he'd say yes."

"Hmmm. Yeah, maybe not." Morgan waved a hand. "Maybe your girls could blackmail him into it."

"Nah. I'll just take you." He checked his horse's girth strap before mounting up. "We gonna rope?"

"Hell yes, we are. I didn't come out here to just let you admire my gorgeous ass." Morgan flexed, and Sawyer cracked up. Silly fucker.

"Well, get that mare out and we'll turn a few steers." That was way more fun than talking about his failings with Liam, or how that was never going to happen, even if he wanted them to get back together so bad.

"Sounds good, man." Morgan opened the gate on the trailer so he could back the mare out, and then they were both mounted and ready to rope, their game faces on. This he could do. Cowboying was the easy part. Interpersonal shit was not.

He had to get his shit together. This whining bullshit was for the birds.

Liam couldn't stop staring at the fancy RSVP card on his desk. He still didn't know how he'd finagled an invitation, but he had, and dammit, he was going to go.

Especially if Sawyer was going with a date.

Would Sawyer go with a man? Would Barb set him up with a beard in a sparkly belt?

How was Liam even going to find time to get a date? A suitably cowboy-ed-up date who would make Sawyer gnash his teeth in pure rage.

Someone tall and studly—a Tim McGraw wannabe who would seem mysterious and charismatic and intensely sexual. Or maybe the ultimate in cowboy next door, a fresh-faced, aw-shucks type with a heart of gold. Nah, that would make him seem old and jaded, and he wasn't either.

Back to creating the perfect date. Tall, dark, brooding, maybe a faint scar on his bottom lip. No chest hair, even though he loved a man with a nice bit of fuzz, because this wasn't for actual use, this was a cowboy action figure, the formal date version.

So, smooth with defined pecs. Maybe one tattoo—something dangerous, but not scary. Tight jeans, great ass, could play guitar, fix the plumbing, and appreciate the importance of a perfectly pitched roof.

"Where am I supposed to find such a paragon?" he asked the envelope with his name on it.

Liam sat back in his desk chair, grabbing his phone for a touch of scroll time, if for no other reason than because his brain was refusing to work. He went to his Instagram, because he might get inspired to do some damn work if he pored over everyone else's shit, but man, it was depressing to see how the rest of the world was moving around him.

Dog stuff. New building plans. Gymnastics stuff. He had a sneaking suspicion that was Emily messing with his—

"Cowboy Wanted?" He squinted at the ad, which he thought must have popped up through his chamber of commerce like for the Roaring Fork area. "Is it a reality show?"

No. No, it was a help wanted deal.

Seriously.

"I need part-time help with my heifers."

"Hunting for seasonal labor moving herds."

"Need a cowboy to speak at the library for Tales for Tots."

"Need model for photo shoot. Romance cover. Bring your own hat and buckle."

Jesus, this shit was amazing.

There were also listings for cowboys one could hire.

"Twenty years' experience in ranch settings. Foreman experience. References available."

"Former rodeo cowboy willing to do appearances and photo shoots. Will travel."

Huh. That was what he needed. Just a date. Nothing pervy. Well, okay, he could perv a bit on his imaginary cowboy cut-out date. That was fair, right?

A man had needs.

He hovered over the phone number on the ad. Was he really even contemplating this? Yes. He was. This wasn't Grindr. This seemed to be a legit business where he could get an acceptable date to the cowboy ball who would make Sawyer swallow his teeth.

It had to be easier than calling Darin in Denver and asking him to phone a friend. Not only that, Liam knew Darin. He would send a flaming queen with a sequined hat and matching chaps.

Assless ones.

He clicked the damn number and called, since there were no kiddie ears around to hear. What the fuck? The worst that could happen was they would turn out to be skeezy, or they would tell him no.

"Cowboy Wanted! This is Tom."

"Hey, Tom." He inhaled deeply. "I'm Liam McMartin and I need to put in an ad. I need to make my ex blind with rage."

There was a soft chuckle. "Well, you came to the right place as long as this feat requires a cowboy."

"God yes. The cattleman's ball in Aspen. I need the ultimate hot date. I promise to return him unscathed."

"I see. That's a good promise. So that tells me our timeline. I might be able to help without you having to place an ad. Your ex. Local?"

"Yeah. Sawyer Canton of the Double Rocking C ranch?" If the guy didn't know Sawyer, he'd know the ranch.

"Oh, my." That wasn't dismay, he thought, so much as anticipation. "Yes, I'm familiar with Mr. Canton. So, let me see. Something along the lines of Cowboy wanted for escort to cattleman's ball... what's your age range?"

"Thirtyish?"

"Right. Twenty-five to thirty-five. Not well-known in the area."

"No. And I want someone hot as hell, you know? I want to be impressive when I walk in the door." Liam wanted Sawyer to be so jealous he wanted to scream.

Petty? Hell yeah, but he needed to believe he had something going on.

"I understand." There was a wealth of humor there, but oddly, he didn't feel laughed at. "Okay. And they have to be smart enough to play along."

"God yes."

"All right. I'll work up a quote for you for the evening, and we'll go about getting you someone for your ad."

He took the plunge, because something about Tom made him feel like he could trust this service. "Just invoice me and call me when you have someone."

"I can do that."

"Thank you. I can't tell you what this means to me." It meant getting a little of his own back, because he needed to.

"Let me just get all of your information."

Twenty minutes later he was a registered user of Cowboy Wanted LLC, he had an ad mocked up, and Tom had an email address to send his invoice to. "We'll find someone perfect for the job. It'll be my mission," Tom said.

"You rock. I owe you a coffee."

"Honey, when I pull this off, you'll owe me chocolate."

Chapter Five

"Rosie, stop kicking your feet. Do you want French toast, a waffle, or the pancakes?" They were having brunch at the Village Smithy in Carbondale, because Sawyer figured that would be a safe place to go. Liam didn't really go there now they'd broken up. "They have mixed berry pancakes today."

"What are you going to have, Daddy?" Emily asked.

"The spicy corn cakes."

She wrinkled her nose. "Oh. Then we won't share."

"No?" He grinned, because that was why he ordered corn cakes with green chile, bacon, and cheese. The girls liked sweet for brunch, and that way he got a whole meal.

"No. That's nasty. I want a cinnamon roll and a sausage."

"Sausage makes you fat," Rosie pronounced, and he blinked.

"Does it? Daddy?" Em's eyes went wide with horror.

"No." He gave Rosie a frown. "Eating too much of anything might make you gain weight, but a couple of pieces of sausage are fine now and again. And people gain and lose weight for a ton of reasons, Rosie. So that wasn't kind." He'd had that drilled into him by his momma, and he wanted his girls to get that too.

Cowboy culture could be pretty crazy when it came to what people weighed, but his girls needed to be free to be who they were.

"I wasn't mean! My teacher said it!" Rosie gave him a thunderous frown. "I promise, Daddy. I wasn't mean."

"Ah. Well, your teacher isn't always right, kiddo." He reached over to pat her hand. "I mean, you need to respect her, but sometimes people have what we call issues." Lord, help him, this dadding thing was a minefield.

"Issues. You have to worry about being fat if you do gymnastics, maybe, but my coach says we work our bodies hard and not to stress."

"It's always better to be strong and healthy." He'd always been lucky he was a better roper than he was a roughstock rider, because those poor guys had to watch every ounce they put on.

"You folks ready to order?" Their server refilled his coffee while she waited.

"I think so. Rosie?"

"French toasts. And sausage!"

Em offered her sister a rare, approving grin. "A cinnamon roll, please, and sausage."

"And I'll take the Santa Fe corn cakes. And a side of hash-browns, please."

"You got it, folks."

He grinned, because the girls had gone back to coloring, so he grabbed his phone to text a few folks, losing track of all the people passing by.

"Da! Da, we're having brunch!" Rosie waved over, bouncing in her chair. "Da!"

His head snapped up so fast he almost gave himself whiplash. Shit. Sure enough, that was Liam.

"I—hey. I thought y'all were going out with your granny this morning." Liam was edible. Totally edible.

"Nope. She's puking. She has to stay away."

"No puking!" Rosie announced at the top of her lungs.

"Oh. Ew."

Momma was going to be so pleased. She would start getting calls in about ten minutes.

"Hey." Sawyer cleared his throat. "We just ordered if you, uh, want to sit with us."

"Oh, I don't want to disturb—"

"Here, Da! Have my seat. I'll move." Em was almost vibrating, and Sawyer saw Liam's expression melt.

"Thanks, sweetie." Liam sat, turning over the coffee cup that had been pushed aside.

The server came to fill it. "You need a menu, hon?"

"He'll have the McHuevos." Sawyer said it without thinking.

Liam shot him a quick glance but nodded. "He remembers well."

"It's only been a year, Da."

"I know, baby girl. I know."

Sawyer didn't say anything, but he did put a hand on Em's arm to remind her to back off. This was a huge victory, Liam sitting with them. They needed to be gentle.

"Are you guys having a good morning?" Liam asked.

Rosie nodded. "I drawed you a picture!"

"Did you?"

"Uh-huh?" She thrust her color paper at Liam, and Sawyer caught her drink before it went over. Sippy cup or not, it would spill.

"Good catch," Liam said, taking the picture. "Oh, is this our Daisy?"

"Yes! You knew!"

"Of course I knew! I know that ribbon on her neck."

"She's so pretty."

She's a purse dog, he thought. Though she was cute, he supposed. He wisely held those thoughts back too. He'd let the kids drive the conversation.

"Well, thank you, Rosie," Liam said. "So, what all are you up to today after this?"

"Daddy's taking us to the library and then to jump on trampolines!"

"I'm going to practice tumbling on them, I think."

"Sounds like fun." Liam chuckled, the sound soft as feathers falling, and shook his head. "Such a relaxing afternoon."

"Mmm." Sawyer grinned at him. "I have books at my disposal there, at least."

"Yes, and ear pods, hmm?"

God, that smile. He loved that smile.

"Yes." And case in point, Rosie shrieked when her food came, the noise happy but shrill. "Inside voice, kiddo."

"Sorry. Sorry, Daddy. I'm just so hungry!"

"It does look good, huh?" Liam blinked at his plate as if he hadn't remembered he was getting food.

"It is good, Da. Eat." Em handed Liam a fork.

"Thanks, love." Liam tucked in, so Sawyer relaxed and grabbed his own fork to dig in. He would probably end up finishing Rosie's too.

They didn't talk a lot, but it wasn't bitter, cold silence. It was eating. It was being together as a family.

This was what his soul missed the most. And he knew it would end soon, but for right now, he could pretend.

"Da, what are you going to do today?"

"I'm going to do some online classes and work, I think."

"Oh." Em frowned. "Are you going to take Daisy to the park?"

"Of course. She loves her walks. She slept with me last night, because she missed you two."

"Show Daddy her picture, Da! She's so pretty and soft." Rosie grinned at Sawyer. "She's a doll baby."

"Is she?" He took a dutiful glance when Liam showed him. Okay, she was adorable with her squished face and happy puppy smile. "She's beautiful. Tiny."

"She's only fifteen weeks old. She's a baby." Liam shrugged and smiled. "She's great company."

"Yeah. I bet she is." So Liam was potty training her and everything. Damn. That was quite a commitment for him. He must be lonely.

That thought gave him cause to stop, to suck in a deep breath and sit with himself for half a minute. Was he glad Liam was—might be—lonely? Did he feel bad about it? Both? Neither? Christ. He wasn't an asshole. He wasn't.

But he wanted Liam to feel the same way he did. He didn't want them just getting on with their separate lives, and if that made him selfish right now, so be it.

"Daddy? Do you need another cup of coffee? You keep picking it up and putting it down."

"Thanks, Em." Dammit. "I guess I do."

Liam gave him a knowing glance. "You two are a wonderful distraction, Em. Sometimes we forget what we're doing."

"We are wonderful!" Rosie sang. "Me and my sister!"

Em rolled her eyes. "So. Embarrassing."

"No she's not." He grinned at Em. "At least not to me. But you have the older sister's prerogative to feel that way."

"Are you mad at me, Sissy?" Rosie asked, her eyes filling with tears, and both he and Liam glared at Em, who rolled her eyes.

"No, silly. Why would I be mad?"

"Because you're so mean." Rosie sniffled. "I like to sing."

Come on, girl. Please. Don't be a bitch to her. She loves you so much.

"Singing's cool. You could be in choir when you get bigger. Kylie's sister is in choir in middle school."

"She is?" Rosie sniffed. "That sounds fun."

Whew. Crisis averted, he hoped. It was a minefield with two girls sometimes.

"Yeah. And then we can all come to your concerts and stuff. You get to dress up."

Liam smiled at Em, giving her the barest nod, and Em sat up straighter, even as Rosie bounced in her chair.

"I like to dress up! Da! Did you hear about dressing up and singing?"

"I did! Your sister is so smart, to know all this."

"She is!" Rosie finally dug into her food in earnest, and the singing and chatter stopped.

"Heaven help us when they start more activities," Liam said, smiling at Rosie.

"Tell me about it." At least Liam was right there in town.

He peered down at his plate to find it empty, but then Rosie shoved the rest of hers at him, so he had something to keep him busy.

"I guess I should go and let y'all have your time together, hmm?" Liam put his napkin on his plate.

"Oh." Em's face fell. "You don't want to sit and have coffee?" Such a smart girl. She knew Liam loved his post-meal coffee. "Please, Da. We're having fun, huh, Rosie?"

"Yep! I'm coloring."

"Okay. I can sit another minute."

He took comfort in the fact that Liam didn't glance at his watch or his phone.

"Do you mind?" Liam muttered, keeping his voice low.

"Nope." He checked around. "I don't think they need their table back, and I'm good with a cup."

"Cool. Good deal." Liam almost smiled.

They sat in relatively companionable silence while the girls talked and had little bowls of ice cream for brunchert, as the server called it. The coffee was damn good here. And he and Liam weren't snarling. Or frowning.

It was a win-win.

He didn't know what do beyond drink it in.

Which was exactly what he did until the coffee was gone. And then Liam did check his watch. "Okay, guys, I need to go."

"Aww."

"We love you, Da."

"Thanks for hanging out," he told Liam. He meant it.

"Thanks for letting me enjoy them. I miss them when they're gone."

"I know." He didn't sigh. He met Liam's eyes, thinking crazy things like *I miss you. I want you back.* "You're welcome," was what he came up with.

Liam nodded, then stood and kissed Em and Rosie. "I love you. I can't wait to see you again."

"Soon, Da!" Emily called.

He realized Liam had taken the bill a few minutes after he'd walked out. Butthead.

He did grin, though. That was very real progress. He would take it.

I can't do this Dare

Sure you can. It's a business meeting. Not a
date. You know how to do business.

Right. This wasn't a date. This was him hiring a man to make him look good at the ball. Like Cinderella's fairy godmother in jeans and a Stetson.

Bibidi-bobidi-goddamn-boo, motherfucker.

So he took a deep breath and tucked his phone away before ducking into the coffee shop. It was one he never went to, and he didn't think most of the cowboy crowd did either, so he would be pretty safe having a meeting there.

The last thing he wanted in the world was for someone to know he had to hire a date. It was embarrassing, but it was more important to not go stag, because—

"Mr. McMartin?"

"Hmm? Yes."

A mid-twenties, clean-cut cowboy stood and came to shake his hand. He looked far less like Tim McGraw and far more like George Strait or one of the bull riders Liam still watched on TV. "Terry Logan. Pleased to meet you."

"Mr. Logan. Pleased. Would you like a cup of coffee?" He needed a latte in the worst way.

"I would. And please, call me Terry." They walked up to the counter to order, and to his credit, Terry Logan paid for his own coffee, not expecting Liam to do it for him. That already put him in a good light.

This was the weirdest situation on earth. He'd never have believed he would do something like this—but then again, he'd never thought he'd get married to a cowboy, he'd never imagined he would get divorced, and he sure as shit never intended to date until his girls didn't need him so much, so this was logical, right?

The musical lover in him thought, of course right, and he grinned as they got their coffees and sat down.

"Oh, now that is a good look on you, I swear." Terry wasn't flirting, he didn't think, and if he was, it came naturally.

"Thanks." He cleared his throat. "So, I'm a little wigged out."

"Oh, now." Terry leaned forward over his coffee, his brown eyes earnest as hell. "There's nothing to be wigged out about. I'm not a skeezy escort, and you're not the kind of feller who would hunt for that. You need someone to go to this fancy dinner thing with you, right?"

"Yes, sir. I'm going to be honest. My ex is going, and—I don't want to go stag. I'm not ready to date, at all, but I want to appear like I'm a functional adult."

A knowing expression appeared on Terry's face. "I understand. So, we need to be newly dating, then?"

"Yes, please. I've been divorced a little over a year, so everything is new and raw." He sipped his coffee, shook his head. "I have two little girls and my own business, so I'm always running."

"That sounds like a lot. And the ex. Are we expecting some friction?"

Sawyer? No. Sawyer was working hard at reasonable and peaceful. "I don't think he cares that much anymore."

"Ouch." Terry winced for him, and that made Liam just like the man more.

"Right? And we broke up because he thought I was cheating on him. I mean, that was the straw that broke the camel's back." Liam couldn't believe that Sawyer would believe that about him. He was a lot of things—anxious, stressed, desperate to prove he was able to provide and contribute—but he wasn't dishonest, and he had meant every one of his vows.

If Sawyer could believe he would fuck around, betray his family? Then Sawyer didn't believe in Liam, on a soul-deep level.

So, when all of the other little hurts and problems had added up to the point where they were a mountain, and then that issue had dropped like the proverbial turd in the punch-bowl, well... He'd left.

"I'm sure sorry." Terry shook his head. "So, we're not out to make the ex jealous."

He snorted. "Oh." He pondered that. "Yeah. I mean, of course I want that. That's why I didn't ask someone I knew to come with me. I wanted a cowboy because it will make him nuts. I hope." He grinned wryly. "I'm just vain enough, you know?"

He wanted Sawyer to regret doubting him. He wanted Sawyer to...mend the tear that ran down the center of him.

He wanted Sawyer.

Eventually that would ease, or that was what all the shit he read said.

"Shit, I'm a rodeo cowboy, Mister McMartin. I understand vain. I can work with that. And lord knows I won't turn down a steak dinner."

"It's supposed to be amazing, and you'll be able to talk with some high-dollar folks. There's an open bar, and I promise not to drink more than a beer. I have to pick up my girls at noon the next day."

"Well, I can be a designated driver, as well. I'm not much of a drinker." Terry was the one to offer a wry grin now. "Rodeo fighting weight doesn't much leave room for alcohol if I don't want to get stupid."

"I get that. I don't intend to get even loose. This is my chance to find new clients, you know?" He was recovering from his ex-business partner Erik's bullshit, and he'd be damned if he let that fucker win.

"Yes. There's a good bit of crossover, from what the boss says. These guys are movers and shakers."

"It's a touch intimidating, but—" He shrugged, then he straightened. "But I have a business to run, so I'm going to shake hands, smile, and make all the contacts."

"Sounds good. I'll be the quiet, smiling, newly dating guy. Hold open doors and get you a drink kind of thing, huh?"

He liked this guy. He got where Liam was going and was a quick study. "Yes. Exactly."

"No problem." Terry grabbed his phone. "Give me the basics—girls' ages and name, pets, name of your business. That sort of thing."

Liam cracked up, but he had all that info. "Emily and Rose, almost nine and four. I have a shih tzu puppy named Daisy. I'm an architect, my business is Roaring Forks Studio. I have three tattoos—a tree, a chrysanthemum, and a rose."

"Nice." Terry gave him a genuinely appreciative glance. "What's the best thing about being a dad?"

"Watching them become everything they can. Em's so

fierce—competitive, determined, stubborn. Rosie's more creative, but she's got a temper and a half. She gets that from Sawyer." He chuckled, because even though both girls were biologically his, Rosie was Sawyer, to the bone.

"Yeah? You don't have the flashpoint temper?" Terry watched him, those brown eyes shrewd.

"No. I have the icy freeze-you-out temper, and I can say the worst thing at the worst possible moment, too. It's a charming character trait."

They both cracked up.

"Well, you seem pretty reasonable to me," Terry finally said when they stopped chortling. He sucked down the rest of his coffee. "Would you like another one? I think I might get one and a treat. I'll work out like a fiend, but it's worth it."

"I remember that's a rodeo thing. I mean, Sawyer is a roper, so it was never an issue for him, but some of his friends always had to be chicken breasts and egg whites."

Terry made a face. "Yeah. It's a thing. But we love the game, right?"

"That's the rumor. At least you're not losing fingers at an alarming rate." He winked over. "What would you like for an indulgence? I'll join you, and it's my treat."

"Hey, thanks." Terry chuckled. "It's always doughnuts for me. I saw they had maple logs."

"Maple log it is. And just a black coffee?"

"Yes, please."

He nodded and went up to make their order, including a chocolate croissant for himself. This was going surprisingly easy.

It was shocking, but cool. He could make friends. After Erik and Sawyer, it had felt like maybe he'd lost his ability to do it, and maybe his judgement as well.

The jury was still out on his judgement, he guessed, but he

was having a non-work-related conversation with another adult and enjoying it.

Maybe there was hope for him.

"Thanks. Can I call you Liam?" Terry asked when he sat down.

"Might as well. We need to be familiar, I guess. Practice for the big day. Assuming you're taking the job."

"Are you kidding? This one will be too much fun. My last job was mucking stalls in Glenwood."

"Oh, this is way easier. I'm totally a better conversationalist than a pile of manure." He winked, and a grin stretched his lips.

"Totally. And the smell is way less intense too. So, you're an architect? Is that like what you see on TV?"

"It's a surprising amount of math." That was the thing he found most people were surprised by. The sheer amount of math.

"So, it's not all blueprints and squinting manfully at work sites." When he raised an eyebrow, Terry laughed. "My sister was obsessed with watching old TV, and she loved *The Brady Bunch*. The dad was an architect."

The Brady Bunch? Lord. That was a throwback. "Ah. I remember watching the movie and cracking up. I do have a hard hat in my truck, but I have sunglasses, so...less squinting."

"Gotcha."

"So, what events do you ride in?" he asked. Terry's hands weren't all scarred up like Sawyer's, so not a roper.

"Roughstock. I suck at the bulls, but I ride both bronc events."

"Bareback is hard on a body. Good for you."

"Have you ever rodeoed?"

He huffed out a laugh that sounded way more like a snort and shook his head. "Not a chance. I can ride and rope well enough to be a help and not a hinderance on a ranch, and I love the critters, but I'm not an adrenaline junkie. I'm more of a constant, steady stress type."

He was going to turn into a diamond one day.

"I can see that. Just make sure it's not like a pressure cooker that makes you explode at some point." Terry bit into his doughnut, and his expression went almost sexual. "Oh my God."

He chuckled, tickled as a pig in shit. "Lord, man. You deserved that bite, if it made you that happy."

"Sorry." But Terry didn't seem sorry, his grin just infectious. "Yeah. It's so good." He polished off the doughnut in relatively short order.

"I—Thanks for taking this job, and you rock for making me comfortable. I'm actually looking forward to this thing now." Not because of anything but that it was going to be new, and he had company.

"Hey, I think you're a good guy, Liam. I was a little worried it would be weird too, but it's totally not. We'll make a splash, for sure." Terry shared a conspiratorial grin with him.

"Yeah. We will. So, tell me about your life, man. Do you love it? Rodeoing?"

"I do." Terry chuckled. "It's a young man's game, so I got to do it while I can. But it's good." He sipped his coffee, and it seemed like Terry was settling in for a conversation.

And it wasn't like he had anything to do before he picked up the girls but work.

Maybe he could play hooky for a bit and just... relax. It was good to know he could still be friendly.

To feel like the good guy for a change.

Chapter Seven

"Hey, now! You behave, Tempest!" Sawyer loved working the horses. Loved it. Hell, he lived for it.

Oh, he knew he was supposed to be all about the reining champ horses. And he did adore them, but they were like thoroughbreds, for all that the best breeds were the traditional working horses: quarter horses, paints, and Appaloosas.

But the bucking horses were his heart.

And they were cantankerous as hell when he had to bring them into the pen from the big-ranging pastures.

They didn't mind their jobs, and they loved being out to range, but they hated being rounded up and tried to make his life a living hell.

He was sure that was fair somehow, but he wasn't feeling that today.

"Come on, Lila. Let's get them in. I need to sort out a few of them. Tempest has a cut on her hock I need to cast my eyes on." He always took a chance letting the horses out to pasture like he did, since his land was a little less than manicured.

Injuries happened, and he checked every horse before they went to work.

"On it, boss." Lila whistled to the drovers, getting them all moving.

She was a solid hand, that one. He'd hired her on as a day worker a few years ago, and now she rode for his brand full-time, proud as punch. He admired her work ethic. And the horses trusted her.

That didn't mean they didn't kick and bite all the way to the big pen.

He waded in to catch Tempest before she got in the pen, grumbling under his breath as she tried to avoid him. She knew he had that halter in his hand, and she didn't want it. She wanted to be free and unencumbered.

"I need to check you out, sweetie. C'mon. We'll get you over and out, no sweat."

Tempest was gonna live up to her name today, he could tell. She tossed her head, giving him the flat ears and the rolling eyes.

"Look here, you. Don't make me bite you back." Like he could. Or would. He was talking and letting some steam off and the lid on his temper.

He heard Lila chuckle from outside the pen. "Need a hand, boss?"

"Yeah. Come distract her while I slip the halter on her."

"You got it." She started waving her hat, laughter filling the air.

He waited for Tempest to focus on Lila, ears and tail flicking, before he slipped the halter over her head. He was just thinking how well he'd done when Tempest lashed out with one hoof and cracked it right against his shin bone.

"Fuck!" He kept it at less than a shout, but he almost went down right in the middle of the herd.

"Boss!" One hand reached down into the mass of horse-flesh, grabbing him and hauling him up and out.

Tempest shied away, and he staggered, Lila half dragging him to the damn gate.

"You okay, man? You're about white as a sheet."

That didn't surprise him one goddamn bit. He felt pale, and the hurt, when it showed up, was going to be a stone-cold bitch.

His lips were stiff when he answered. "I need to sit, Lila."

"Sure. Come over here by the water trough. There's that bench." She helped him limp over and sink down.

"Bobby! Eduardo. I need Tempest caught."

"Yessir."

His leg was already beginning to swell, the calf pushing against the denim of his jeans, the shaft of his good work boots. Dammit, that wasn't great.

"You need to go to urgent care, boss?"

He gritted his teeth as everything started to throb. "I might need an X-ray." He hoped to hell she hadn't broken his damn shin.

"I'll get the truck. You sit." She knew him well enough to not even ask whether to call his momma.

"Thanks, lady." Jesus. His— shit. Shit, what time was it? He tugged out his phone. Okay. Okay, he needed to call Liam.

The girls were at school and daycare, and he needed to leave to pick them up in an hour. There was no way he'd be done, even if his leg wasn't broken.

Dammit.

Lila pulled up in the truck, and the maneuvering to get him in left him feeling queasy and sweaty. Lord. He was a cowboy, damn it. He needed to cowboy up.

"Sit tight, boss. I'll get you there."

"Uh-huh." He clicked Liam's name in his contacts.

It didn't even ring twice. "Sawyer? What's wrong?"

"I got kicked." He was fighting not to gag as the truck started moving. "Lila is taking me to urgent care, but I won't be able to get the girls from daycare. Do you think you can go get them, or do you need Momma to?" He knew Liam would rather pick them up, so he was giving him the first chance.

"I'm on it. No problem. How bad is it? Do you need clothes?"

"I don't know. I will...yes. Hopefully it's not broken, but something sure feels like shit." He had a bad feeling that somewhere in there a bit was cracked.

"I'll grab sweats and get the girls." The immediacy of Liam's attention made him shiver.

"Thanks—" He stopped the *babe* that tried to pop out. "I really appreciate it. I know you're busy as hell." He hoped Liam took that the way he meant it. In an olive branch sort of way. They had been at a point pretty recently where everything they said was like a spark on a pile of dry leaves.

"I'm not that busy. I'll be there in a bit. You're not driving, are you?"

"No. Lila is, but she'll have to head back to the ranch. We just rounded up the green remuda. I'll call Momma when I'm ready to come home."

"Okay. We'll deal with things in an hour."

"Yeah. I'm sorry, huh?"

"Like you asked a horse to kick you."

He had to grin at the irony in Liam's voice. He'd always had that way when stuff went wrong. He always made Sawyer feel like they were in it together. "True. I'll call you when I know something."

"I'll have my phone. Good luck." Liam hung up, and it still stung, the lack of an I love you. It hurt, but right now, not as bad as his leg did.

"Everything good?" Lila asked. "He getting the girls?"

"He is, yeah. And he'll bring me some sweats, so you can

drop me off and get back to the herd." He needed Lila there to tell the newer hands what to do. She knew his method.

"If you're sure."

"I am." Liam wouldn't let the girls swing in the wind. He knew that. And when it came down to it, Liam wouldn't leave him hanging, either, if nothing else because they were dads with shared custody. He was a good man, even if Sawyer wanted to say otherwise.

Hell, Liam had never even suggested he'd take the girls away from Sawyer. Not once. And Liam was their biological dad. At the time, he'd thought it wasn't important to him, that Liam wanted kids and he would have the ranch. But he'd fallen in love with their girls, and Liam had never doubted that.

Fuck, this hurt. His leg throbbed like some miniature dwarf hammering away for jewels.

At his balls.

In fact, it hurt from his left pinky toe to his right ear, just like a kick in said balls.

Lila pulled up in front of urgent care twenty minutes later. "I'll get a wheelchair."

He gritted his teeth. "I can do it."

"I'm getting a fucking wheelchair, boss. I don't need you making it worse." She hopped out and grabbed a transfer chair from right inside the door. She got him into it, then took him in so he could sign in.

"You need to get back, Lila," he said once he was sitting off to one side of the desk, waiting to go back to an exam room.

"Fair enough. I'll get the horses doctored. You call me if you need a ride back."

"Will do." He gritted his teeth some more, the sweat turning cold and hot in waves. Lord.

They got him back in relatively short order, and to X-rays

after that, and by the time he got back to his bay, he heard. "Daddy! Are you breaked?"

"Broken, Rosie."

"I said brokden, sister!"

"Well? Are you?" Emily crossed her arms and stared at him.

"Uh-huh. My shin bone is cracked." And wasn't that a damn bear of a situation?

"Oh, Daddy." She came to him and held his hand. "We brought you a pair of pants and house shoes."

"And Da bringed you a cookie and a coffee because you hurt."

Liam handed him an iced caramel latte and a slice of lemon pound cake without a word.

"Thanks." He needed the coffee more than he needed his next breath, and the lemon might not make him barf, so it was all good. "You all make it better."

"I'm sorry you hurt, Daddy. I'll make supper tonight. I can make sandwiches." Rosie went to touch his leg, and Liam caught her hand, thank God.

"Y'all might want to stay with your Da." He wasn't sure he could take care of the girls at home if he was laid up.

"Daddy! We're not babies anymore. We can help."

"My brave girls." They were amazing.

"Da says that he'll help us however we need him to, and we want to help." Em kissed his cheek. "It'll be okay."

"Thank you." He said it to the girls, but he also addressed it to Liam, who he knew was taking time off to help deal with this. "I sure didn't expect this today. Tempest got spooked."

"No one can expect accidents, right? That's why they're accidents." Liam shook his head at him, smiled at him, and it felt so damn right.

"Yeah." It was almost like old times, and for a moment he could let himself believe. But Sawyer knew better.

"Do you get a cast Daddy? Can we sign it? I'll help Rosie write her name." Em squeezed his hand. "How are you going to ride with a broken leg?"

"I don't know, baby girl. The docs will tell us all that." How was he going to get all his damn work done with a leg in a cast? He had a good crew, but he needed to put his eyes on his horses.

"I'll stay home from school and help, Daddy." Rosie patted his chest, her little eyes so very serious.

"Mmm." He glanced at Liam, appealing to his ex. He was always the voice of reason.

"I tell you what, I'll let you make Daddy supper, then I'll come pick you up tonight for bed, then tomorrow after school, I'll take you back to help again. Fair?"

"Can we take him breakfast too?" Em asked, and Liam sighed and nodded.

"I bet Granny can do that, honey. I don't want your da to have to drive all the way out here a million times, okay?" He would spare Liam that, at least.

"No. Da can. He said so." Emily nodded as if that was that.

Liam rolled his eyes.

"Well, Sawyer," the doc said as he came in. "You did a number on that shin. It's cracked."

"Does he get a cast?" Rosie bounced, so excited. "I readed a book about a little girl with a cast and her best friend drawled a sun on it."

"He can have a walking boot, but it will be pretty good-sized." The doc grinned. "But if you get a silver Sharpie, you can sign that too."

"Yay! Sister will write my name and I'll put a sun on it!" Rosie bounced and beamed. "Did you hear, Daddy?"

"I did." He gave the doc a look. "Do I get some Tylenol now?" He was about to throb apart.

"You do. You even get a Tylenol 3, if you have a ride home."

"He has a ride," Liam muttered.

"Yeah?" He glanced at Liam. "Cool. Then bring it on, Doc." He would have argued, but he needed that pain pill.

"Good deal. I'll get you booted up. You'll need to see the orthopedist in Aspen in a few days. It'll be about an hour, sit tight."

Liam lifted an eyebrow, that expression brooking no argument. "The meds first, please."

"Yes, sir." The doc gave a mock salute. "You're right, though. Meds on the way."

"Thank you."

Why was that so goddamn hot? Liam was so freaking... capable. Maybe it turned him on because for everyone else in his life, he was the one who had to do shit like that. Liam was the one who thought of him. Or had been.

No. No, he still did.

Liam knew that. Even if it wasn't as much as before, Liam cared about him. And Sawyer, well, he was still so deep in love he didn't know whether to scratch his watch or wind his butt.

"Can I sit on one of the chairs to do my homework, Da?"

"Yeah, honey. Get it done so you can make your daddy supper."

"Okay!"

"I'll sit with you, Daddy," Rosie told him. "Can I?"

"Uh-huh. Can you lift her up here, Liam?"

"Sure. You be crazy still, okay? Daddy's hurting bad." Liam lifted her up and carefully eased her down on him.

"Thanks." He wrapped an arm around her, keeping her on the side opposite the injury just in case she kicked.

"Here you go, Sawyer." The nurse was a friend of his mom's, and she seemed tired, but she was smiling. "Tylenol 3."

"Oh, God bless you."

"No problem. It'll ease things, so will the boot. Here's some water for you." She handed him the silly paper cup with a pill in it.

He sucked it down, then closed his eyes, leaning back against the backrest of the bed thing.

"You're lucky they didn't send you up to the hospital," Liam said quietly.

"I am. I'm glad. That's a much longer drive."

"Yeah. It is, and it's a crazy wait. It sucks that you're hurting. I'll ferry the girls for the next day so you can see them."

"You're a star, babe." He was so tired, and his head pounded. Rosie was like a miniature furnace against him. She always was.

"Shh...Close your eyes. I'm not going anywhere. I promise. You and Rosie nap."

"Okay." He had to let the rest of his worry go, because Liam was there, at least for now. Tomorrow he was sure it would go back to sucking, but for now, he would try to rest.

"Good man."

He chose to imagine that Liam kissed his forehead, easing him down to sleep.

Chapter Eight

Liam dragged himself out of his car. He'd been taking the girls up to Sawyer's every day to see him, but it was Sawyer's days now, and it was Friday night. Sawyer's mom was there to help out, so no one had to worry about Sawyer driving. That worked for him, because he could stay home for the weekend, get some work done, clean.

Try to get back the time he'd lost driving.

He didn't begrudge Sawyer the injury. Sawyer loved those horses, and he was good, careful. Animals had minds of their own, and that was part and parcel of the whole cowboy gig.

And Liam had to admit, he hated seeing Sawyer hurt. It didn't matter whether or not they were divorced, it sucked to be hurting, and the girls hated it too.

Still, he had a job and a life, such as it was, and he needed to... He looked at his office, which his condo sat above, and shook his head. Nope. He decided to wander down to the bistro that was only a block away and get some kind of comfort food.

Fries maybe. And a beer.

He was greeted by name as he walked in, and it felt amazing. It had taken an eon for people to accept him as a local, as someone who wasn't only going to stay until he got an offer in Seattle or LA.

"What's the special today?" he asked as he was seated.

"We have the chicken meatballs with creamy mustard sauce, the dip duo with guac and queso is half off, and the cooks are playing with trying out poutine." The hostess, who was talking about going back to school for landscape architecture, grinned. "How are you today, Liam?"

"I'm good. Really. I'll totally try the poutine. I learned to like it in Ottawa during an internship."

Holly led him to a table. "I applied to CU. Thanks for the recommendation letter. I appreciate it."

"No problem." He liked Holly, and he'd let her come into the studio and ask questions about being a startup versus joining an established practice.

He'd done both, with varying levels of success.

"I'll get that working for you. You want an IPA? We have one called Juicy Bits today, and it has a nice citrus base."

"Works for me, yeah." He settled in, running through his emails, his texts. There was one from Dare, with a picture of his growing family. Then Terry had texted with a picture of a sponsor shirt that was filthy and torn at the shoulder with a note that said,

work for the ball? :D

What a butthead. Liam did like the son of a bitch a lot.

There were a couple of work emails he filed under Open Monday folder, and then there was an email with the subject line of *Inquiry re Erik Mathers.*

Fuck. Nothing about his ex-business partner was ever good.

Liam had been so proud to be hired by the Greune firm,

and prouder yet to buy in, be a part-owner. Too bad Erik and he were at odds about literally everything from hostile architecture to cutting corners to personal politics.

His eyes widened when he read the email. No fucking way. Erik had put him down as a fucking reference for a job.

It had to be a mistake. Shit. What was he supposed to do? Ignore the email? Refuse to recommend? God, he didn't need this shit.

His beer landed on the table. "Everything okay?"

Liam nodded. "Just a work email. Nothing major."

"Ah. Well, you give 'em hell." Holly also put a water down for him. "That poutine will be up in no time."

"Thanks, lady. I appreciate it." He grinned and just hit reply.

> I'M SORRY, BUT I NO LONGER WORK WITH MR. GREUNE, AND I CANNOT SPEAK TO HIS WORK ETHICS. THANK YOU. LIAM MCMARTIN.

There.

Done.

The urge to call Sawyer and tell him about the nerve of Erik using him as a reference was huge, but he was divorced, dammit.

So he texted Terry.

> Seriously? That's way too fancy for the ball...

Three dots appeared, then a laughing 'til you cry emoji. He sent back,

> bows

"Liam! Hey." Fallon Jackson, one of the local contractors he knew, stopped by his table. "How's it going?"

He stood, without spilling his drink, thank you very

much, and shook Fallon's hand. "Good. Good, I've been running my butt off. How's it for you?"

"Busy as a one-legged buttkicker." Fallon shifted from foot to foot. "Look, I don't like to stir up trouble…"

"Oh lord…" He waved to the empty chair at the table. "Have a sit and talk to me."

Who was being an asshole now?

"Thanks." Fallon pulled out a chair to sink into. "So, Erik is telling everyone y'all are sending business each other's ways. Like if there's a job you don't want, he has your blessing and approval."

He felt his lip curl, and there wasn't a damn thing he could do about it. "No, sir. Not even a little. I'm not working with him. We're not on good terms." Not even the tiniest bit.

"Well, I didn't think so. But one of my junior guys mentioned it yesterday, so I was going to come by to see you. I don't work with him at all anymore."

"Well, he's full of beans. I won't recommend him. We're diametrically opposed." He didn't do hostile design, he didn't believe Aspen was only for the uber-rich, and he wasn't interested in cutting corners.

"I'll spread the word." Fallon was relieved, that was written on his face. "I mean, there's a lot of folks who would use him, but I'd prefer to work with you."

"Good deal. You know I like working with you, man, and we have a good relationship. I don't want to mess that up."

"Ditto."

"Oh, hey, Fallon. Did you want something?" Holly put the poutine in front of him. Everyone said she was the hostess, but she always waited on him personally.

"No. No, I was just having a chat while I'm waiting for Sarah. No worries."

"Well, let me get you a table and I'll send her back when

she gets in." Holly winked at Liam, then led Fallon away, who lifted a hand as he rose.

"See you later, man."

"Absolutely. Kiss Sarah for me." He stared at the poutine, trying to decide if he even wanted it now.

God, this nightmare with Erik was never going to end, was it? Not if he didn't leave the valley, which he refused to do because of the situation with the girls.

Erik had been everything he'd thought he'd wanted to be—respected, successful, well-known—but it had been on the backs of slimy business deals and cut corners, and when he had figured it out, he'd been convinced it was simply a mistake.

It hadn't been a mistake.

An audit had proven they weren't compliant on three jobs with either safety or ADA requirements. Then there had been the park reno downtown with the no-sleeping-here-you-bums benches, and finally, the gay people shouldn't be allowed to adopt that explained why he and Sawyer had stopped being invited over for supper when Emily was born.

Which didn't make sense, because Em and Rose had been carried by a surrogate, but whatever. It still made him blind with rage. How many broken homes had straight parents been responsible for over the years? And it made his business partner a bigot, to him, all of a sudden.

Erik always had been, he just hadn't known it.

He hadn't been able to take it, so he'd left, after turning Erik in to the ethics commission.

A text popped up on his phone, and he was afraid to look, especially since it was from Sawyer's mom, but it was a picture of the girls painting Sawyer's toenails, his toes hanging out of the walking boot and toeless sock thing they'd given Sawyer in case his feet swelled. That image put a smile on his face and restored his appetite.

He sent back a quick,

ty. So. Cute.

He did love how those girls made him feel as if everything was worthwhile.

Well, that and Daisy. And a good IPA. And poutine.

Which was pretty yummy, after all.

Chapter Nine

"Why on earth would he put those girls in their fancy-assed Easter dresses to come to a damn egg hunt at the ranch?"

Sawyer sighed, his leg throbbing as he hobbled over to the window to peer out at where Emily and Rosie were embarking from Liam's Escalade. Emily wore a turquoise dress that was like one of those 1950 poodle things in the skirt and had a sweater a few shades lighter that went over it. Rosie wore pink, her raven's wing hair and freckles really set off by the color. It was... sparkly, too, shot through with silver glitter.

"Momma, you know Liam had nothing to do with what they're wearing. Neither one of us have since Rosie turned three. You be nice." The girls chose their own clothes these days. Period. And they were both wearing cowboy boots.

He limped to the porch, the damn boot better than a cast and crutches, at least. "Hey. Thanks for coming all the way out to drop them off," he told Liam, who was carrying backpacks to the house.

"Of course. Happy Easter." Liam handed him a card attached to a bar of ruby chocolate filled with passionfruit. It was his favorite, and the gesture meant…well, it meant the fucking world.

"Granny! Look at my dress!" The girls ran inside with nothing but quick hugs for him.

"Thank you. Uh. Do you have someplace to be, or did you want to hang out for the hunt?" He had to ask. Had to.

"No. No, this is for you, and you have your family here. How's the leg?"

"Sore. But better." He knew it was healing because some days it absolutely itched like crazy. That was always a sign of healing, in his experience. And he wanted to tell Liam he had been Sawyer's family, but he wouldn't believe it.

"Good. Happy Easter. I— The brisket smells great."

"Yeah?" He grinned. "I'll send some home when you come to get the girls if you want." He loved smoking stuff.

"If there's any left. Do you need me to pick them up for school Tuesday morning? They have Monday off."

Were they having a conversation?

"Would you mind? Momma is leaving for Denver Monday midday." Look at them. Wow.

"Of course. I'll be here at seven thirty Tuesday morning."

"I really appreciate the extra effort." Good thing he had to hold onto the porch rail for balance, or he'd be reaching for Liam.

"You'd do the same for me." Where had Liam discovered this new, Zen attitude? It was as if Liam was…at peace.

A pang hit him right in the center of his chest. Fuck, he wasn't there at all, and for a moment, he had the crazy urge to shout at Liam, ask him how he dared. But he let that shit go fast. "I would. I guess I should let you go, huh?"

"Yeah. I'm going to meet Darin in Vail for the night. Have a few drinks. Chat." Liam shrugged. "He needs to meet Daisy."

"Sure." Daisy. Lord. "Gordie and Hammy are out with

one of the hands. I bet they sniff around for you for an hour."
Those heelers missed Liam.

"Aww...they're good boys. I miss their faces."

I miss you. He did. Like a sore tooth. Like a third of his life was missing. But what was he gonna say? Bring Daisy out for a playdate?

"All right. I'm off. Enjoy my babies. Don't let them eat all the candy."

"I won't. They'll have to work for it." He watched Liam go, his heart hurting all over again.

"Daddy! Granny says we can't wear our dresses to hunt eggs." Em came out, putting her feet down hard.

"Why not? Will they not wash?" He knew better. Liam always bought machine wash, even if it was line-dry.

"Of course they wash," Em and Liam spoke together.

"Da, why are you still here?"

"I'm just about to go meet Uncle Dare. I was just telling Daddy about some things." Liam came to the foot of the stairs. "Give me kisses."

"I love you, Da. Tell Uncle Dare that we can't wait to meet the new baby."

"Another baby?" Didn't any one of them have a brain in their head?

"They say it's their calling." Liam rolled his eyes. "You heathens be good."

"Promise, Da! See you Tuesday!"

Liam lifted a hand, heading back to the car, and Sawyer looked at his girls. "So. Eggs."

"Yay! Eggs! Are we going to have Easter baskets too?" Rosie jumped up into his arms, damn near toppling him over.

"We totally are. Granny even got me one." He did the dance of the wounded bear, keeping them upright, mainly by bouncing off the porch rail.

"Rosie! Daddy's foot!" Em pulled Rosie off. "Don't break him again!"

"Oh! Oops. Sorry, Daddy." Rosie shimmied down, all hangdog. "I didn't mean to hurt you."

"I'll be just fine. I'm just glad you still love me," he teased. "Come on! We got chocolate to find, though I just promised your Da not to let you eat too much."

"Da won't know," Rosie explained. "We won't tell."

When he came in, Momma glanced up from where she was making mustard potato salad. "Y'all were out there a bit."

They had been.

"Liam dropped off the girls. I wanted to make sure it was okay with him, coming to get the girls."

"Granny! Chocolate."

"I know. We'll get there. We're waiting on some of the hands' families, ladies. Gemma and Leo Oliver are coming."

"And Kacey and Monie?" Rosie liked the kids who were more her age.

"Yes. And there are a couple of teenagers too."

"Yay!" Rosie twirled, her little dress floating out as she spun. "I like to have other kids."

"That is kind of the sucky thing about Da's. There's no kids except at school."

"You go to the community center," Sawyer pointed out. Still defending Liam.

"There are trampolines there!" Rosie started bouncing, right there on the kitchen floor.

"Rosie, I am trying to cook," Momma snapped.

Rosie stared at his mom, eyes wide. "Sorry, Granny."

"Em, can you take Rosie to the den and get your baskets and all?" Sawyer asked gently.

"Sure, Daddy."

When they were out of the room, he glanced at his mom. "You're in a shit mood."

She scowled, opening her mouth, but then sighed. "I just don't feel very well today, son. I have a terrible headache."

"You want some Tylenol or something? I have sinus pills." He hated that she was hurting, but that wasn't a good enough excuse to snap at his daughters.

"I'll take them. Maybe the sinus pills will help. I'm sorry, son. Can you take over here for a minute? I'll go tell Rosie I love her."

"Sure. Sure, just breathe, Momma. Everything is going to taste amazing."

Sawyer would bet it was sinuses. They could do a number on a person. He headed to the cabinet above the sink where he kept a little box of meds and pulled her out a sinus tablet blister pack.

He stirred in all the spices for her salad, then peeked at her list to see what else she needed. Pea salad. He could get that started.

Em wandered in, barefoot now, her curls escaping her French braid. "Granny's loving on Rosie. Can I help? Why's everybody here mad? Did you fight with Da outside or something?"

"No. No, your Da and I had a good chat. And Granny is just really not feeling good. I got her some sinus pills out. Do you want to get the peas out of the freezer and the ham out of the fridge for me?"

"Pea salad!" She laughed, grabbing stuff for him, including the cheese.

"That's right. We need onion and celery, mayo."

"Da bought light mayo. It's not nice."

"Ugh. No, I bet not. Better to just eat the real stuff in moderation, right?" Sawyer had to grin. Liam went on these kicks where he ate all healthy, and then binged on gooey yummy stuff.

"Yes. He's working out. He says he's getting a belly. Silly Da."

"Mmm." Did that mean Liam was ready to start dating? Sawyer might just curl up and die. Lord help him. "Well, if he needs to work out, he can come help with horses, huh?"

"He likes the horses. He always asks about Peaches." She handed him the bowl he pointed out.

"Yeah? I know she misses him." Horses were so damn smart, and Peaches still hunted for Liam, even after over a year of him being gone.

"He misses her too. He says, if he'd thought—" Em stopped, shaking her head. "It doesn't matter."

"You can tell me, kiddo. I promise I won't get mad." He knew she worried about telling tales and him and Liam fighting.

"He just says that if Peaches hadn't stayed here, we might have bought a house with room for her, but since she belongs to the ranch, he couldn't bring her to live with us."

That was the truth. Their marriage had come with a prenup, and what belonged to the ranch, legally belonged to the corporation. It hadn't been set up specifically to deny anything to Liam; it was just set up the way it had been for a couple of generations.

Protect the land.

And God knew his momma could meddle. That had been one of their problems, and a big reason Peaches had stayed right where she was. She was determined to protect what she considered Sawyer's birthright at all costs.

"Legally, that's true,"

"But she's his horse, right?" Em tilted her head.

"Yes. And he can come ride her anytime."

"I wish he wanted to."

"Me too, kiddo," he admitted to Em. "And there isn't a lot I can do about that."

"No? Can Granny?"

Fuck.

"Okay, here we are, ready to make stuff." Momma brought Rosie in, who was wearing her little jeans and a T-shirt that said, *We all know I'm hilarious.*

For once, his mom's timing was great.

"We started the pea salad, Granny," Em said.

"Oh, thank you, my loves." Momma beamed at them.

"I'll go change into jeans. I'll be back." Em's voice was flat, not angry, not really, more...disappointed.

He watched her go, biting back a sigh. Damn it all. He hated that Em was unhappy, but he couldn't say anything, especially about the dress or— No, you know what?

"Did Da get pictures in your dresses, Rosie?"

Rosie bounced once, then shot Momma a glance and stopped. "Uh-huh. We all dressed up together and took pictures with our baskets and our bunnies and even Daisy had a fancy bow and a fuzzy chickie! We wanted to show you how pretty we looked, but Granny said we'd just get dirty, and you'd saw us."

"No reason to ruin your pretty clothes, right Rosarita?" Momma asked.

"Uh-huh."

"Well, I think you're the two prettiest girls on earth. So thank you for wearing them so I could see." He didn't ruffle her carefully done hair, though the urge was strong.

"You're welcome!" She gave him a smacking kiss. "Can I stir?"

"You can." He did love that she was still his sunshine. Em was so much more complex with her emotions.

It took a good half an hour before Em came back out, wearing an old sweatshirt and a pair of shorts. The sweatshirt was about as long as the shorts, but he wasn't going to mention it.

"What can I do, Daddy?"

"How about we go decorate the porch, huh?" There were pastel streamers and a couple of inflatables he hadn't gotten around to putting out, and she would love to help him with something like that.

"Sure." Her shoulders moved under that huge sweatshirt, and he led the way out, opening the big bunny that would light up pink and blue and get almost six feet tall.

"The streamers can go on the railings, kiddo. And the balloons."

"Okay, Daddy."

They worked together for a few minutes before he glanced at her sideways. "I'm sorry about the dress, kiddo."

"It's okay. It doesn't matter. I have two lives. That's cool."

"I'm not sure it seems all that cool." He wanted her to believe she could talk to him, but was he just encouraging her to bitch about stuff? God, he felt like he was in a minefield half the time.

The other half, he was fumbling around in the dark.

She stared at him, her bright blue eyes sharp. "I miss when we all used to hang out together and do stuff like go riding."

"Oh, baby girl, I miss that too." That was the God's honest truth.

"Then why are you and Da not together anymore?"

"Well, we've talked a little about that." He'd explained how he'd made some dumb mistakes and hurt Liam's feelings, as he called it, so bad that things couldn't be fixed. And he knew Liam had explained that he'd worked too much, and how the situation with his job had been so bad that it had made him want to fight all the time...

She flapped a hand. "But you still love each other so much. I can see that! And you love us."

"Never doubt that for a minute, kiddo. Not one little bit."

"Then I don't understand!" She crossed her arms and stared at him.

"I don't know how to fix it, Em. I'm sorry." He knew that absolutely wasn't good enough, but it was the best he could do right now. "Okay, plug me in, huh? I still need to do the big blow-up egg."

"Okay." She sniffled, but she was being super brave, and he loved her so much right then it hurt his chest.

"I love you, Em."

"I love you too, Daddy." She came to hug him. "Happy Easter."

"Happy Easter. Now let's sneak a piece of chocolate before everyone gets here."

"So that's it? You love each other, but we're all just going to be divorced anyway?"

Ouch. "Sort of, yeah."

"Boys are *stupid*." She rolled her eyes, seeming so much like Liam. "Let's finish decorating. Easter's almost over, and Rosie's excited."

"Okay, Em. Sounds good." He wasn't sure how, at eight, she wasn't excited about Easter, but he wasn't sure he could fix it.

He just had to keep struggling on and praying he did this right.

Chapter Ten

"Da! Come on!" Em called out.

"I'm coming!" Liam shook his head as he locked the car. "God save me from demanding daughters."

"We have to get your suit for the ball! I think you should wear blue."

"Blue? Not black?"

"No. A vest and a white shirt. Something that makes your eyes big as saucers."

"'Big as saucers', huh?" That sounded very... anime. "I guess that could work." Em had very definite ideas about what she liked in fashion, for her and for him. She'd given up on Rosie.

"Yes. And fancy boots. Not plain work ones. *Fancy*." She twirled, beaming at him. "Oh, and a hat. A gray felt."

"You've given this a lot of thought, honey." He had to grin at her.

"It's your first big party, Da! You have to sparkle, but in a boy way. That's the hat and boots." She opened the door to the western wear store, "Come on!"

He chuckled. "I'm coming." He did love walking into a cowboy haven like this one. The smell of leather smacked him in the face, and the racks of Wranglers and Stetsons seemed to make a guy travel back in time.

He hadn't been into cowboys until Sawyer had walked into his life, but he was hooked through the balls now, and there wasn't any going back.

"Hi, there. How can we help you today?" The lady who came out from behind the cash wrap to ask that was very sparkly in the Aspen sort of way. Boots, a suede skirt, and a fringed top with cut-outs in an intricate pattern paired with a bunch of silver and turquoise jewelry screamed let me sell you a pair of three hundred-dollar boots.

"Da needs an outfit for the big cowboy ball!" Em's excitement was a tangible thing.

"Oh, well, now. You came to the right place. Let me show you our formal wear area, and then you can holler if you need help." She led them to a side area with racks of men's jackets and pants, rows of hats lined up along the wall.

"No jacket, Da. I like the vests. They're snazzy."

Snazzy? Seriously? Was that even a thing?

"Well, we have to remember this is business too, baby girl. I need to come off as serious enough for people to want to hire me."

"But kinda artsy too, Da. You're not like, a cattleman. You're an architect." She waved a hand like that was that, dammit.

"You're too grown up for your own good, baby girl. Now, let's pick some things out, and I'll try them on. Fair?"

"Totally fair." She bounced some more, beaming. She did love to shop. "I like this one here, it's silky and neat."

The collarless white shirt had dark buttons, and he wasn't sure, but he'd try it on for Em. It did have a look to it that he kinda liked...

The vest she picked out was also pretty cool. Maybe this would work.

He put the clothes on, and he surprised himself with how sleek and trim he came off. It was western without being rodeo, interesting without being gaudy. He kind of loved it.

Emily clapped her hands. "Da, you look amazeballs."

"Em, I sort of feel amazeballs!" Now he needed boots. "Gray boots, baby girl?"

"Uh-huh." They headed for the boot rack. Once he had those, he went to pick out a hat. Even if he wasn't super cowboy, the hat was mandatory at an event like this.

"Gray felt, please, ma'am, with a pinch front."

All the adults in the store stared at his incredibly sure, smart, amazing girl.

"Whatever the lady says." He would give her this. He loved the pride in her expression.

"What size?" The saleswoman eyed him. "Let's try this." She plucked a glorious hat off the rack to hand to him.

"Oh, Da. Da! You look like a movie star!"

He bowed, giving it all the drama he could with his sweeping arm, and Em applauded.

"Do my eyes look big as saucers?" he asked.

"No, but they're so blue. I would go to this ball with you even."

"That's high praise."

She nodded. "I know, because I am a good dancer, and you are...whoa, Da."

"Yeah, yeah, yeah. There will be no dancing. Networking, making a good impression."

"But what if someone asks you to dance?"

"We'll see." No. He felt like his dances still belonged to Sawyer, and that was his shit to work out, not some stranger's.

Besides, he'd have a date who knew he wasn't a dancer.

"Uh-huh." She crossed her arms, her head tilting.

"Oh, don't give me the Granny Canton stare. I can't bear it." He grinned to soften that a bit.

"Uh-huh. You did good, Da. I'm proud." She grinned at him, green eyes dancing. "Now, go change back."

"You in a hurry?"

"I don't want you to get it all dirty."

He knew that line too but wasn't going to say it. He went to change, and they boxed and bagged up boots, hat, and clothes.

"You ready for lunch, girlfriend?" he asked.

"Yes, sir! Can we have tacos?"

"Have I ever said no to tacos?" That was like saying no to air, to breathing.

"Nope." She boogied. God, it was great to see her in a good mood.

They put the stuff in the car, then headed for their favorite Mexican place. Las Montanas had all kinds of tacos, and he loved the chicken tomatillo monstrosities, while his girl could get her crispy beef.

"Thanks for your help today, baby girl."

"You're welcome, Da. You want to cheers?"

He grinned and raised his iced tea glass. "To us?"

"To us!"

"No, Daddy! Come on. We need to go to the store in Aspen. Not the Boot Barn." Em waved him toward town instead of toward the highway that would take them to Glenwood Springs.

"Baby girl, that place is expensive."

She gave him an arch look, one so like his momma's that it

hurt. "Daddy. It's not like you don't have money. This is important."

"Ugh." He took them into Aspen though. This was her daddy and daughter date, right? He parked as close to the western store as he could, then grabbed her hand to walk to the shop.

"Help me balance, huh?"

"I've got you, Daddy. Don't worry. I was thinking dark gray or black for you. A jacket."

"Yeah? But not those shiny, weird pants, right?"

Now her expression changed to one of horror. "Oh, no, Daddy. Good Wranglers. Dark wash, cowboy cut."

He chuckled. She knew her shit.

"I'll wear my best boots and hat, okay?"

"You mean your best boot, Daddy."

"Right." He scowled at the boot which was decidedly not cowboylike as they walked into the store. "Ugh. Yes. Looks like I won't be dancing."

"You could, just nice and slow is all."

"Do you think there are slow dances at the ball, sweetie?" She made him grin, all the time.

"It's a ball! I saw it on that show. About the Regency ladies."

"Tell me you did not watch *Bridgerton*." His momma had, and there were a million naked butts.

"No, Daddy. Um, it was Sandytown."

"Huh." He would look that up on his phone when she wasn't watching. His Regency knowledge was pretty damn deficient. "Well, cowboy balls tend to have two-stepping."

"Still, that's dancing. We like standing on one foot and swaying, right?"

"We sure do."

"Can I help you folks?"

"Hi, Cassie. I'm Emily. Do you remember me?"

The saleslady grinned wide. "I do. What are we doing for dress-the-cowboy today?"

Sawyer shot Emily a curious look, but she just soldiered on.

"He needs a western cut jacket, please. In black. And he needs a bolo tie."

"Of course. For the ball?"

"Yes, ma'am." Em beamed. "And a white button-down. And those fancy wrist buttons."

"Oh, I like that." Cassie the saleswoman pulled out some shirts and jackets for him to try on. "And what size on the dark wash Wranglers?"

"You read my mind!" Em clapped, happy as a pig in shit.

"Thirty-thirty-four," Sawyer said.

"Daddy's tall."

Sawyer snorted, keeping it soft so as not to hurt her feelings. "Thank you, honey."

"You are." She grabbed his hand again. "Come on and try these on."

"Yes, sweetheart." Demanding girl. It made him a little dizzy. But he clomped after her, and he stepped into the dressing room to try on the shirts. The jeans he would just buy. He knew what fit, and he wasn't dealing with the damn boot.

He hated the stupid thing.

"It will get better soon, Daddy."

He glanced at Em. "I know. I'm just not used to being laid up."

"Yeah, but you're a cowboy. You've been hurt a lot. You could lose a finger!"

"I could, I guess. Good thing I'm a pretty good roper, huh?" What do you think of this one?" He held up a shirt.

"I like the fancier one but try them both." Emily sat as he tried on the first shirt, and she shook her head. "Nope. Try the other."

"Okay." He tried on the one she liked, and she went all sparkly on him.

"Yes! Now put that jacket on."

"This one?" He teased, picking up an awful camo one he'd grabbed as a joke.

"No. Ew. The black one." She tapped her foot and waited, which made him want to hoot.

If he could, he would tape this, to watch it over and over, but he guessed his job was to pay attention. She was on a roll.

"I like this one, kiddo," he told her. The cuffs went all the way down. The shoulders fit like a glove, but they weren't too tight, and he liked the single-button style and the black-on-black embroidery.

"I do too, Daddy. It makes you all handsome and classy." She turned her finger in a circle. "Let me see the back?"

He spun so she could judge him from that side too, dutiful as all get-out. She was cracking his shit up.

"I like it. You're like a rodeo champion. I like it very much."

"Aw, thank you, sweetie. Do I need a new hat?" He had said he'd wear his good black one, but she was having such a great time.

She lit up like a Christmas tree. "Oh. Oh, we should look. First the tie, then we'll decide, okay?"

"Okay."

"I brought a selection." Cassie came over with a velvet-lined tray holding four bolo ties, everything from a simple silver arrowhead to a fancy-ass turquoise thunderbird.

"What do you like, baby girl?"

"None of these. We need a green stone, please. Is there a green one?"

"Would you like to come with me and look? That way your dad can sit a moment." Cassie gave him a wink, and there was a little padded bench in the dressing room, so he plopped right down.

His phone buzzed, Morgan's name popping up.

U ropin 2day

Nope. Still got the boot on and I'm shopping with the eldest

fun fun. she excited about a daddy/daughter date

she's ordering me around like a drill Sergeant

Man, Sergeant was hard to spell. He should have gone with SGT.

LOL! Good deal. You deserve it, man. enjoy

He could hear Morgan laughing at him.

You better look good for this shit too

Stunning. Promise.

Uh-huh

"I found it, Daddy!" Em came running back to show him a really nice bolo with a black, braided leather string, silver caps and a silver setting, and a polished piece of malachite set in a natural shape.

"Wow. I like that one, baby girl."

"Me too! Try it on so I can see?" She bounced, so much like her sister, all of the sudden.

He pulled it on over his head, then pushed up the slide so it laid along the placket of the top button of the shirt.

She turned his face, one way and the other. "Perfect. Very nice. You like it?"

"I do."

"It goes with your eyes."

"My eyes are hazel, kiddo."

"This makes them more green than gold, Daddy." Now she was back to duh face.

"Oh. Okay. That works for me. Hat?"

"Let's go!" She dragged him out, still in his finery. His decent but far from new jeans seemed pretty shabby in comparison, but he looked good, he had to admit.

Her face wrinkled up. "New band? Is that a thing?"

"It is." That could work. "We can totally get me a new hat band. And I can get my good hat steamed and blocked."

"Oh, that's cool. That's frugal and really classy too."

"'Frugal'?"

"Yes. It means good with money. I learned it at Girl Scouts."

He went all dramatic and wide-eyed. "How in the heck do you have time for Girl Scouts and gymnastics and all else you do?"

"You know, Daddy! Girl Scouts is at the community center, so I can do that and then swim with Gracie." She grinned. "After all, you were the cookie dad, and we're going to camp this summer!"

"We are." He loved to tease her. "I should be healed by then."

She frowned, that worry in her lived right under the surface. "Did the doctor say it was still bad?"

"No, baby. I'm just being a turd. It seems like it's taking forever."

"It's only been four weeks. I've been marking the days off."

"Why?"

She shot him a grin. "Da says that your leg will be all weird and skinny and super hairy, and I want to see."

"Oh, man. That's mean." But true. Not as bad as if he was in a cast-cast, but still. He was wearing a wrap and a heavy walking boot.

"Da says it happened to his arm when he was a little boy. He said it was stinky."

"Yeah, but I don't have a hard cast, so it'll be less gross."

Her face fell. "Bummer!"

"I'm sure it will still be suitably gross. So is this the outfit?"

"It is."

What had he done to deserve his girls? "Okay. Let me change, and we can go have lunch. what do you want today?"

"Tacos?" she asked, grinning like the Cheshire cat.

"You and your tacos. You're on." He liked the enchiladas at the place she wanted to go to.

"Yeah? You getting enchiladas, Daddy? Can we have chile con queso?"

"We can. You know I never say no to that. And yeah. Chicken and green chile, huh?"

"Da gets tomatillo tacos." She wrinkled her nose. "Sour."

"Mmhmm." Liam loved tomatillo sauce. "He loves that weird stuff."

And Sawyer loved the taste of it on his lips.

"He does. But I like crispy be-eef."

"Are you folks going to La Montañas?" Carrie asked. "We have a coupon."

Emily beamed. "We are! Can we please have the coupon, ma'am? Oh, and can we have a fancy sock for Daddy's sticky-out toe boot? We don't want people to gossip."

"You got it." Carrie winked at him, chuckling all the way

back to the cash wrap, and he and Em followed. Sticky-out toe boot. God help him, he'd never call it anything else.

She made him laugh, and he knew he was lucky to be able to have this sort of day. They would become further and further apart. She was already so busy, and as she got older, well. Eventually she would be a teenager, God help him.

"You're going to be great, Daddy. It's a good outfit."

"Thanks, baby girl. I'm happy you got to come pick it out for me." He handed over his card once they were all totaled up, and then they were off to lunch.

They settled in their booth, and he ordered an iced tea and a Sprite for them. She bounced to the music that always seemed to be playing in her head, grinning a little.

"What's so funny, missy?"

"I love this restaurant. Da brought me here on our date. What did you do on your date with Rosie?"

"We went riding, and then we headed out for ice cream. Your sister will take sweets over tacos anytime, you know that." Rosie wanted whipped cream and sprinkles.

"Ice cream is cool." Em giggled softly. "Cold even."

"Icy." He snorted with her, laughing at her wild laughter as it started up.

"You two are having too much fun." That was the server, and he knew her by this point but couldn't remember her name to save him.

"My fathers always have fun with me," Em pronounced, eyes dancing.

"They do! Crispy beef tacos?"

"Yes, ma'am. And this daddy will have beef picadillo enchiladas, please!"

"Chips and salsa."

"Please. Sorry, uh…"

"Erin."

"Thanks, Erin."

"Anytime." She grinned at them. "I'll bring the chips. Be right back."

Em lifted her glass. "You want to cheers, Daddy?"

He grinned and raised his iced tea glass. "To us?"

"Yes, sir. To us!"

Chapter Eleven

Liam met Terry outside his studio the night of the ball. The hotel was within walking distance and, even if it weren't, it wasn't worth sixty dollars to park. They could Uber it for a quarter of that, if they needed to. He simply didn't see the need to waste money. He'd rather just give it to Terry, to be honest.

He applauded as Terry walked up, seeming for all the world like an all-around champion. "Don't you dress up nice?" he called.

"Why thank you." Terry gave him a slow once-over that managed to be flattering but not weird or skeezy. "You look pretty snazzy yourself. I like the hat."

"Thank you. My eldest picked it out." He smiled, tickled as all get-out. "The whole outfit, in fact."

"She has good taste. You said they were both girls, right?"

"I did. Good memory." He fell into step next to Terry. "So, what have you been up to?"

Terry made a face. "Digging fence post holes for a tiny ranch outside of El Jebel." He shuddered. "That's crappy work."

"It is. But it gives you great muscle tone."

"Yeah, yeah. This is going to be way more fun."

"Lord, I hope so! If I'm less fun than digging holes, I'm in real trouble." The last few weeks, he was beginning to believe he might be okay, he might be someone folks wanted to see.

"Oh, I bet you can be damn entertaining." Terry gave him a sideways look. "And I'm supposed to act real interested right?"

"Yeah. I mean, I'd take attentive and focused. I don't even know if he's coming. He cracked his shin. He may stay home."

"Mmm." Terry didn't sound convinced. "This is a big deal for the cowboy who gets invited. Even a rich one. It's usually more about visiting businessmen and movie stars. He'll be here."

"Well, so am I, but I'm here to make a great impression and to hang out with a...new friend?" Who he happened to be paying to be here with him.

"Hey, I know I'm on the payroll, but after this is over, I am totally willing to go for coffee and pay my own way. Or, you know, tacos."

He had to laugh. "Em loves tacos."

"She's the one who picked out the outfit.?" Terry asked.

He nodded. "Yep. Rosie would insist on a fuzzy coffee and a doughno, as she calls it."

"Oh, that's charming as anything."

"She's funny. She wants to be her sister's age, so badly." And Liam loved that she was her own bubbly person.

"But you want her to stay slow and steady, huh?"

"God, yes. She's at such a good age. I mean, Em is just as amazing, but they're so different." One was light and airy, and one was deep and a pure mystery. He was a lucky bastard.

"Spoken like a true dad. No taking sides."

"Well, you'd have to meet them, but they are like chalk and cheese. Completely separate, but both so damn cool."

"That's awesome." Terry stared up at the hotel with a hint of awe in his eyes as they approached. "Always thought it would be neat to stay there but could never afford it."

"Right? It's fancy-pants." It wasn't Sawyer's vibe, and they tended to stay in a more mid-range hotel, no matter how much money they were making. His man wanted to spend money on different things.

"It is. But it will be fun for a night, right?"

"Especially since we don't have to park." Because that was an unreasonable cost.

"God. It can be murder down here."

They got to the door and headed in, Liam showing his invitation.

"Oh, fancy." Terry glanced around. "So very."

He leaned in to murmur, "So much studded leather and woven wool and felt hat."

"Right?" They grinned at each other, and damn, he was glad he was here with someone he liked. "Banquet room?" Terry asked.

"Yep." He laughed when Terry offered his arm but took it.

The room was full, and they walked around the outside, searching idly for their table, for the bar.

"There it is." Terry nodded at their place settings. "I'll go grab us a drink. What would you like?"

"I'd like a light beer, please. I'm easy to type." He just didn't want to stress it.

"You got it." Terry held his chair, a true gentleman, then headed off.

He sat there, glancing about, curious to see if he recognized anyone, if he had any clients attending. There were so many people moving, shifting around. He and Terry had been a little early. He hadn't wanted to be seen walking up, though. Walking home? Sure. They could write that off as too much beer and needing fresh air.

A few folks nodded, one lady he recognized from the Chamber of Commerce raising a hand, but as yet, no one seemed inclined to come chat. People were too busy seeing and being seen.

It was fine, because he'd be doing the same thing soon. He needed to get off his new boots for a few before he got going.

"Here we go. Light beer." Terry returned with a Coors Light and some kind of a dark lager. The bar was included in their ticket, so he didn't have to worry about it. He would reimburse Terry for any tips he left.

"Thank you. I appreciate it." He lifted his glass. "To a successful night."

"To the best night ever," Terry agreed, and clinked their glasses together.

He grinned, but he knew that was probably so not true. His wedding night with Sawyer. The days his girls were born…

Liam felt a terrible pang at all the water under that goddamn bridge. So he kept that smile on and nodded. "You know it."

There was no way this was even going to be in the top hundred days, but it was going to be fun and lucrative. He'd made up his mind.

"Liam! So glad to see you." A barrel-chested man in a big boss of the plains-style hat and a pair of boots that cost more than the rent on his condo stepped up beside him. Hank Bell was a mover and shaker in Aspen, and he offered a hand to Liam, smiling broadly.

Boom. He'd evinced his will to the universe.

He stood and shook hands. "Mr. Hank. Good to see you! How's the world treating you?"

God, don't fuck this up.

"I'm doing well. Doing fine. Look, I heard you had to hang your own shingle. Is that true?"

He kept eye contact, made sure his posture was solid and

straight. Pun intended. "Yes, sir. I have my own studio now, and I'm really enjoying the creative freedom."

"Well, good for you. I know the last little while has been hard." Those shrewd brown eyes sharpened. "Listen, I have a project I want to talk to you about." Hank handed him a card. "Give me a call on Monday."

"Yes, sir. I'll be happy to. Enjoy your evening. It looks to be a good one." Oh, fuck.

Fuck yes.

He wanted to pump his fist and whoop like the world's biggest redneck, but he didn't. He smiled and nodded and was polite and Zen as anything.

"You too, Liam." Hank clapped a hand to his back and was off.

"Is that good?" Terry asked, smiling.

"That is amazing. Seriously. That is the best plan."

Terry lifted his beer, and they clinked. "Cool. I'm tickled that you already have a line on something."

"I should have introduced you..." Shit, where were his manners?

Terry waved one hand, dismissing the thought. "Dude, he didn't seem interested to meet me. It's no biggie. I promise."

"I still feel bad. Pinch me next time, hmm?"

Terry chuckled, eyebrows gyrating as if they had minds of their own. "You got it, boss."

"Hush." He took a pull of his beer, his nerves jangling, but in a good way. In fact, they kept on at high alert, because before they rang the triangle to tell them dinner was about to be served, three more high rollers stopped by to check in with him.

Hoo yeah.

Liam was soaring, overwhelmed by his good fortune. He grinned at Terry and blew the man a kiss. "You're a good luck charm."

"You think so? You just wait until the dancing starts." Terry's eyes twinkled, and he chuckled, his cheeks heating a little.

"I haven't danced in so long. I hope I remember how." He hoped he could figure out who was leading.

"I bet you're a natural."

"The ex always said I was." His cheeks heated again, but for a totally different reason. He and Sawyer had danced all the time, and it had often led to shenanigans.

"Well, then. You gonna let me lead?"

"Sure. I'm all over it." Terry raised his glass.

He had to nod, because he never had. Sawyer had taught him to two-step.

The servers started coming around, serving plated dinners with big, fluffy potatoes, some sort of green bean thing with almonds, and steaks. Enormous steaks.

"Now that's worth the price of admission, huh?" Terry asked.

"Yep." Damn. That was a mountain of food. "This is some damn fine beef."

They dug in, making conversation with a young starlet on a sitcom with her manager, a celebrity chef and her wife, and one of the cowboys he knew from Sawyer, but whose name he didn't remember.

The guy was kind enough not to ask.

He couldn't see Sawyer anywhere, but that didn't mean he wasn't in the room. There were a ton of tables, and the din was kind of amazing.

Still, it didn't matter, did it?

Sawyer would see him, or he wouldn't, but everyone would see he wasn't simply spinning his wheels but had moved from the new architect with the rotten boss and suspicious husband, to a man with a new business, a new lease on life. Dammit, he was making his way.

And if it was lonely, well, Terry was interested in a beer now and then. Or a coffee.

Friends. He needed a few who didn't know Sawyer, who he could be new and fresh with. New. No preconceived notions.

Their plates were whisked away at the end of the meal, and dessert came around, along with coffee.

"Damn. This is the life." Terry dug into the cheesecake.

"I would have thought you had to be careful so you could ride."

"Not tonight. I figure, how often do I get to pig out? That steak was so well cooked... Now, I googled the regular menu here, and thank God for catering. They want twenty bucks for some cooked cream with hay in it."

"Hay? Like dead grass?" He could cook cream, he guessed.

"It said "hay infused panna cotta"." Terry shook his head. "I've eaten my share of hay by accident. It ain't yummy."

"Yeah...I mean...Just give me chocolate." That was his vice. All the chocolate.

"The cheesecake is nice."

"Mmm." He didn't love the sour. But the coffee was damn good.

"Do I have to order you a chocolate sundae after?" Terry teased, and he was tempted to flip the man off, but this wasn't the place.

"Nah. I have a big Cadbury bar at home, just waiting for me." He did wink.

They had to sit through a couple of boring speeches over coffee, but then the meal was over, and the real party went into full swing.

"You want to come and dance, Liam? We're here. We might as well cut a rug."

"I say why not?" Liam rose as Terry did, letting Terry take his elbow and tug him out to the dance floor. It was like he'd told Em. This wasn't exactly slow dancing, but they had a nice waltz. It wasn't romantic, but it was…pleasant.

He liked Terry, he liked moving, and he liked feeling as if he was good at this. And Terry did let him lead, which was cool, because he might have killed them both if—

"Who the hell are you?" The dance stopped on a dime, Sawyer right there as if he'd come out of a column of smoke.

Terry's eyebrow lifted, lip curling. "What's it to you, man?"

Oh, lord.

"His husband." Sawyer's voice was as hard as he'd ever heard it.

"Ah. The ex." Terry chuckled, the sound as dangerous as it was soft. "Don't make an ass out of yourself, man."

Liam stood there for a minute, just stunned into silence. Sawyer wasn't a fighter…not like that.

"Make an ass out of myself? No one waltzes with him but me." Sawyer's cheeks had gone a dull red.

"Maybe not before, but he's dancing with me now."

There was no way this was happening. No way on earth. He turned to Terry. "It's okay. Come on. We'll go have a drink."

"Unless he hits harder than a two-thousand-pound bull, I ain't worried." Terry's slow grin was insulting as hell and pointed right at Sawyer. "And you said he's a roper."

"Oh, you son of a bitch." Sawyer hauled off and popped Terry right in the nose.

Terry didn't even flinch, in fact, all he said was, "You want me to clean his clock, Liam?"

"I'm going home." This wasn't…he hadn't wanted to…

Fuck him raw.

"I'll take you." Terry put a hand under his arm, steering him out through the throng of watching people.

His hands were shaking, and he couldn't quite catch his breath.

"Well. I guess that worked," Terry said.

"I guess it did." He was a fool. What had he been thinking? "Let me get you an Uber."

"I can walk you, Liam." Terry chuckled. "Unless I'm bleeding."

"No, but you are bruising up. Do you get hazard pay?"

"Nah. That was awesome." Terry grinned then.

"God save me from cowboys."

"Yeah. It's too bad you like the type."

"No shit on that." He wasn't ever going to date again. "Come on. I'll get you a bag of frozen peas."

"As long as we get you chocolate."

Oh, yeah, he could handle that. After this stunt, he was going to need it.

Chapter Twelve

"Well, that went great."

Sawyer looked up from where he'd dropped his head in his hands, glaring at Morgan, who'd been there for every craptacular technicolor moment of him losing his shit and punching Liam's date. They'd gotten the hell out of town and run down to Zane's Tavern in Basalt, which was open until two, which might be enough time for him to figure out what the hell to do. "You are not helping."

"No? I mean, it wasn't exactly tapping on a shoulder and cutting in…" Morgan was just barely keeping his shit together.

"I said, hush."

"Nope. You said I was not helping. You know your mom will have heard about this by now."

"I know." His phone had buzzed several times, but since none of the texts had mentioned the girls, he'd ignored them. "What was I thinking?"

"That someone else was getting a piece of Liam's ass?"

"I am going to hit you next."

"Then why do you keep asking me these questions?" Morgan said. "You know I can't resist."

"Yeah, yeah." Sawyer sighed. "What am I going to do? I have to be able to get along with Liam for the girls' sake."

"You're going to have to apologize, man. He didn't look like it turned him on."

No. No, Liam's entire body read embarrassed, ashamed, and desperate to escape. Not turned on. And Sawyer couldn't blame him. He'd acted like an idiot, and a violent one at that. He'd just... he'd lost it. And he'd never done that before. Boiled over until he couldn't hold it in.

"I can't just text, though."

"No, you need to show up in person."

"How? I mean, I can't just go in while he's working." He lifted his head all the way and threw up his hand, his knuckles stinging like fire.

"Make an appointment? Go over there tomorrow? He doesn't have the girls until Monday, right?" Morgan shrugged. "You want to go over now?"

The question made him stop short. "I kinda do."

"Okay." That was a quick agreement. "I'll drive you. And I even have mints in the truck. You don't want to show up with whiskey on your breath."

"Some date I turned out to be for you."

"Are you kidding? I'll eat out on this for weeks." Morgan's eyebrows went up and down.

"He just...he looked amazing, man, but the dances are supposed to be mine."

Morgan watched him, eyes quiet, focused.

"I know. It was jealousy that—"

"No."

"No?" Sawyer stared back at Morgan, lost as fuck.

"No, you never believed he was cheating on you. I was around then, you know. You were feeling unloved, sure. And ignored. But not jealous. So, you need to be very clear when you go talk to him, or he's going to just write you off."

"Jesus. You hit hard."

"If nothing's changed, why should he even hear you out?"

Sawyer's chest clenched. "You're right."

"Listen. You love him. He dropped everything when you got hurt. He brought you food. He drove the girls to you every fucking day. You two need to...you need to fucking talk to each other."

"We have!" They had, and it hadn't mattered. Liam had said so.

"No, I think you talked *at* each other. You need to apologize, and you need to listen. Or you need to let him go."

"I don't want to let him go."

"Then fight for it." Morgan slapped his hand down on the table, drawing a few stares. "You're a cowboy. We don't just give up."

"I'm scared I'll lose my girls," he admitted.

"Bullshit. You're scared you won't get him back." Morgan never let up. "You know he never so much as threatened to take those girls from you. Not once."

"Morgan."

"Are you gonna sit here?"

"No. No, take me back to town." He threw a couple of twenties down and pushed to his feet, his shin aching. "I need to see him."

"I can do that. I'll even grab a hotel room in town in case you need to head back to the ranch."

"Thanks, Morgan. Really."

"Don't thank me yet. This will be hard." Morgan got him into the truck, got them moving. "He's pissed, and it's late."

"Yeah."

But he knew Liam. Liam would be up and pacing, livid.

Thank God the kids weren't there.

Morgan drove him into Aspen, and he reminded himself to breathe. There was no more pep-talking. Just a quiet, "Good luck. I'll be at the Durant."

"Lord. At least stay at the W. Tell them to put it on my bill."

"Oh, I can totally do that." Morgan winked. "Call them and let them know, and I'll even let you out of the truck."

So, he set up a room for Morgan—even though they'd said it was full until he told them who he was—who let him off at Liam's place, and he limped up the stairs to the condo above Liam's office.

The lights were on, the music was too—Ed Sheeran, which was so Liam—the sound bleeding through the door.

Shit.

Sawyer took a deep breath, then went ahead and knocked. Morgan was right. He owed Liam an apology, and he owed them both talking about this shit full out, not tossing things at each other and running. That had been jealousy. That white-hot hurt feeling he'd had tonight. Before had been about feeling neglected. Like they weren't together anymore, even if they were.

It had been about hurting and not knowing what the fuck to do about it. It had been like clouds, not fire.

He knocked, hoping he didn't get the door slammed in his face the moment Liam opened it.

Liam yanked the door open. "What do you want? Why are you here?"

"I need to talk to you, Liam. Please. I— can I come in?" He knew Liam didn't have anyone there. Not with Ed Sheeran on the speakers.

"You want to make sure, what? That I'm alone? I am. But it doesn't matter! We're broken up!"

"No. No, I want to apologize. I was way out of line, and I'm sorry."

"Yay." Liam started to close the door. He didn't grab for it, but he made a plea.

"Liam, please. Can we actually talk about something? This? You deserve a real apology. An explanation."

"I am—do you know what time it is?"

"Eleven thirty. You weren't in bed. Please, Liam. Please, talk to me."

Liam stared at him, bright blue eyes serious as a heart attack, then he turned and simply walked back into the condo.

But he didn't shut the door, so Sawyer followed him inside, breathing a sigh of relief that he'd gotten over the first hurdle. That wouldn't be all there was to it, and he knew better. But he felt a spark of hope.

He closed the door and stood in the living room, trying not to twitch.

He'd never been in here, and it was fascinating, how different it was to the home they'd made at the ranch.

The ranch still had the decor it had always had — his grandparents', his mom's. Liam's house was cozy, but classy, filled with warm Santa Fe colors, lots of maple wood.

"I'm not offering you a drink, but you can sit."

"Thanks." He took another deep breath and limped to the couch. "I appreciate it." It was way easier to think off his feet the way he was throbbing, but that was his own fault for rushing over to hit some guy he'd never even seen before

Some cowboy who took the hit without even flinching. The son of a bitch had to be a roughstock rider. Had to be.

Liam didn't sit. He stood with his arms crossed, staring.

Right.

"I'm sorry, Liam. I was completely out of line. I lost my shit, but there's no excuse for it." That was a good start.

One eyebrow rose, arching right up into Liam's hairline. "You're right. There's no excuse. This was a business outing for me. I was—God, all they're going to remember is the two of you fighting!"

"I never thought. And I know. I should have. I just—" He took a deep breath, trying to organize his thoughts. Something told him this might be his one last chance to really get Liam to listen. "Look, I knew— I've known all along that you didn't step out on me. I was hurting and casting about for a way to get back at you. And I'm so damn ashamed of that. But seeing you with someone else tonight, dancing with him… That told me how I would have felt if all the shit I was unloading on you was true, and I just boiled over. I'm not proud of it, but it sure put things into perspective."

Listen to him, using his words.

Liam stared at him, and Sawyer could sense the war bubbling inside that brilliant mind. Liam didn't have a poker face, never had, and Sawyer saw fury, agony, shame, and a few emotions he didn't recognize and was fairly sure cowboys didn't have.

After an eternity, Liam sat in one of the dining chairs without saying a word.

He'd take that as a win.

He took a deep breath, determined not to babble. Morgan had told him simply to tell Liam the truth. "I still love you. I know that might not count for a lot. A bunch of divorced people still love each other. But I can't— It's not working. Trying to get past you."

Liam stared at him, shaking his head. "Why now? Why pick a huge, fancy party for this?"

"I didn't pick it." Sawyer spread his hands. "Shit, Liam, I even knew you'd be there. It just never occurred to me that you would go with someone, or that it would hit me that way." He was just gonna lay it out.

"Well, I guarantee it won't happen again. Thanks for the apology."

His shoulders started to stiffen up, but he pushed them down. "Don't do that. Don't just dismiss everything and shut down."

"I'm not!"

He stared at Liam until his gaze dropped.

"Okay, fine. I just—I don't know what to say. You tell me you accused me of cheating on purpose? You broke my fucking heart, Sawyer."

"I know." He did. "At the time I would have said it was because I thought that." Sawyer sighed. "No matter what I say I know I was a dick. And I've been trying to let you go, because you deserve to be better off without me. But dammit, I can't."

"Why the fuck were you a dick, though? I was underwater everywhere!" This wasn't quiet or unemotional, not at all.

"Because I was alone all the damn time. Because I felt like nothing I did was right. Because you were so damn miserable. I wasn't real self-aware, but I sure was pissed off." He sighed, shaking his head. "I mean, I've had a lot of time to think about it now."

"I was miserable. Erik is a fucking asshole, and he's dangerous. I was trying to contribute to our family, start our life, and everything was falling apart."

Dangerous?

"Dangerous how?" He needed to know this. How did he not know this?

"It doesn't matter. It's not your problem anymore."

"Liam." He thought about invoking their kids, but he didn't. "I worry about you."

"He's an evil son of a bitch, and when I refused to cut corners, he started on the attack. I know I told you some of this." But Liam hadn't told him all of it. Clearly not.

"Tell me?" He made it a request instead of a demand. Maybe that would make Liam less defensive.

"He's an asshole, and I caught him cutting corners and suggesting hostile architecture. When I called him on it, he informed me that there were no poor people in Aspen. Then he started the rumors about me sleeping around, hoping to 'bring me into line'. The whole thing is ridiculous. Childish."

"Holy shit, b—Liam. I didn't know. I mean, I thought he was a dick because he was jealous of how much more talented you were."

"To be fair, a lot of it happened while we were so rocky, so you didn't know." Liam said grudgingly. "But I thought you were buying his hype."

"He brought it up to me more than once, and I told him he was full of shit. And I didn't let that get to me at all. It was us being apart so much."

"I'm not like you. I didn't start with a functional business. I feel like I've been—" Liam's lips clamped shut.

No. God, no. They were finally saying things to each other.

"Feel like what?" He was an impatient bastard, but he wanted to listen. He needed Liam to tell him shit.

"Running to keep up from the second I met you."

"What?" Wait, what? What had brought that on?

Liam held up his hand, ticking off points. "You have a ranch. You're an amazing horse trainer. Your mom thinks you hung the moon, and never let me live it down that I wasn't quite as amazing enough to be with her beloved son. You didn't go into business with some asshole who tried to cheat you out of everything."

"Hey. I— I know the ranch is a lot. But it's not even totally mine yet. I mean..." He stopped at the expression on Liam's face. "Okay, that was hella defensive. But I've always admired you for making your own way."

"I don't feel admirable. I feel tired."

Sawyer stood, holding out his hand, trying not to sway on his booted foot. "Then you should get some rest. Seriously. It's late." He had a lot more to say. A lot more to hear. But Liam was deflating like a balloon, so he knew he needed to let the man go to bed. It had been a shit night, and that was on him.

Liam didn't stand but took his hand. "It's midnight. Do you have your truck out there?"

"No. Morgan dropped me off. He's a roper friend of mine. Gave me a stern talking-to."

"Then what? You're going to walk home?" Liam shook his head. "I don't think that's very decent."

"Well, I'm not sure how many more hotel rooms there are downtown, Liam. I can get an Uber." He should have just called Morgan to come right back and get him, but he didn't want to. He squeezed Liam's hand. "I'll figure it."

"No. No, that's... You can stay here. You can't just...no."

"Babe."

"No. You can have the couch—" Liam blinked down doubtfully at his boot. "You can have the bed."

"I can sleep in Em's room."

"And have her bitch about dad smell?" Now Liam's mouth curved into a tiny smile.

"She would, but I don't want you to be uncomfortable."

Liam blew his lips and stood. "Let me grab you some sweats."

"Thanks." Relief made his knees weak. It was like Morgan said: Liam had to care if he was still willing to be so damn good to him. Sawyer could work with that.

They would figure it out, one way or the other, dammit.

He headed down the short hall to Liam's bedroom, and the scent there was so familiar, so very right. He breathed in deep, wanting to hold it in his lungs. Inside him. Sawyer did love that lemon balm and musk smell.

"Take your boot off. These were yours. They ought to fit." Liam passed him a pair of old, gray sweatpants.

He blinked, biting back a grin. "Did you steal my ratty old sweatpants, Liam?"

"They were in some laundry, so you gave them to me."

"Oh, that definitely qualifies. The girls give me shit all the time," he teased. "Pink socks. Tiny tank tops."

"Yes. Itty bitty jeans." Liam smiled, and the expression was warm, happy.

"Millions of hair doolies." The girls didn't lose shoes like they did when they were toddlers, but they sure lost hair things.

"Lord yes. Glitter. Glitter everywhere." That smile. That smile offered to *him*. The girls were something they agreed on. They both loved them with a single-minded ferocity.

"Do you want a T-shirt?" Liam was in a sweatshirt and a tiny pair of workout shorts.

"Uh. Yeah." He didn't need it. It was plenty warm in the condo, but he wanted Liam to feel comfortable, not like Sawyer was coming on to him.

"Sure." He was handed a soft, well-worn shirt that smelled like his lover.

He was gonna spring wood. But that wasn't what this was about. This was about being here. What did the therapist his mom went to call it? Being present.

He needed to prove to Liam that he was trustworthy, that he was learning.

So he changed into the clothes in the bathroom, leaving his stuff folded on the chair by the hall to the front room, his one cowboy boot under the chair.

"Do you want a bottle of water or a juice, Saw?"

"I'd love some juice." The tart and sweet would be great. "Is there anything I can do?"

"No. I'll grab you some juice."

"Hey, where's your puppy?"

"Daisy? She's at the dog sitter's. She's not ready to be on her own, you know?" Liam's voice faded as he headed down the hall.

"Ah. Yeah." And he would bet Liam had been too mad and tired to go get her. Or he didn't want to deprive the sitter of her check. He could see that too. "I'll have to meet her sometime."

"She's a hoot."

"Cool. I wonder if she would play with the ranch dogs."

"She'll have to grow some yet." Liam chuckled. "And I'm not sure which one would be more jealous. She's a Da's girl."

"That doesn't surprise me. You inspire loyalty."

"Ha." Liam came in with a glass of juice and a bottle of water. "Here you go. I'm going to crash on the sofa so you can rest your foot."

"Hey. No. I mean, I don't want to be all weird, but there's no sense in that. Unless you suddenly decided to be a monk and go to a single, your bed should be big enough for us both. No hanky-panky."

"It's big enough. I just don't want to hurt your leg."

"I sleep in the boot. I'm way more likely to kick you." Sawyer rolled his eyes. "Not fun."

"You'll be careful." Liam put the water on the far side of the bed and slipped under the covers.

"I will. I won't move, most likely." He was so damn tired. But he wouldn't hurt Liam again for the world. So he would be dead-careful. "Do you usually sleep in the middle?"

"No, Saw. I can't seem to figure that part out."

"Me either." He took the side of the bed he always had and settled in, smelling the sheets, he hoped surreptitiously.

"They're fairly clean. I didn't expect company."

The urge to go, not even the roughstock rider, was huge.

That was an asshole thing to say, so he didn't. But he thought it, and not without a measure of satisfaction.

"I'm not worried about your sheets. I like how they smell."

"Oh." The glance he got was surprised, and maybe a touch pleased. "Oh, good to know."

"Yeah. I always have. Liked the way you smell." Sawyer sighed. "Your pillows are for shit, though."

"You kept the good ones." That was dry as dust.

"Oh." He chuckled. Liam always was faster than him with a comeback.

"You're a turd, you know? Hitting my date. Terry is a decent guy. You'd like him."

Unlikely. Truly unlikely.

"Uh-huh." He kept the sarcasm out of it, but yeah, no. He'd maybe blown that bridge right up. "Where'd you meet him?"

"I—at the coffee shop, the first time. It was just a business arrangement. I had an invite, and he was free that evening."

"Well, I'm sorry I ruined it, babe. I really am. And if I see him again, I'll apologize to him as well. I'm ashamed of myself."

"I wanted you to wish you were with me, but—" Liam chuckled and shook his head. "It backfired on me."

"Shit, babe. It made me nuts." He snorted a little. "But you always did do that."

Watching Liam all dressed in his finery, dancing with another cowboy had been like waving a cape in front of a maddened bull. And he knew he'd been a dick. He'd probably be in the newspaper tomorrow. Lord help him. But he wasn't the kind to wake up and choose violence most days.

"I wanted you to not be able to take your eyes off me." Liam sighed softly. "I bet your date was pissed."

"You were stunning, babe. And Morgan was pissed, but

mainly because I screwed up so bad. He's a buddy I met roping. Not a date-date."

"No? I—cool." Liam snuggled down in the bed, turning off the bedside lamp. Sawyer tried not to sigh, because it was over, this chance to talk, to try to connect, when Liam spoke. "How mad is your mom?"

"I'm avoiding her until tomorrow morning. So I know she'll have a good head of steam by then, but I just can't deal with her until then." Sawyer had let her calls go to voicemail and texted her that he was staying in town tonight.

"Yeah, she's busy with the girls, so you're safe for a few hours."

"I am. I can hang out and sleep. And my date got a nice hotel for the night, which is way better than sleeping in his horse trailer RV."

"Yeah." Liam turned his head to peer at him in the darkness. "I've—this has been the weirdest day."

"It has." Impulsively he pressed a kiss to Liam's cheek. "Get some sleep, babe. I'll be good, huh?"

"Uh-huh. Sleep." Liam inhaled and let the breath out in a long, slow sigh.

"Yeah." He watched Liam, because he hadn't been here, in this situation, in more than a year, and he didn't want to give it up.

But at some point he did close his eyes, and that was all it took. He fell into dreams in a heartbeat.

Chapter Thirteen

Liam hummed and snuggled in to the warm body next to him. God, his head hurt. Maybe a migraine. But the heat and feel of Sawyer made things better.

It had to be Saw. No one else smelled so damn good. Maybe he would stay in this dream and not get up and let the headache tear at him.

Except that he wasn't on his side of the bed being all quiet and shit. He was wrapped around Saw like an octopus or a vine, cheek on the fuzzy chest.

That was going to be a problem.

"Morning, babe." Saw nuzzled the top of his head. "How are you feeling?"

"I have a headache, and I want to cry because I have to wake up." That was as honest as he knew how to be.

"Well, we can hang out for a bit. It's Sunday."

"Yeah." But they couldn't simply stay here. He had been drooling, he bet, and he had a piss hard-on.

"You're getting all tense." Sawyer started massaging the back of his neck, a motion guaranteed to ease his headache. The man had a knack.

"I'm in bed with my ex-husband, and I have an erection. It's a bit of a situation." In fact, it was wonderful and awful, all at once.

Why was he in love with Sawyer? Why couldn't he fall in more than like with someone like Terry?

Possibly because you already have the cowboy you want? That little voice in his head was so sarcastic.

"Mmmhmm. I kinda like it." Sawyer wiggled a bit closer, if that were possible.

"This is a mistake." But Sawyer's body knew his, and he loved the way they moved together, fit together.

"Is it, though? I don't know, babe." Sawyer kissed his temple. "I think it might be the best idea we've had in a long time."

"It feels—I need—fuck, kiss me." Who was he kidding? Sawyer knew how to touch him, knew how to make him come, and he wanted it. Now.

Sawyer moaned, then kissed him, lips and tongue finding his with hot intensity. The need was immediate, like gasoline and matches.

Part of his brain was insisting this was monumentally dumb, but most of him was insisting no one had ever made him come so hard in his life. Only Sawyer.

"I love how you taste," Sawyer told him. "Damn, babe." Then he dove back in for more kisses.

He whimpered, straddling Sawyer, pushing into their kisses, tongue-fucking his lover with all he was. He was so damn hungry, not just for touch, but for this touch. For this man.

"Babe." Sawyer gasped the words out, hands on his ass, squeezing his cheeks.

"Uh-huh." He didn't want to talk about it. He wanted to get off.

Sawyer rubbed them together, cock hard against his. That

was almost enough, but not quite.

"Too many clothes, Saw." He yanked his shirt off, letting Sawyer see him, his new six-pack, his hunger.

"Uh-huh." Sawyer took plenty of time exploring his chest and belly before pulling off his own T-shirt. "Need help with the pants."

"I can do that." He scooted down the bed. stripping his own shorts off before attacking the man's sweats.

"Easy," Sawyer warned when he got to the boot.

"I won't hurt you."

"I know. I do." Sawyer was watching him like a hawk, but not with worry. No, this was all heat.

"Good. I just want to make us both feel good."

"You only ever made me feel good when you touched me, Liam." Sawyer yanked him back into place as soon as he crawled up that body again, their cocks rubbing together.

"Fuck." His eyes rolled, his lips dropping open in pure lust.

"Uh-huh. That's the idea. Do you have stuff, babe?" Sawyer stroked his cock, hand traveling up and down. It felt so good it took him a full thirty seconds to form words.

"Nightstand?" He thought. Lube, for sure. "No condoms. Haven't been...you know."

"Neither have I. I keep stuff for when I jack off, but that's it."

"Not even with your buddy?"

"God no. You?"

He shook his head. "It's not like that. Not at all."

"Good." Sawyer sounded altogether too satisfied for his own good.

"Asshole." He grinned, then leaned to grab the lube, because Sawyer was on the bottom and injured, so it was unfair to expect too many acrobatics. Liam wanted to save those for him.

"I think I'm dreaming," Sawyer groaned. "I don't ever want to wake up. Ever."

"We don't have to think about that." He didn't want to think about it.

"We don't. Jesus, babe. I want you so bad. Open the lube for me. My hands are full right now."

And Liam could feel that. One was on his ass, and the other was on his dick. It felt so good he wanted to go on this ride endlessly.

He managed to get the lube open, his heart going ninety to nothing. Liam panted, handing it over when Sawyer let go of his ass, hoping that Saw could take it from there. He heard the crazy little squirt noise, then hot fingers coated in cool gel pushed between his ass cheeks.

He opened his mouth to ask again if Saw wanted this when Sawyer's fingers stroked him, just like he needed it. His legs tried to draw up, but he arched his back instead, pressing back into those probing fingers.

"Hot. So damn tight, too."

"Been so long," he moaned out the words, his muscles fighting, then loosening.

"I got you. We'll make sure you're ready," Saw said.

"Okay. I—Please don't hurt me." He wasn't talking about his body. He was begging for his soul.

"I won't." Those green-gold eyes met his, that gaze serious as a heart attack as Sawyer dipped a finger inside him, going deep, opening him up. "You got my word. I'm going to make you fly, babe."

He wanted to believe it. He wanted to fly. So he bore down and let Sawyer in. Those fingers worked and moved and got him wet, his muscles massaged open, and then Sawyer pulled free to lift him.

"Gonna be inside you now, babe."

"Fuck yes. I need…" *You. I need you, you fucking amazing bastard.*

"You got me." Sawyer arched and yanked and grunted and arched and the tip of that hard cock slid inside him, making him moan, because nothing else in the world felt this good. Nothing. Sawyer's lips parted, and he huffed out a hard breath. "Fuck yes. Perfect."

'Uh-huh. Oh, God." He sank as low as he could, taking Sawyer in. He had to grit his teeth against the need to come, and he clenched, letting Saw have him.

Saw bucked underneath him, driving them together. He was going to feel this for days. And that was going to be both good and devastating, and he knew it.

It didn't matter. This was a fantasy for Liam. He needed to believe, right at this moment, that Saw needed him. Cared for him.

Loved him still.

"Where'd you go, babe? Stay here. Stay with me." Sawyer cupped his jaw, eyes focused.

"I—I'm here." He nodded, smiling at Sawyer because he had to. Because he was flying.

"Good." Sawyer winked at him, then dragged him into a fierce kiss.

He threw himself into it, really pushing down and grinding with his hips, his whole body on fire. Sawyer answered each and every motion with thrusts of his own, filling Liam with that heavy cock, and that was what he craved.

"Fuck, yes." He braced his hands on Saw's chest. "That's — more."

"Definitely more." Saw grabbed his hips and yanked hard.

He grunted, rocking back and forth, giving them both heat and friction and the most perfect fucking thrill. Sawyer rolled up to bite at his chest, freaking all teeth and cock, and it was enough to send Liam right over the edge, his shout ringing in the air. "Fuck yes."

Sawyer's expression was pure need, and it sang in Liam. Sawyer thrust a few more times, then answered with his own jets of wet heat, filling him so deep and hard. He could have cried, it was so good.

"I have you. Fuck, you feel just right." Sawyer reeled him in, held him close.

"I—"

"Shh." Sawyer stroked his back as he came to Earth. "It's okay. Me too."

"Mmhmm." He had to think. In a minute. Not yet. He was still having random muscle spasms.

Sawyer chuckled, nuzzling under his ear. "Damn."

"Tickles..." His eyes crossed, and he fought the urge to giggle.

"Mmm—" Sawyer's phone rang, jolting them both. "Dammit."

"You need to get it?"

"It's my mom. Just let me make sure it's not about the girls." Sawyer grabbed the phone. "Hello? Is everything— No, I texted and told you I was staying in town. No. It's... Well, if they're still asleep, then what does it matter? Uh-huh. I'll be home later this morning. No. Not now. Mom, please. Okay, bye." Sawyer sighed as he hung up. "Lord."

"Yeah." Awkward. He pulled himself up and off Sawyer's cock, heading for the bathroom. God, seriously?

Sawyer's mom had fucking radar. *Is my son's dick in some-one? Yes? Fuck, I'd better call.*

"Hey." Sawyer followed him. "I'm sorry. I just needed to make sure nothing was wrong."

"No. Of course. I just..." *Didn't ever want anyone to be able to sound so calm with his cock in my asshole?*

"Just what?" Sawyer came to put hands on him, rubbing his shoulders.

"It's always your mother." That just popped out. "Always."

"Liam."

"No." He spun around. "Don't *Liam* me. I get that you have to make sure our kids are okay, but your mom always seems to come first."

"I'm sorry."

"What?" Liam felt a little deflated at that. Sawyer had never apologized without a "but" before.

"You're right. When I put my mother before you that wasn't fair at all, and I'm sorry."

"Oh." Okay, weird, but also pretty cool, when you get right down to it. "Thank you. Seriously, thanks."

"I know it's not like, all hunky-dory and everything, but it's important." Sawyer dropped a kiss on his nose. "Did you want me to clear out, or should I hang out for breakfast?"

"I have frozen biscuits?" he offered. "And the best coffee."

"I could stay." Sawyer grinned, reaching past him to turn on the water in the shower.

"Is this weird?" Did people do this? Have affairs with their exes?

"Maybe a little, but I'm willing to go with it. I've decided just to be honest with you. I want you. So I'm willing to give you space if you need it, but if I can stay for breakfast and a shower, I will."

"You can stay for a shower and breakfast." He didn't want to say no.

Not at all.

"Good deal." They stepped under the spray together, and Liam decided he wasn't going to think too hard about this right now.

He could always overthink it later.

Chapter Fourteen

"**W**e're going to eat lunch with Da-a-a."

"Sheep say baa-a-a," Emily teased her sister.

"I know that."

Sawyer grinned, because their chatter always made him laugh.

"Okay, hooligans. You got all your bags?"

"Yes, Daddy," they chorused.

"Where are you and Da taking us?" Em asked.

"We're going to make pizzas." The girls loved their local pizza place. It let children make their own pies, with chef's hats and all. It was friendly and easy, and he didn't worry about the kids making a mess.

"Oh! Really!" Em's eyes lit up. "Rosie, come on! We can make pizza!"

His mom stopped to stare at him as she came out to tell the girls goodbye. "You're going to lunch with Liam?"

"Yep. We're meeting him for pizza." *Don't start, Momma.*

"You mean your ex. The one whose date you punched at the Cattleman's ball. That Liam?"

"Yep. That's the one." He stared her down, daring her to say anything else.

"Son…"

Nope. No. This was a chance to get back what he wanted, and he wasn't losing it.

"Momma, I need you to butt out." The girls were putting their stuff in the truck, so he didn't worry about them hearing. "I know you mean well, but I listened to everyone too much when it came to Liam. Now I listen to me."

"This is a stupid mistake. He broke your heart."

"Yeah." And he'd broken Liam's. He knew that. But there was still something there, right? Even if it was simply friendship, there was something there. "Doesn't matter."

"If it's about the girls."

"Momma, what did I say?" he snapped. "I don't want to get into this."

"Fine. Just remember when you're crying in your beer that I warned you. You two are gasoline and matches."

"We are. And I'm ready to light the fire again."

"Ready, Daddy!" Em called.

"Coming!" His girls were excited, and so was he, so they were on the way. "Are y'all ready to pizza?"

"Oh, yes!" Rosie bounced. "I want pineapples."

"Ugh." Em gave her a look.

"Hey, it's make your own. You don't have to eat Rosie's."

"I know. I'm just playing with her. She can eat all the pineapple."

"Come on, Rosie-tosies." He got her in the truck in her seat. "What do you think Da will have on his pizza?"

"Saursages and onions. He loves saursages."

"He does, huh?" He loved all the stuff. Like a loaded supreme.

"Uh-huh."

"We share pepperoni sometimes, though," Em pointed out.

"Sometimes," Rosie said, sounding doubtful. "But we each get our owns."

"Yes. You get to *make* your own," he reminded her.

"Yay! With Da!"

"Yep."

"I'm glad you're going to eat with us too, Daddy," Em said.

"Are you?"

"Yes. It was nice the other day, having breakfast, and you and Da smile at each other when you drop us off now."

"We do, don't we." He had to grin at that. Liam was still being very cautious, but they had improved. A lot. They could talk to each other. Laugh together.

And when they'd made love? It had blown his mind. It always had, but knowing he might have another chance at something he'd thought was gone forever had made him that much damn happier.

"Yes, Daddy. It's nice to be friends." Rosie was very concerned with being friendly these days.

"It is." And more, he hoped. Friends with benefits or ex booty calls wasn't enough.

He intended to help Liam fall in love with him again. Good thing he was so damn loveable.

He coasted into town, hunting a place to park. He would see how much of the day Liam wanted to spend, so he wanted a good spot.

"I see Da's car! It's over there!" Rosie bounced in her seat, legs kicking.

"Cool. Let's see how close we can get." Astonishing as it was, he found a spot not far away. "We'll move your bags over after we eat, huh?"

"Okay, Daddy." Em was in the best mood. It was a little

scary. She was so... changeable most of the time. But this whole thing with him and Liam seemed to put her in a sunny space.

Rosie rolled down her window as he killed the engine and waved. "Da! Da, we're going to make pizza!"

Liam came up to the truck to get her out. "We so are. Hey guys. Don't forget to roll up your window, Saw. It's going to rain."

"Gotcha." He turned on the truck to push the windows all the way up. "How're you today?"

"Good. Good, staying busy." Liam smiled at him, then hugged Em tight. "Hey, gorgeous girl. How goes?"

"Perfect, thank you. Pizza smells so good, and—" Her eyes went wide. "I see Liliana in there! Can I go say hi?"

Liliana? That was a new one. Em seemed to know everyone.

"Yes, but don't be rude and interrupt if they don't want her to chat, okay?" He watched her trot off, chuckling when Rosie demanded her hug from Liam.

Liam swung her up into his arms. "I missed you, my angel baby. My little baboo. My sweet sugar lump."

"I missed you, my Da! My silly-billy. My potatofishy face!"

"Oh, wow. Good one." Liam kissed her cheek, then glanced at Sawyer. "They have a good time?"

"Yeah. Em might need a little help with math. I think she's afraid to ask you, since you're math dad, but I don't want to steer her wrong."

"I'm on it. She's got her multiplication tables mostly, but she hasn't grasped them in reality."

"Yeah. Practical application." He smiled when Liam bumped shoulders with him on the way into the restaurant.

"What's practice applicable?" Rosie asked, her word jumble hilarious.

"When you learn to use it in everyday life," Liam said.

"Oh. Like one pizza and one pizza is two pizzas!"

"Yes, ma'am. And how many pizzas do we need?"

"Me and sister and Da and Daddy. One, two, three, four!"

"Exactly. I'm so proud of you."

"Me too, kiddo. So smart."

"Hey, guys! I saw Em come flying in, so I got a table ready for you."

"Thanks, Sydney." The hostess was awesome that way, and Sawyer thought it was good to be a regular. "She saw a friend."

"She knows everyone. Hey, Rosie. How are you?"

"We're going to make pizzas!"

"I know! How cool is that?"

Rosie giggled, and they got seated, ordering drinks. He got one Sprite for each of the girls. Then they could switch to water.

"Did you want to share a pie and a salad, hon-Saw?" Liam's cheeks heated. "We could share a deluxe."

"Sure. If you're good with that." He grinned. Liam must be in a good mood. "You know I'm down for all the toppings."

"I do."

"You must be friends," Rosie pronounced, and Sawyer tilted his head, fascinated to hear this. "If you don't love chocolate ice cream, and your friend loves chocolate ice cream and it doesn't make you barf, then you eat it to be nice so that next time you can have strawlberry!"

"Well, yeah. Next time Daddy will have sausage and onions for me." Liam nudged him under the table on his good leg, though he was damn near healed up.

"I so will. You have my word."

Em came up to the table with a grin on. "Can we get in line to make our pizzas? Liliana's going up with her big sister, and we can all do it together?"

"Sure, baby girl. You sit, Sawyer. I know you're still

sore." Liam took both girls with him, and Sawyer got to sit back and watch them. His people. It made his chest hurt. He loved them all so damn much, and having them all together, all smiling, no one giving him worried glances and wondering when an argument would start. Yeah, this was the good stuff.

The drinks came and he ordered their deluxe and Caesar salad with extra croutons, along with some cheesy bread, because the girls loved it, and they could take anything they didn't eat home.

"Sawyer. Hey, man."

"Morgan. How goes it? This doesn't seem like your kind of place."

"I'm here with my niece. My brother and sister-in-law are in town."

"Fun. I'm here with Liam and the girls."

Morgan's eyebrow lifted. "No shit."

"Right over there." He jerked his chin to the line. "How long is your niece in town? My girls could take her swimming at the community center."

"She's just here for the weekend. They're going camping for a week."

Camping, huh? That sounded like fun. They used to camp a lot. "Well, we should get together and do something, huh? Let me know if she has time." Sawyer figured Liam wouldn't mind. He loved to have the girls be social.

"I will. Maybe we can all go play minigolf or something?" Morgan glanced at Liam. "Three or four, it's cool."

"Yeah. Okay, that works. I'll talk to them, and I'll holler."

"Awesome. I'll leave you to it." Morgan gave him a broad wink, then headed back to sit with a guy who looked like Morgan, a cowgirl who had to be a barrel racer, and a little girl with amazing blonde curls and a huge, sparkly bow on her head.

Liam came back with two happy girls with their chef's hats. "Everything okay?"

"So, what did we make?" he asked, to see if they went with what they had said they were going to. Rosie could be as this way and that as the wind. Em was pretty constant.

"Pepperoni, for me, and Rosie did pineapple and ham."

"I told you, Daddy."

"You did, Rosie. I'm proud of you for sticking to your guns."

"I'm not stuck." She frowned mightily.

Liam snorted. "He means you didn't change your mind. So, who was that?" Liam nodded toward Morgan's table.

"Roping pen buddy. His niece is visiting from Texas. I told him maybe the girls would like to get together."

"Oh, that's nice. It's supposed to be a beautiful day out there, once the rain blows over."

"It is. How do you feel about mini golf?" He held his breath, hoping against hope that Liam felt good about it.

"Is that a lot of time on your feet?"

"They have benches, babe. I promise to be good."

"Well...I could, yeah. I mean, if you want. If the girls want." Liam's cheeks were pink, but he was smiling.

"Oh, please?" Em gave Morgan's niece the wide eyes. "I love her bow. I bet she's in cheer."

"I want the pink ball," Rosie said. "Unless the guest wants it," she added.

"Oh, that's very nice, Rosie!" Liam praised her. "That's super friendly."

Rosie's smile went from pleased to thousand-watt. "Can we go say hi?"

"Only if they're not eating yet. And if our food comes, you have to come back, okay? No running." Liam watched them go, grinning. "They're good girls."

"They are." He had to smile back. "So...mini golf is cool?"

"If you don't mind…"

"I don't." Hell, he was over the moon. He was in heaven. This was his fantasy. "Full disclosure, Morgan was my date for the ball. But he gave me a stern talking-to and sent me to you. We're just friends."

"You told me. The roping pen. I didn't hit him, so he may not remember me."

"Ha. I'm sure he does." He gave Liam a look, but he was teasing. "Have I mentioned I'm sorry?"

"Couple of times." Liam paused. "Some of the apologies were more impressive than others…"

"I like to strive for my best." Sawyer batted his eyelashes at Liam, who winked.

"Da! Brielle's parents said her uncle Morgan could bring her to play golf. Then their food came." Em came over, almost running, but not quite.

"Brielle, huh?"

"Yeah, she's in cheer, too. They're going camping. I'm so jealous!"

"Yeah? You haven't been camping in a while, huh?"

"Forevers, Daddy." Rosie draped herself over her chair, dramatic as anything. "Maybe never, since I was so young last time." She opened her eyes very wide.

"Oh, she's very good at that," Liam drawled.

"I think Em's been giving her lessons."

"Your daddy should take you guys camping. It's the perfect time of year."

"Daddy?" Em turned to him.

The pizza arrived just then, the girls squealing over cheesy bread.

"We'll talk about it, okay?" He watched Liam, needing him to understand he wasn't being glib. "All of us."

One of Liam's eyebrows lifted, but that was all he got.

He'd take it. It wasn't the immediate refusal he would

have gotten a few months ago. Baby steps. That eyebrow, a curious expression, maybe the barest hint of a nod. Liam was giving him all the things, and he wasn't going to take it for granted.

"Okay, Daddy." Rosie was munching already, losing interest.

But Emily watched them like a hawk.

Liam stayed relaxed, though, and he followed those cues. They were going to be okay—nice and casual.

The pizza tasted perfect, crisp and hot with lots of cheese. Just like he liked it. And he couldn't ask for better company. So, Sawyer pondered his strategy for a camping trip while he munched.

The girls chattered, merry as magpies, and Em didn't tease her sister, which was a blessing. This was when he was his happiest. Well, that and when he and Liam were in bed alone. But when they were together and loving, and everyone was smiling. This was the damn life.

Liam reached for the salad at the same time he did, and their fingers met, lightning shooting up his arm.

Sawyer jumped a bit, but it was a good shock, one that made heat curl in his belly.

"Sorry. I was going to grab one of the croutons. They're my favorite."

He knew. "Take it. Then let me have the olives."

"They're all yours." Liam grabbed an olive and picked one up, offering it to him.

Okay, that was hot as hell.

"Thanks." He took it, the salty brine of it making his eyes cross.

"Daddy is a weirdo. Olives are nasty."

Emily rolled her eyes. "Olives are yummy!"

"Om nom," Sawyer said. "Though I didn't like them until I was Em's age, kiddo."

"Really? I might like them too?" Rosie asked, and he nodded.

"Someday."

"Just like mushrooms, Rosie. I like those now too, and I didn't used to." Em patted Rosie's arm.

"Ew. I like pineapapapapapples!"

Liam chuckled and ate another piece of cheese bread.

"Well, you know what you like, kiddo," Sawyer told him. "Do we want dessert here, or ice cream when we play mini golf?"

"Ice cream! Please, Daddy!" Rosie bounced, and Liam chuckled.

"Me too, Daddy?"

"Ice cream it is. I bet Bri likes it too."

"Does Mr. Morgan?"

"I don't know, kiddo. I know he likes beer."

"Beer is stinky," Em said.

"It so is," Liam agreed. "Pee-ew."

"Pee-ew! Pee-ew!" Rosie giggled, sing-songing the words.

Lord help him. She would be on that now for a week.

Thank God she was Liam's for the next three days. She could make those noises at him.

They were finishing up when Morgan stopped by with Bri. "So, when did y'all want to go?"

Sawyer glanced at Liam. "Want to come play?"

"Sure. Why not?" Liam shrugged and nodded. "It's been a good long while."

"Yay!" Em bounced. "Both dads!" She high-fived Rosie. "Which car?"

"I'll drive. Your daddy's still broken." Liam shook his head. "We just need to settle up."

"I'll get it. You all go load up."

"We'll follow. Thanks. My brother and his wife appreciate the alone time," Morgan said.

"I'm sure. Hey. I'm Liam." Liam held one hand out to Morgan.

"Morgan. Nice to meet you. I hope you don't hold it against me that I know this guy." Morgan jerked a thumb at him.

"Ha-ha."

"Of course not. He has amazing daughters, you know." Liam winked over.

"I know! He tells me all the time." Morgan winked. "And this is Brielle."

"Hello." Bri smiled a grave little smile.

"Hello, Brielle. It's nice to meet you. Would you like to go play gooney golf?" Liam was so gentle, so good with kids.

"Uh-huh. And Em says she's in cheer."

"She is. And I like camping," Rosie piped up.

"Me too. Are you coming camping with Uncle Morgan?"

"No. We have to stay with Da." Rosie beamed. "But we might go later."

Morgan acted as if he were watching a tennis match, lost in the rhythm of little girl speak, eyes bouncing like mad from Em to Bri to Rosie and back. It was a fascinating phenomenon, Sawyer had to admit.

"Okay, ladies, let's get this show on the road, huh?" He stood, and the server came to take his card.

"Did you want me to get half?" Liam murmured, and he shook his head.

He could take his family to lunch.

"I'll get the golf," Liam said, then started herding kids toward the door.

And it was just like old times, and it squeezed his heart some.

"You good, buddy?" Morgan asked, expression one of concern bordering on worried.

"Lost. Totally lost. He's letting me in, a little bit. I just have to not fuck up again."

"Well, if you need an ear, you just holler."

"I will. I'm not walking on eggshells or anything, but I'm working hard."

"I ran into the guy that Liam took to the party. All-around rider. Nice guy."

"Yeah? Did he have a big old bruise?"

"Not anymore." Morgan chuckled. "Don't be mean."

"Uh-huh." He tucked his card back into his wallet. "I'm sure, given some distance from the event, I won't be."

Still, he sort of wanted to know where the dude had come from, how Liam knew him. So maybe he would poke that a bit.

"Did he say anything about Liam?" he asked as they walked outside.

"Not really. Something about coffee." Morgan shrugged the question off.

"Mmm." Sawyer let it go, because who wanted to sound like a bitter old bastard? "Well, I'm glad you and Bri happened along."

"Me too. I wasn't sure how to occupy her, but she seems to fit with your girls just fine."

"They're a friendly bunch, really. And she has a common ground with Em already, so it helps." They met the rest of the family on the sidewalk, and Liam led them to his Escalade to get everyone settled.

It felt normal to sit in the passenger seat, to hear the 90s alternative on the radio while Liam drove them to the venue. They all sang along with 'Rain King', which Em loved as much as Liam did, and Rosie always got the words wrong.

Liam glanced over at him. "Do you want me to drop you off at the entrance, and then park?"

"That would be great, babe. Thanks. I'm just a little sore, but I can make it."

"No problem. I'll drop you off and then we'll meet you in a second." Liam eased up to the curb, careful as could be.

"Thank you." He stepped out, making sure not to stumble. God knew he didn't need to go down in front of all the kids. And Liam. And Morgan.

"Be careful. We'll be right there." Liam pulled off, and he waited, standing there and trying to focus, to breathe.

He felt like the world had been spinning a little fast, and he was just a damn cowboy. He needed to let things slow down.

Then he glanced up and watched Liam and the girls walk up to him, and he knew he couldn't. He had to grab this with both hands.

Chapter Fifteen

"Em, are you done with your shower?"

"Yes, Da."

"Can you help your sister brush her teeth?"

"Can I stay up a half hour to read my book?"

Little bargainer. "Yes."

Liam shook his head and gave Rosie's birthday cake a once-over. He hadn't done a half-bad job. He would put it away until tomorrow, but he really liked how it had come out. He glanced at Daisy, who was sitting up on her butt, staring, and he grinned.

"Good thing you're too short." He found her a cookie, and she snapped it up and ran off to her crate. She was getting old enough to choose to go in there when she needed time away rather than being put in there when Liam needed a nap.

"We're ready for kisses, Da!" Rosie called. "And a book. I want *Octopuppy*!"

"Yes, ma'am. Grab it and hop in bed." He grinned at Em on the way by. "Love you, baby."

"I love you, Da. Sleep well. I'm going to read." She waved her book.

He got *Octopuppy* off the shelf so he could read it to Rosie. "Happy almost birthday!"

"Happy birthday!" she parroted back. "I'm going to be five! I'm so big! I go to kennygarden next year.

"I know. I think that's amazing." He got her tucked in after checking out her hands and teeth surreptitiously. Both clean. Yay.

"Me too. I will be in the same school as Em. I will be *big*."

"You will. But first you have summer."

"Camping, Da."

"We'll see. That's a very big trip."

"Uh-huh. But if you *and* Daddy went, I would never be scared."

And he liked to camp, but Saw had been the one to always plan it. "Like I said. We'll see. *Octopuppy*?" He held up the book.

She listened for about half the book, and then she was out like a light.

He headed back to the kitchen to clean up, smiling as he saw his phone light up. Saw.

Hey, babe. Is Rosie excited?

So excited.

He took a deep, deep breath and jumped.

We're having cake and ice cream at 2 w/a handful of her friends at Herron Park if you wanna come

Yeah? She would love it if she got all her presents at once. Well, all but momma's. I'd hold it.

He got a crazy face emoji.

I'd love to.

Cool. I'll let you surprise her.

He started doing the dishes, amazed at himself. Another text popped up. Terry.

Wanna coffee 2morrow

Cant. Rosies bday Sorry! Monday?

He and Terry had coffee once a week or so, and they were becoming good buddies. No chemistry, no heat, but good friends.

Oh cool. Well, tell her happy happy

Sawyer's next text came up right after that.

What are you up to?

Doing dishes. Fixin to sit on my butt.
Wanna see the cake?

He shot a photo and sent it.

That's too cool, babe. She'll adore it

That felt good to hear. It wasn't fancy — a purple cake with fairies and sparkles — but it was cute and fine for three five-year-olds and family.

Thanx

NP. I'm just sitting. It's kinda nice.

Damn.

No one bothering you? I should leave you
be, huh

Nah. You can bother me any time.

Was Saw flirting with him?

Poke poke poke

He'd just fake flirt right back and see.

His phone rang, and he grinned, picking up on Sawyer's call. "Hey."

"Are you poking me? Better watch that."

"Poke poke poke." He finished up the dishes. "How's the foot?"

"I am out of the boot. I still have a brace inside a wrap, but that's mainly to keep me honest."

"I'm glad. I know you were getting tired of it." He'd never been in one, so he couldn't imagine.

"Yeah. It was really cramping my style. I want to be able to get athletic."

His cheeks heated, because he had a feeling Sawyer meant with him.

"Are you going to...take up basketball?" he teased.

"Nope. I prefer full-contact sports."

"Oh..." He couldn't stop his smile. "I hear that. I'm into wrestling."

"Tussling, even." That voice was low, husky, and perfect.

"Uh-huh. Dancing is also up there with my favorite things." Maybe he should lock up the condo and head to his bedroom...

"Oh, babe, I always love dancing with you. With or without clothes."

"Yeah?" He did lock up the house, grab a glass of wine,

and head back. He peeked at Em, who was sound asleep, book on her chest. Then he settled in his bedroom, his door shut.

All the while, Sawyer kept him revved up. "Yep. Horizontal is the best, but the tease of two-stepping with you makes me hot."

"I miss that. Dancing with you. It was always so magical." Should he admit that? Maybe not, but it was true.

"We'll have to dance soon, babe. I would love that. No strings." He knew Sawyer meant it, but was it true? Really? They had a lot of tangles.

"I don't know if we can have no strings, honey. I don't know if I can."

"Well, I would try for you. But I really don't want no strings either."

He chuckled, not knowing what to say exactly. He guessed he needed to just enjoy this and go with it for a while.

"So, what are you wearing?"

"You dawg. Such a cowboy."

"Hey, I heard your door close."

"Stop it, now." He leaned back against his headboard, a huge smile on his face. "A T-shirt and a pair of shorts."

"Mmm. Your old ratty shorts?" Sawyer's voice went all raspy.

"You know I love them. They're comfy." And he wasn't going to admit that he was wearing Saw's old T-shirt.

"I do. I love them too. Easy access." Saw sighed. "If it wasn't so late and the kids wouldn't get up and freak out, I would ask to come over. But I can wait to see you until tomorrow and dream about you tonight."

"Yeah. We probably need to be sensible, but it's a good thought." And he would admit to being a touch disappointed, but only in private.

"It is. And, you know, I'm alone at the ranch, and it is pretty lonely."

"Yeah, I bet it is. If you were here, we could...watch a movie."

"Oh, we could have a movie on, sure. I'd be watching you."

God, Saw was on fire.

"You're going to make me all...caught up."

"Well, you know what to do about that. I mean, I'm not opposed."

"Saw..." He chuckled soft and low. "Listen to you. I—I'm glad you're coming out tomorrow."

"Me too. Not just for Rosie, babe. And I have some things to talk on. Not bad things. Good shit."

"Yeah? Like what?" He put his phone on Facetime so he could see Sawyer.

"Like camping." Sawyer grinned at him. He was lounging in bed now too, and he was shirtless.

"Yeah? You want to take the girls?"

"I do. I think Rosie is just old enough for a nice two-day trip now."

"You should take the fifth wheel and go for a week. It's going to be gorgeous up in the mountains, if you can find a place to park." He thought it sounded like a ton of fun, in fact.

"Yeah." Sawyer licked his lips. "I was hoping you'd come."

Whoa. "Are you sure? That's...I was intending to take the girls to Denver, but I can pivot, if you're serious."

He caught himself holding his breath.

"I am. I know you don't break ground on that project you got at the ball—"

"No thanks to you," he teased.

"Yeah, yeah. But you don't start that until mid-July."

"Yeah, Hank wanted to wait until after the fourth." And he could just take his laptop for emails, but...what if they fought?

"So I was thinking we could go on and just really take some time, if you were willing. I mean, I can take the girls myself for a long weekend, but to take the trailer out and stay, I would want you with us. I mean, I do anyway, but this is a total family thing."

"So, let's do it. Let's just go. I mean, we'd have to share a bed, but if you can handle that…"

"Oh, kill me, why don't you? Of course I can. Now, the lack of privacy might be bad."

"Yeah. Rosie will end up between us every night, and you know it." But what about Em? Would this confuse her?

Should he just be honest with her?

"We can talk to the kids together, if you want. I don't know what to tell them, exactly, except I want you to come with us, and that's where we sleep." Sawyer's smile went rueful.

"That's true enough, huh?" And it might work. Em would get her hopes up, but then again, he was doing that right now, wasn't he? He wanted… something with Saw. Something more than an every-three-days exchange.

"I'm going to make things better, Liam. I swear to God, I'm going to work on us." Sawyer was staring right into him, and the intensity damn near hurt.

"I believe you." He wasn't sure what else to say, because he had a lot to unpack, but he did believe that with his whole heart.

"Thank you." Saw's smile was transcendent. "If I was there, I'd kiss you."

"If you were here, I'd let you."

"Mmmm. Damn. Tomorrow. I'll sneak you off for a good one, huh?"

"Maybe we can have a discussion after. A…planning session." He'd love that. It was a Saturday, after all.

"I think so. We need to do our camping trip up right, huh?" He could see the desire in Sawyer's eyes.

"I'd like that. I'd like to simply—be four of us. Together."

"Yes. No one else, no distractions. Hiking. S'mores."

"Bacon in the mornings. Long walks. Cards. Laughing."

"I love it. I want that." Sawyer leaned back on his pillows a little more. "Holding you."

He found himself close to tears. He hated sleeping alone. Hated it.

"I know, love. I do too," Sawyer said.

God, had he said that out loud?

"Do you want me to come, babe? I can."

His eyes went wide. "Would you? If I said yes?"

"I would. I'm not teasing. I know I said it would be more sensible to wait until morning, but I'm not even talking sex. I want to be with you."

"Bring enough clothes for a couple of days?"

"I will." Sawyer's smile was... astonishing. Just amazing.

"I'll make us some popcorn for that movie we're going to watch."

"Sounds fantastic. I'll be right there." Sawyer waved, then hung up, and God, they were really doing this.

He went to make sure that his bathroom was clean, that his sheets were all right, and then to see if he had popcorn. It would be hard to Door Dash at this point. Thankfully, he did.

Sawyer did love popcorn.

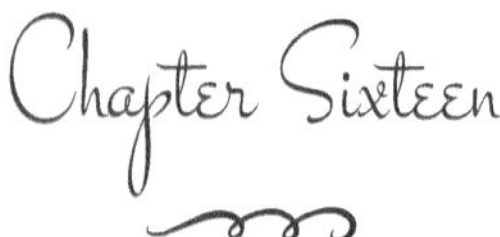

Chapter Sixteen

"Well, Rosie-girl, did you love your cake?" Sawyer asked as he put plates in the dishwasher. "Your da worked so hard."

"Best birfday! Best one ever!" She stopped short, as if a light bulb had gone off. "Have you been here before ever?"

"I came over once to talk to your da when you were with your gran." He wasn't going to lie.

"Oh. It's nice. Your house is better, but we have Daisy."

Yes. Daisy the most adorable purse dog in history. He wanted to dislike her, but she was great.

"Hey, I have dogs."

"But they work. Daisy just plays." Rosie beamed at him. "And she's the cutest puppy ever."

"She is pretty adorable." He had to laugh, because Daisy did a silly dance like she knew they were talking about her.

"See? She knows. Let's go outside and go potty, Daisy! It's time!" Rosie opened up the back door that led down the stairs to a small enclosed patio. "Da! I'm taking her out!"

"Be careful! I'll be right there."

"'Kay!"

"I'll go," Em said. She clattered down the stairs too.

"Thank you, Em!" Liam called from the back of the house.

"They like to be with her, huh?"

"They do. And they're very careful not to let her out." Liam came to stand next to him, close enough to feel his warmth. "But she gets tired heading up those stairs."

"Does Em carry her?"

"Yeah. Rosie isn't quite old enough yet."

"I love how they adore her." He'd always thought ranch dogs were enough, but now Sawyer got it.

"They do, and she makes bad days better."

"I'm glad." He hated the idea there were a lot of bad days.

"Me too. Did you want to sit and discuss camping? When did you want to go?"

"I was thinking before the fourth." Sawyer shrugged. "It will get weirdly busy after that. I know you have that project in Vail, and then the big fireworks thing at the ranch, and Em has sports she wants to do."

"Yeah. All of the above. I'm flexible. I can answer emails remotely, and I'm in a bit of a lull until some jobs fund, so let me know."

Okay.

Okay, that was good. Now he was going to see if Liam would come for a week. In the RV—it was fancy as all get-out, and they could spend some quality time in the mountains.

"So, I was thinking we'd leave on a Monday and come back Sunday?" He kinda held his breath, because he was pushing, and he knew it.

"How about Friday to Saturday? That gives one of us a chance to get them ready for daycare Monday."

"That's fine, babe. If it works for you, I'm all over it." Hot damn. Look at that. Liam was going camping. With him. For a week.

Eight days even.

"I was thinking Glacier Basin."

He tilted his head. "In Estes? We can try, but it fills up bad..."

"I—I sort of reserved us a spot, because it was filling up." Liam's cheeks were bright red. "I know one of park rangers there. He was a frat brother of mine, and he had a cancellation."

"Oh, wow." He laughed outright. "Sneaky monkey."

"No. No, I just—I mean, I could cancel it, but I wanted to know..."

"No way. That's perfect." The girls would love that. And it was pet-friendly, so Daisy could come too.

"So, we can bring anything specific—that store in Estes is hellish. Understocked, filthy." Liam wrinkled his nose, and Sawyer wanted to kiss him.

"Yeah. Not my idea of a yay." He swore people on vacation just acted like total assholes. They tore through the grocery store in Estes and left a huge mess, as well as empty shelves. And of course, getting a manager up there who would stay more than one season was hella hard. Still, he'd bring meat from the ranch, spices, and mac and cheese. They'd cook out and laugh and go for walks.

Like a family.

"We'll have to be sure to make tacos."

"God yes. Em won't come unless we do," Sawyer teased.

"No. We'll need bacon, eggs, potatoes—"

"Country ribs?" Liam had always loved those when Sawyer made them, and he couldn't imagine Liam making them for himself.

Those bright blue eyes lit up. "Yeah?"

"Yeah. I'll grill them if you make the sauce to dip." He did love that he'd put that expression on Liam's face.

"Okay. I can make do that. Will you make me one of them burnt cheesecakes to take along? With the blueberry syrup?"

"A Basque cheesecake? Sure. I can make it Thursday, and you can eat on it all week."

"Yum." That was a good trade. God, he'd missed conversations just like this. That trade-off, the feeling of what they liked about each other. "It means a lot to me, that you're into this. I am too."

"I can't promise we won't fight, but I want this to be good for all of us."

"Me too. I know we can't ever promise we won't poke at each other, but I swear, Liam. I'm trying hard. I want you to believe in that, at least."

"We both are. That'll be good for now, right?"

"It will." He held out his hand, and Liam took it, so he squeezed. "It's amazing."

"Yeah."

"Why are you holding hands?" Rosie asked. "Are you being friends?"

"We are, kiddo. Did Daisy do her thing?"

"Uh-huh. Em is carrying her up the stairs."

"Go hold the door for her, please," Liam said.

"Okay! Em! Daddy and Da are friends again!"

"Yay." Em only sounded the tiniest bit sarcastic, which for her was a great feat. So he was going to take that as a win too. For Rosie, it really was that simple, he thought.

"Girls, can you come into the kitchen for a sec?" Liam called, and they both came running in, Em still carrying little Daisy. "I was wondering if you two would like to go camping."

"Camping?" Rosie squealed, running around in a circle. "Now?"

"Next weekend. Friday. Does that work for y'all?" Sawyer

asked. Daisy started barking at Rosie, so Sawyer caught his youngest in his arms, blowing on her neck.

"Who are we going with?" Em asked.

It felt good to answer her for once. "The four of us. Your Da got us a campground space up at Estes. We'll take the fifth wheel and go." He knew how important having a flush toilet was to Em.

"Is Daisy coming?"

Liam grinned. "Yes, but she has to be in her harness, and we don't open the trailer door unless she has her leash on or she's in her little pen, okay? This is her first trip, so she's not used to traveling."

"Yes, Da," the girls chorused, so serious.

"Can we bring our tablets for nighttime?" Em asked.

"Can we go fishing?"

"Can we make s'mores?"

"And hot dogs?"

"And burgies?"

"And—"

Liam held one hand up and grinned. "Yes, to all of it."

Em nodded then, before zinging them with, "Is Daddy spending the night here? Again?"

"I think we'll see what happens today, honey. I might have to go back out to the ranch, but I'd like to stay." Sawyer figured it was better to be up-front. They were still feeling all of this out.

"Okay, can we have Chinese food for dinner tonight?" Rosie loved her sweet and sour chicken.

"Sure, kiddo. It's your birthday." Liam reached out to tousle her hair when Sawyer let her go.

"Ooh...can I have an egg roll too? I like those now." Em's question made Liam grin as if he knew a secret, and Sawyer wanted to know too.

"Oh, man, I like those too," Sawyer said. "Yum."

"Then you can have three, Daddy." Rosie stood tall like a little princess. "Since it's my birthday."

Oh, she was totally into bestowing grace on her faithful subjects. "And lo mein?"

"Uh-huh. If you share it with Da."

"I promise. I'll share with your Da." Sawyer didn't so much as glance at Liam, because, if he did, he'd lose it.

Liam's foot touched his under the table. It was enough to make him want to die with laughter.

And that was it, wasn't it?

There was still laughter.

There was still hope.

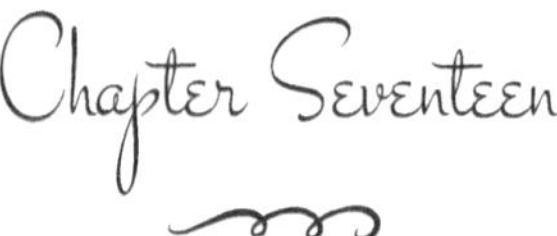

Chapter Seventeen

"You did not!" Terry stared at Liam as if he'd grown another head, and Liam wasn't sure whether to blush or grin, so he did both.

"I so did. I mean...you saw him." Sawyer was hot—even when Liam was mad at him, the son of a bitch was gorgeous.

"Well, sure. I mean, I don't need a guy like that. I am one." Terry gave him a broad wink. "But he is gorgeous."

"Yeah, and I agreed to go camping with him and the girls for a week."

"Oh, wow. Now, there can't be much privacy while camping..." Terry waggled his eyebrows.

"Nope. No danger at all. None. Just a family outing..." He met Terry's eyes. "This is the first step to forgiving him, isn't it?"

"It is. Danger, man. Danger." Terry shook his head in mock sorrow. "Now I have no chance."

"Bah. You weren't into me, and I knew it." It worked out, because Liam needed a friend. Just a good, solid friend.

"I could have been, man, but it was in the contract. Make

my ex jealous. I knew you still had it bad for him, and you're a good guy. I want to be friends."

"I think we are, huh? I just want to know that I'm doing the right things for all of us." Hell, he needed to know he wasn't fucking things up.

"I get that. It would be harder on everyone a second time around."

"Yeah, and I'm trying to figure out what the best choices are. I guess that's what this camping trip is, huh?" A chance to see if they could breathe, see if they still needed one another.

"Yep. Because familiarity really can breed contempt. You spend a week together and you're at each other's throats? You know to back off." Terry munched his pastry.

"True. You know, I don't remember a lot of fighting. A couple of snarls about his mom redecorating the house. Then the one big fight."

"Things got pent-up." Terry nodded sagely. "My folks said it was better to talk. A lot. About everything."

"Yeah. I was having terrible trouble at work—bad enough that I didn't even know, you know? —and he was feeling like I didn't care enough. It just exploded, and I walked out with the girls."

"And you said you fought about his mom?" Terry gave him one of those piercing looks.

"Yeah. I guess I felt as if he didn't care enough to go against her." Liam fiddled with his coffee cup. She'd raised Sawyer in that house, Sawyer's dad had died in the house. She didn't want anything to change. He'd needed to make something his own. "She is a force of nature—she's not evil, at all, but she knows she's right. About everything."

"Mommas." Terry rolled his eyes. "I bet. Her little boy needed to listen to her."

"Yeah, but—I wanted it to be our home. Mine and Sawyer's and the girls'. Not us living in her house."

"What did Sawyer ever say about that?"

"Well, she moved to another house on the ranch, but that was it. She was always there." And it had been like a burr under his saddle. He hadn't managed to work it out—partially because he cared for Barb. She wasn't evil, just sure about what she wanted. And he liked her and vice versa, but he was no shrinking violet. He'd been vocal.

Vocal. He'd been demanding. He'd wanted what he wanted too, dammit.

Sawyer had, no doubt, been caught in the middle. But then, Liam had been caught between work and Sawyer and all the stuff with the girls. They hadn't talked.

Terry nodded again. "Yeah, that had to chafe, her just letting herself in."

"I'm sure it chafed seeing me in her kitchen."

"But it wasn't her kitchen anymore, buddy." Terry's voice was steady as anything.

"No. I mean, legally, maybe. More than it was really mine, for sure." He blew out a sigh. "I tried to convince Sawyer to build a new house, but... hell, I can't blame him. That's the ranch house."

"Are you going to tell him that? That it bothered you?"

If he did, did that mean Saw would tell him all the things that were a problem?

"I should, huh?"

"Yeah. You should have an amnesty discussion."

Liam frowned. "A what?"

"Tell each other why you got butthurt. Agree to give each other amnesty for it. No added butthurt. Just listening."

"This is a thing? Really?" He knew he had to seem poleaxed.

"Yep. I know it sounds pretty new age for a guy like me, but my mom is a yoga teacher." Terry chuckled. "She has lots of coping shit."

"That's a great idea. I mean...have you ever done it? Did it work?" He wanted...he wanted better than they'd had. He wanted to be at peace in his heart, either with Saw or without him.

He was tired.

"I have. It's worked. Now, the relationship ended, but not because we couldn't talk." Terry's expression closed up. "But it works."

"That's good to know." Okay, that was a sign, right? Like that was a friend thing, and he should ask? Or maybe he ought to ask if he should ask... "You want to talk about it?"

There. That had to be the appropriate answer.

"I don't want to bring you down, man." Terry's sunny smile had gone behind a big old cloud.

"Dude. I booty-called my ex. Like, a lot."

"And good for you." Terry winked, the grin returning.

"I just want you to know that you got a friend. If you want to get it off your chest, I got your back."

"Thanks." Terry grimaced. "It's just a crappy story, and I don't want you feeling sorry for me."

"Okay, I'm a little unsure, am I supposed to push or back off?" He could do either one, but he wanted to do the *right* thing.

"I'm not sure." Terry shook his head, then glanced around before shrugging. "Gabe died."

"Ah." He winced in sympathy. "Was he a roughstock rider too?"

That was a hard, harsh life, and guys died way too often.

"Yeah. He was a bronc rider. Got kicked in the head." There was no emotion in Terry's voice. Which meant it had to have been horrifying.

"Jesus, I'm sorry. That sucks for you. That's a terrible situation." And it had to just hurt and hurt.

"Yeah. I mean, we were on our way to something permanent, but... well, it's been a few years now. I'm okay."

"Still, I'm sorry for your loss. That's a terrible thing to have to go through."

"Thanks." Now that grin was back full force. "I think Gabe would have wanted to go out that way. Maybe not that young, but still."

"Well, please don't follow his example. We're just getting to know each other. You haven't met Saw or the girls yet." And he didn't want to lose another friend in his life.

"Yeah, no. I'm getting long in the tooth for the bigger shows, which is why I was hooking up with Cowboy Wanted." Terry waved a hand. "I'll hang out here."

"Good. Good. I know a few ranchers, if you want to cowboy."

"The last one I saw with you hit me."

Liam nodded. "And he so owes you an apology."

"He does. Maybe a beer. Depends on if your kids are around." Terry chuckled. "And if he still sees me as a threat."

"I didn't tell him I was desperate enough to hire a date." And he was sort of loath to do that right now.

"Well, we're friends, right? Invite me to the Fourth of July cookout or whatever y'all do."

"I can do that." He did have to grin at the idea of introducing Sawyer and Terry officially. "In fact, you're invited. No matter whether at the condo or the ranch. You're welcome."

"Thanks, man. This is the first cowboy Christmas in ages I have nowhere to ride."

"Well, we'll make a brisket and the regular sides. It'll be fun." And he'd love to see Sawyer have to make up to Terry a little.

"Just tell me what I can bring."

"I'll holler at you when we get back."

"Good deal." Terry leaned back and picked up his coffee cup again. "When do you head out?"

"Friday morning. I'm going to spend the night at the ranch Thursday night."

"Cool. You need me to check on your place while you're gone?"

"Do you mind? I'll be home the Sunday after." And he'd feel better if someone had an eye on things.

"Not one bit." Terry winked. "And I won't even invite anyone over."

"I trust you, man. You took a left hook for me."

"I did." Terry hooted, drawing a couple of smiles. "Have so much fun."

"I hope so. I may call."

"I hope you don't have to." Terry patted his arm. "But if you need to, call."

"Thanks." He found a real smile. "For the coffee and the support."

"Ditto, cabbage head." Terry grinned back, then hoovered up the rest of his pastry.

Liam's phone buzzed, a picture of the girls riding in the pasture popping up, along with Saw's text.

Thinking about you

His grin widened, and he texted back.

Yeah? Good deal. They're so damn cute.

Perfect.

"Wanna see my babies? They're out riding."

Terry peered at his phone. "Cowgirls, man. The littler one is going to be a barrel racer."

"You think so?" He watched Rosie on her horse. "God help me. Her sister's a gymnast."

That was scary enough.

"Barrel racers are worse." Terry gave him another pat on the arm. "You still hungry?"

"Worse than gymnasts? Heaven help me. You know, I want something cold and light—you want to go to the diner?"

"Yep. And sure. I would totally dig a burrito while you nibble rabbit food."

"Ooh…I like burritos…" He grabbed his coffee cup and trash. "Let's go."

"Yeah. Later, Janie."

"Bye, guys!" The barista waved them out.

"Come on, man. We'll eat, and then I'll go clear off my desk for my vacation in the boonies." He was ready, for the most part.

"Sounds like a plan. I'll even buy."

"Damn. It's a banner day." Liam liked Terry even more now, knowing what he knew and knowing Terry's attitude about life.

He could learn a lot from the guy.

Sawyer sat in his camp chair, legs stretched out in front of him, ankles crossed, watching the sunrise over Rocky Mountain National Park. He sipped his coffee, the chill up here pronounced, which was why he was layered up in his heavy flannel jack shirt. Lord. This was a reminder of how good it was to be alive.

And out of the damn boot.

Em and Rosie were sacked out, sleeping so heavy it stunned him. They had played and run and danced all evening, eaten like ravening dinosaurs, and crashed. Which was nice for him and Liam, because that meant they'd had some adult time.

The door opened, and Liam stepped out, wrapped in a jacket. "Mornin'."

"Morning, babe. How's it going in there?"

"Still sleeping like babies." Liam sniffed the air. "Coffee?"

"In the pot on the stove." They could cook in the fifth wheel, but he had a Coleman stove so he could do stuff early in the morning without waking the girls.

"Excellent. I need it. Chilly this morning, huh?" Liam poured himself a mug, warmed his coffee, and sat.

"Yeah. But man, look at that sunrise." It was so clear and so damn fine. And sharing it with Liam... yeah.

"Mmm...I should go get my phone." But Liam stayed right there.

"Nah. Let's just watch it." He sipped more coffee. Liam was close enough to touch, so he moved his cup to his other hand so he could reach out. The feel of Liam grasping his hand gratified him in ways he couldn't even begin to explain.

"It's beautiful up here." Liam didn't cast eyes at him, but he didn't let go either.

"It is. This was an exceptional choice, babe. The girls love it, and I look forward to getting up in the morning to see it."

"Yeah. We've got a week to enjoy it."

"Who will we want to kill first, do you think?"

Liam glanced at him, and they both grinned. "Em," they said together.

"She's definitely not the easiest baby on earth," Sawyer admitted, and Liam chuckled.

"She's got an amazing will and a razor-sharp mind. I think she's going to take over the world, if I'm honest." Liam shook his head. "She's fierce."

"She is. But Rosie is going to be our sneaky one. Em will brazen things out. Rosie will plot and plan."

Liam nodded. "She'll have to, I think, to outsmart her sister. Then, all of the sudden she'll figure out that she's creative and wonderful and be on it."

"Yeah." Sawyer pondered that, then nodded nice and slow. "Yeah, I can see that. She'll decide she doesn't have to do what her sister does to be successful. But that takes time, huh? Like, she has to see what else there is."

"Yes, but she will. Em will help her, because as much as

they fight, Em will eat anyone that dares to hurt her." Liam snapped his teeth together. "Munch."

"I know. How did we get so lucky with those girls?"

"My blood," Liam deadpanned.

Sawyer took a long moment to decide if he should get pissy about that. A year ago, he would have taken it like a punch to the gut. But now he saw the little grin playing on Liam's mouth, took a deep breath, and rolled his eyes.

"Yeah, yeah. And my guidance."

"God yes." And just like that, Saw could breathe. He'd read the joke right, and Liam had rewarded him with heartfelt agreement. He wasn't walking on eggshells. That had been his lot in life before the divorce.

What he was doing now was feeling his way in the dark, hands out, not willing to crash into something and knock it down because it had all been moved around.

"Well, we'll just have to go with the flow, right?" Sawyer asked. "The girls will let us know which direction to go."

"They will. They're...pretty damn clear, aren't they?" Liam's chuckle warmed the air.

"Yeah." Sawyer squeezed Liam's hand. "I guess I ought to start bacon."

"Sure. They'll sleep a little longer, if you want to relax, though."

"I do." He wanted to sit and enjoy Liam's company and the sunrise. The coffee. Sawyer was a cowboy. The simple things really were the best a lot of the time. He knew it.

Liam grabbed the coffeepot and warmed them both up. "It's supposed to be pretty today, possible storms tonight."

"Like thunderstorms?"

"Yep." Liam chuckled. "Hopefully not a thundersnow."

"Oh, God." The first time they had camped together, they'd gone to Grand Mesa, and it had thundersnowed on them. It had been cold, wet, and gross, and they'd ended up sleeping in the truck, because they'd been determined to rough it in a tent.

"Hey, at least we have the cushy RV of glamping joy. I'll sleep with Em. You can have Rosie."

Oh, Rosie freaked at thunder.

"Hmmm. That doesn't sound very fun." He was really much more likely to snuggle with Liam. But Rosie was damn important to both of them, and Em could be impatient.

"Hopefully she'll be out before the thunder starts, right? I'd rather sleep with you too."

"We'll just have to see, but I sure hope so." He'd think about a food coma situation where the kids could go to bed early.

"We'll have to go for a nice long walk today. Maybe go up and search for elk in the park. I know Em will want to go shopping at some point..." Liam winked at him. "I blame your mom."

"You know she would totally take credit for that. I think I'll get Em to pick her out some fudge."

"Oh God, that will take an hour."

They both cracked up. Em loved to taste test flavors. By the time they got done, they'd have a sugared-up tween with a temper.

"Perfect." Sawyer winked at Liam. "I'll take Rosie to run in that little park by the creek."

"That sounds great. She loves the ducks."

"She does." Sawyer chuckled some more, and Liam pursed his lips.

"Promise you'll make sure she doesn't fall in." Oh, Liam's voice was dry as dust.

"Hey, she's only fallen in the water a couple of times with me!"

Liam stared at him.

"Okay, one time I might have pushed her." He winked broadly.

"'One time'." Liam sighed in a gusty, exaggerated way.

"I did not tip that little boat over. That was Em."

Liam chuckled, the sound utterly wicked. "She says it was all your doing. All of it."

"Uh-huh. That's because her sister would murder her for blaming it on her." Sawyer grinned at the horizon. "It's about to get warmer."

"Yep. Sun's almost popped out of the toaster."

He reached for Liam's hand. "I've always loved how you taught the girls that."

"Yeah? I try to be a good dad. You're way more fun." Liam held on.

"There has to be a balance. When they're sick or really scared, they want you.' Sawyer shrugged, letting that not hurt like it had in the past. "They trust you so much."

"I love them, and that's so important to me. Being someone they can trust."

"I know." Sawyer tried to think of what to say to not sound whiny butt. "I think I've wanted to be the fun dad to make sure they still wanted to come spend time with me."

The shock on Liam's face was gratifying as fuck. "You were fun anyway. I'm a worrywart. I know it."

"Maybe a little." He winked over. "But that makes you a good businessman."

Liam blinked at him. "You think I'm good?"

"Well, of course I do. You're amazing."

"I don't feel amazing. I feel like I'm always running to catch up. I mean…" Liam stopped and shook his head. "Listen to me."

"Hey, we both feel that way, right? I feel like I'm always running." Sawyer shrugged. "But we can work together a little more on that, right? That's part of what we're doing." At least he thought it was. He wanted Liam back, but he also wanted to streamline things so the girls got the best of them.

"Yeah. If nothing else, we can be friends, right? We all deserve that."

"We do. I don't want to be at odds with you all the time." He hated that, in fact. Now, if he was hoping for more, so be it, but Sawyer was determined to keep his options open, dammit. "I'm just tickled to be sitting here with you this morning, babe."

"I am too. I'm...It's going to be a nice week, dammit. I know it will."

"Even if it thundersnows," Sawyer agreed. "We'll make it that way." And sitting there, holding Liam's hand again, watching the sun break over the horizon? He meant every word.

Chapter Nineteen

"Da! Da, thunder!" Rosie came screaming from the tiny playground at the campsite, and Liam scooped her up without a single thought, shielding her from the rumbles that made her so scared.

"Rosie, baby. It's okay. It can't hurt you." He didn't know how to keep her from freaking out.

He did know her sister was going to give her a raft of shit.

He hugged her to him, letting her hide in his shirtfront.

"Daddy! I don't want to have to go in because Rosie is a baby."

"Em, that's not okay. She's not a baby. She's allowed to be scared." Sawyer kept his tone even, which Liam was proud of. "We'll see what your Da wants to do, but she can always go in and watch a video."

"It's thunder, Rosie. It's just loud." Em had been arguing this for years. "I promise it can't hurt you."

"I'm not a BABY!" Rosie screamed. "You shut up!"

"Rose! You do not scream at your sister," he snapped.

Rosie started fighting him, kicking him in the balls, and he dropped her with a grunt.

"Daaaa!" She wailed, her baby body shaking as she got up on her hands and knees.

"Liam!" Sawyer rushed over to scoop Rosie up in one arm before helping him get mostly for the most part upright again.

"She..." He wheezed. "Is she okay?"

The lightning snapped and the skies opened up, the rain about as cold as ice. Motherfucker.

"Aaaagggh." Emily ran for the RV, her little roar kind of hilarious. She might melt. He'd laugh if he had the air.

"She's fine. Come on, babe." Sawyer hauled him and Rosie the camper, and damn if Sawyer didn't push Daisy back into the RV with one foot, gently, on the way in.

Rosie ran to the loft bed, sobbing, while Em stood there in the middle of everything with her eyes huge in her face. "What do I do? Does Da need ice for his...uh...boy parts?"

Liam was going to die.

Dead.

Boom.

Zombified Father of the Sore Balls.

"It might be chilly for that. I'll have an, um, look." Sawyer was fighting laughter, he could tell.

"Ew! Daddy! No one wants to see that!"

If Saw so much as chuckled, Liam was going to make him sleep outside.

"Why don't you go dry off, baby girl? And can you get Rosie a towel and make sure she changes too? I'm going to take Da to the bathroom." Okay, no laughing.

"Can we have a cookie, Daddy? Please?"

"Pwetty please?" Rosie added.

"Apologize to Da, and yes, you can. And get a dog cookie for Daisy, since you almost let her loose, huh?" Sawyer's tone brooked no argument.

Em nudged her sister, and they parroted, "We're sorry, Da."

"Thank you. Get your cookies after you dry off." He limped to the little bathroom. Fuck, that hurt.

"Do you need ice?" Sawyer asked, following him in.

"I don't think so." He raised his shirt to peer at his belly in the mirror. As long as no bruises were immediately rising up, he should be okay.

"Oh, baby. Your sweet balls." Sawyer winced for him. "You are done having children, right?"

"Don't make me kill you, man." He chuckled though, because God yes, he was done.

All the way done.

"Mmm. I could hold them for you, if you needed me to."

"I think I'll murder you."

"That might be difficult to explain to my mother," Sawyer shot back with a wicked grin.

"No one has ever explained anything to your mother, my love. Ever." He winked to ease any meanness he might have had. Barb wasn't an ogre. Mostly.

Sawyer hooted. "Oh, some have tried. In fact, someone attempted to mansplain something to her at the City Market last week."

"Is he still alive?" Liam waggled his eyebrows.

"She hid the body in the freezer."

He snorted. "She is clever like that."

"How are you feeling? Better?" Sawyer bent down and checked out his boy parts. "You're going to be a little swollen. She got you good."

"Or bad, depending on how you look at it." He grunted as he pulled his jeans all the way off. He would change into jammies. "Really bad."

"I'm sorry, babe. I think she is too."

"It was an accident. Do you think she needs a therapist about this whole thunder thing?"

"I think maybe it can't hurt. I expected her to grow out of

it by now, if I'm honest." Sawyer helped him strip off his shirt, then started the shower. When he raised his eyebrows, Sawyer chuckled. "It will help you relax."

"Thanks. I'll make some calls. She just needs some coping skills that aren't run-like-an-idiot. What if she runs into the street or something?" Just the thought made him queasy.

"Yeah, no. Let's get her in to see someone."

"Thanks." He knew not long ago Sawyer would have argued with him, because Barb scoffed at therapy culture, as she called it, and Sawyer had always kind of had the same cowboy feeling about it. So, this was progress.

"I'll look into it, then we can make an appointment when we can both go?" If they were going to do this, then they could be a united front.

"Of course. You just let me know when."

"I'll text you before I set a time and day. That way we can coordinate."

"Okay." Sawyer got all his clothes off, then helped him into the shower before stripping and stepping in with him. It was tight, but it worked. "This should warm us up."

"I— Are you sure?" He leaned in, begging a kiss. This wasn't going anywhere. The girls were out there. Still, Saw was here and bare and fine.

"I am. I know you're not up for anything, baby. Just let me warm you up, then we'll all snuggle and watch a movie, huh? Maybe have some popcorn and hot chocolate." They'd prepared for all weather, since this was Estes and it could freaking snow and hail in June.

"Sounds good to me." *I love you. Jesus help me, I still love you more than makes sense.*

"Me too." Sawyer soaped him up. "Lord, that was some cold rain."

He chuckled. "And a hard kick." He was definitely going to have to find some Tylenol.

"Uh-huh." Sawyer kissed the back of his neck. "We'll be gentle with your parts for a bit."

"Thank you. Hopefully the front is past us and we can just be wet and cold instead of wet, cold, and hysterical."

"Yeah. Yeah, that would be good." Sawyer chuckled. "I haven't heard more thunder, but I bet Em is keeping her busy." Still, Sawyer rinsed him, and they turned off the water and dried off, because the girls probably needed some reassurance.

They dressed in warm sweats, and Rosie climbed right up into his lap. "I'm sorry, Da."

"I know, Rosie-Posie. That rain is sure coming down, isn't it?" He held her, rocking her like she was a toddler again.

"Uh-huh. Em turned on the TV so I wouldn't hear thunders."

"Well, she's a good sister, huh?"

"Mostly."

"Mostly. She loves you all the time." He kissed her temple.

"I know." She yawned, which was a good sign. That meant the freaking out part was over.

"We were thinking about popcorn and movies."

"Can I go play in the rain?" Em asked.

Liam frowned over. "Wait. What? Didn't you just run in screaming because you were getting wet?"

"Yes, Da, but I wasn't ready!"

Liam blinked. "Ready? To get wet?"

"Right!"

He was never going to understand little girls. Ever.

"You're still not." Sawyer's voice held a note of iron. "That rain is too cold, baby girl. You'll get sick. How about you help me make hot cocoa and popcorn instead."

"Can we have parmesan cheese and black pepper on some of it?" Em glanced at her sister. "Not all. Just, like, half."

"We can." Sawyer held out his hand to Emily, and she grabbed it to go to the tiny kitchen.

"See? She loves you. She knows how you like your popcorn." Liam was proud of her—not only for letting herself be deflected, but for caring about her baby sister.

"She's okay," Rosie said, laughter lurking in her voice.

Daisy whined, and he leaned down to pull her up with them, too. Poor baby had to be freaked out by the crying and shouting.

"Oh, Daisy. Are you scared? I will 'tect you," Rosie said. "It's just hot air sliding over cold air. Sister told me."

Liam's lips curved in a smile, but he made sure Rosie didn't see. It would never do for her to think he was laughing about her. She was just so amazing and resilient. He adored her. Even if she had clocked him in the balls. "That's right. It's science. Science is amazing. Seriously."

"It is, huh? I love science."

"And math. Daddy likes animals."

"But he has to use science too. So he knows which bulls will make good babies."

She pondered that. "Yeah. And he has to know about good food and stuff for the horses."

"Yep. So he uses it all the time."

They heard the sound of popcorn starting to pop not too much later, and the smell of hot cocoa filled the air, competing with the rain. Yum.

"I like camping, Da. I like camping with you."

"I love camping with you, kiddo. But no more kicking, okay?"

"Okay, Da. I promise." She glanced up at him. "I didn't mean to."

"I know. Still, let's not anymore, okay?"

"No more," she agreed. "Love you."

"I love you too." He glanced up as Em brought him popcorn. "All of you."

"Daddy too?" she asked.

"Yeah. Daddy too."

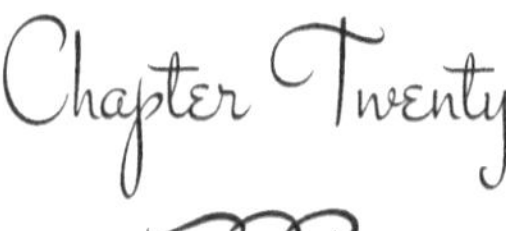

Chapter Twenty

"You want a beer, babe?" Sawyer wasn't ready for their camping trip to end. He'd had the best week, hiking and fishing and going into town with his kids and Liam, feeling like it was old times again. Happy times.

But the girls were in bed, and he had Liam to himself one more night, and they still had a dying fire left in the firepit. So, he was going to sit out there with his husband, who he was so not thinking of as his ex, and enjoy some adult time while he could, before reality crept back in.

"I'd love one, thanks." He'd never seen Liam so relaxed, so easy in his skin. It was damn gratifying.

"Cool." He got two out of the cooler, where he'd loaded them up this afternoon just for this. So, he didn't wake the girls when they were asleep by going inside to grab them out of the fridge. They were worn out, those two, but they would still want to come out and sit if they knew the firepit was still in the offing.

"Do we have to go back?" Liam asked.

"I know. I don't want to. I could stay out here forever."

Sawyer smirked, knowing that was a pipe dream kind of statement.

"You'd miss your horses and your bulls. I know you." Liam winked at him, smiled in that knowing way he had. "I could do this more than once a year, though."

"We could, maybe, huh? Together?" He wanted to ask for a lot more than that, but he wasn't sure if this was the time. They'd been so… in tune. He didn't want to fuck that up.

"I—I think maybe we need to talk, Saw. I need to know what we're doing here."

"So do I. I need to— I'm getting my hopes up, Liam. So, I guess I need to know if there's any reason to." He handed over the beer, moving to sit so he could face Liam and not be restless and wandery for this discussion.

"Me too. For us, for the kids, everything. I don't want to be… I don't know. Lost. Worried. Alone." Liam spread his hands; his body language pretty open for how serious the words came out.

"Okay." Sawyer met Liam's gaze head-on. "How do you want to do this?"

"I don't know. I mean, we're divorced. I miss you. I still love you, but we broke up for a reason, didn't we?" Liam searched his face, those bright blue eyes sharp in the firelight.

"We did. I mean, a lot of reasons." He sighed, popping the top of his beer. "I miss you so much, though. And I've been thinking. And I'm not asking this because it will be easier on the girls, or because I'm just selfish. I want us to live together again. Just to try it."

"Why?" The word wasn't mean, but he knew how important it was. Liam questioned everything. That was how he coped.

"Because I think we've both worked on things. I think we still have what it takes to be a family. Because I love you so damn much."

"I never cheated on you. I never even considered it. You're the one I wanted. From the first time I saw you."

"I know, baby. I knew it when I said it. I just... I saw red when the rumors started, and I used it against you. I'm ashamed of it." That was the truth.

"I didn't even know. I was so shocked. I was buried under Erik's bullshit, and I just didn't know what to do."

"And I was feeling like you didn't want to even come home." Sawyer sighed. "I think we'd have to commit to talking for sure."

Liam's eyes rolled like dice. "God forbid. At least I'm not fighting so hard to build the business back up. Where would you want to live?"

He needed to step carefully with this one and not just pop up with something glib. "Ideally? The ranch. But I'd be willing to split our time, even. And I would want to sit down with Momma before we did anything and explain the rules. I know that was an issue, and I never dealt with it like I needed to." He understood his mom was a source of stress. If the trial time worked out, he would suggest them building a new house, maybe. Liam was good at that kind of planning.

"Yeah. I—If we decide to be permanent, I want to design a house for us. We deserve that—something that's ours. Both of ours."

"We do. Somewhere where we set the ground rules and make the memories. I mean, I'm not saying I don't have a lot of complicated feelings about that house, but I would want a place that we made together." The ranch was plenty big enough, and had enough resources to support that, and his mom could move back into the old house if she wanted to.

"I'll be eco-conscious. I know resources are finite, but— Saw, that's always going to be your mom's house. She fussed if I moved the plates in the cabinets. I felt trapped. Like I was a teenager again. I mean..." Liam glanced down into his beer bottle. "I never got to walk out of our bedroom naked, even before the girls. I never got to feel like I wasn't a renter."

He'd never heard Liam be so specific about what he'd disliked about living in that house. "Then we'll make our own place. And in the meantime, I'll talk to Momma about what we need from her to make it work."

"Yeah? Because I care about her, and I don't want to hurt her, but I need a door that locks, huh?"

"Yes. And she needs to know that she has access to the kids whenever she wants, but she needs to ask first, huh?" That was fair. And he could do that.

"You mean it? I don't intend to hurt her, but—"

"But you need to know you're my priority." Sawyer nodded, catching Liam's gaze. "I do too. I need to know I'm important, babe. I need to know that from you."

Liam nodded. "I can do that. I can leave work at work."

"I would rather you brought work home, though, and worked in a home office sometimes, rather than have you gone so many hours. Does that make sense?" Sawyer waved his beer in the air. "If you have to work after the girls are in bed, I can do accounts or read at the same time."

"So long as we're together, huh?"

"Yes, and it's not because I don't trust you. It's because I miss you."

Liam nodded. "No, I believe that. And it's hard to talk about things when one of us is always gone."

"Yeah. It creates miscommunication. See me use my twenty-five cent words."

Liam's lips curved again. "Maybe fifty."

"Right?" This was good. They were using their damn words no matter how much they cost.

"So...are we doing this? Are we really doing to try to be a family again?"

"I want to. How about you?" He held his breath, hoping and praying inside.

"I love you. If we fuck this up again, I'm never going to forgive us, for all our sakes."

"I love you too, baby. I really do." He got all choked up about it, in fact, so he sipped his beer, the sour and hoppy flavor of it making him almost cough. "So, what do we tell the girls?"

"That we want to try and be a single family again. That we are going to work on our problems like adults. That we made a mistake, and we want to make it right?"

"That sounds like the truth, and the simplest way to say it." He chuckled. "How do you think Daisy will like ranch life?"

"I think you'd better get used to an indoor dog, because she's not living in the barns."

"No, I think that's wise. Hell, I would have had a dog inside long before now if not for Momma."

"I know." Liam rolled his eyes. "Trust me, I know."

"She's—"

"No. No, I'm sorry. That's unkind. I need to watch my mouth."

"We'll get there, baby. I'm not mad." Sawyer got it. His mom had hard limits. She was allergic to dogs, so they'd never been allowed in the house.

"Maybe I should stay at the condo, though...I mean, I can't leave her..."

"Nope. She can come to the house and stay. Momma can deal." Hell, he would buy his mom stock in allergy pills for a while.

This was part of the deal, wasn't it? Them, working together to find an answer.

"Okay. Okay, cool. I just can't see leaving her at the office or making the girls give her up now."

"Or you. You love that silly mutt."

"I adore her. She's so smart and funny. She is great company, and I've been so lonely."

"What about the bull rider? You two are friends, right?"

"We've just become friends. Just."

"Oh." Sawyer blinked. "How did that happen? I mean, you don't go to the rodeo anymore, right?"

"No." Liam rolled his eyes, cheeks bright red and damn near glowing. "It's embarrassing, man. Like a lot. I hired him from Koby Foster."

"Koby? Like, Cowboy Wanted?" Now he tilted his head, trying to figure that out. "What for, baby?"

"Isn't it clear?" Liam stared at him as if he had two heads.

Sawyer wracked his brain. "No. I mean, it's not like you need a hand to work... Wait. You hired him for the ball?"

Liam just stared at him, expression still as if it had been carved from marble.

"Shit." He tried not to let his lips twitch. But damn. If Liam had been trying to make him jealous, it had worked. "And I clocked him one."

"You did, and we're not going to speak about it again."

"Okay." Nope. Not until their twenty-fifth anniversary or something. Oh, damn, that was hysterical. He let it go, though. He would laugh about it when he was alone. On the ranch. Out on the range where Liam would never hear him.

His sexy lover had to *hire* someone to date? Seriously? Sawyer didn't believe it.

Then again, if his intention had to been to get a cowboy who Sawyer didn't know, he would have had to reach pretty far. Lord. He was going to have to call Koby.

He wanted to know all the dirt. Every single detail.

"Stop it."

"What?" Sawyer asked.

"The mental and facial gymnastics."

"I don't know what you're talking about."

Liam stared him down. "Look. I know. It was pitiful and lame. I just wanted you to believe I wasn't a loser, okay?"

"Hey. You are not a loser. I had to ask a friend to go with me. I just didn't want to go alone. Kind of ruined his night too."

"Yeah, I found myself a little short on friends after leaving you, and Erik's firm."

"I hear you, baby. I just made a few new ones. Well, Koby for almost a year, but Morgan has just been a close friend for a few months. Roping pen."

"Terry's a sweetheart. I like him a lot. I sort of wish I'd been into him, but...he's not you."

"No, he is not." Sawyer scowled.

"Hey. I said it. I just couldn't even. I still have it so bad for you."

"I'm selfish enough to be glad."

"I wanted you to just need me, so badly. It was a dumb thing to do."

It had been, but it had caused him to go to that condo and apologize, hadn't it? "I think of it as the thing that made me look in the mirror, baby. I can't complain."

Liam's lips pursed, his lover obviously fighting a grin. "I invited him to the Fourth of July. You and the girls can meet him."

"Oh, yeah?" Sawyer pursed his lips. "I'll invite Morgan. They can keep each other company."

"Oh, that would be good. Terry is newish to town and needs friends."

Now wait. That just blew his whole grump out of the water. No fair. "Well, you know he's welcome. If you vouch for him..."

"Thanks, Saw." Liam reached out to touch his hand. "I know it's hard to say it."

"It is. I'm a jealous asshole. But I trust you."

"He lost his partner on the arena floor. He just needs somewhere easy to be." Liam rolled his eyes. "And I wasn't supposed to tell anyone, but you're...my man."

"I am." Jesus, what a piece of goddamn crap that had to be for Terry. "That's awful, baby. I'm so sorry he had to go through that."

"Me too. I mean, we broke up, but I knew you were alive. I knew you were happy. I knew if I needed you, I could call."

"Well, 'happy' is a relative term. But I was good when the girls were around."

"Yeah. Yeah, they...they love you. I never talked badly about you to them. Dare? Yes. The girls, no."

"Well, Dare will gossip about anyone," Sawyer teased.

"They're pregnant again, did I tell you?" Liam glanced over at him, eyes wide.

"You did, and my only real response is, no shit? They know what causes that." He grinned. "Good for them."

"Yeah. He's a little put out with me. I decided I'd rather come out with you than to Denver for a guys' vacation."

"Wow." Sawyer grabbed Liam's hand to kiss his knuckles. "Thank you."

"I've had the best time."

"Me too." Sawyer squeezed his fingers. "I love you, babe. Seriously. I want our family back."

"Good. I do, too. And hopefully that means we'll work harder for it."

He nodded. "God, I hope so. I'm so tired of knowing something so good went so bad."

"I think we just—we let go too fast. Too easy. I know we were both hurting, and we were worried we were messing up the girls. But I want to try again." Liam stared up into the night sky. "What's our timeline? The girls need consistency."

"I think we ought to try to get you in before the Fourth."

Sawyer had given it some thought. "That way you're in before the girls start any of their summer sports, and before you start that new project."

"Yeah. I'm hoping to not be in Vail too much, but I did plan it as if the girls were going to be gone every three days."

"I know. I figure this way they have a good bit of continuity." Sawyer would just keep them at the ranch. They didn't need daycare during the summer.

"Cool. Okay. Well, then I'll call Terry to help move stuff."

"Shit, baby. I can muster up ten hands."

"Yeah? I—thank you. I forget how much firepower you have."

"Terry is welcome. Morgan will come out too, I bet. I'll buy pizza. The guys will love an excuse to hit the town." He felt a little dizzy.

"I'm a little scared, Saw. You have so much power to hurt me."

"I know that now." He'd lashed out, not knowing if he had back a year ago. "And I'll be careful with it."

"I believe you." Liam reached out to him, and he thought there might be tears in his lover's eyes.

He grabbed that hand and held on, knowing they were on the edge of a pretty tall cliff. They needed to balance to keep from falling.

That was all they could do, wasn't it?

Hold on, pray, and keep on their feet.

Lord help them both.

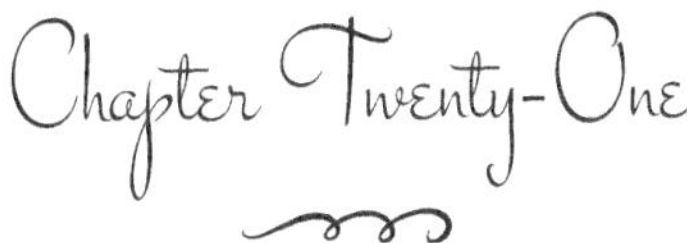

Chapter Twenty-One

L iam felt a little like an elephant was sitting on his chest, the closer they got to Aspen.

Had he really agreed to move back to the ranch? Honestly? Dude.

How was he going to manage it?

How was he going to tell the girls?

How was Saw going to tell Barb?

How—

"Da, are we not spending the night with you? I counted, and it's your night."

Fuck.

He cut his eyes over toward Sawyer, who was driving, and sort of silently asked for help.

"Your Da and I need to talk to you and Rosie about that, kiddo."

"Why? What's wrong? What happened? Did someone rob the condo? Did the building burn down?"

"What? No!" Jesus, that *girl*. She had a hell of an imagination, and she would have Rosie hysterical if she thought too much about it.

"Well, your face is all serious!"

"It is serious, but it's a good serious, sweetie." Maybe they should stop at a burger joint and chat.

"Okay." She seemed pretty skeptical, and he couldn't blame her. She'd been through a lot in her short life.

"I promise. You want to get milkshakes and talk about it?"

"I like milkshakes, Da! Daddy, can I have strawlberry?" Another nation heard from.

"Yes, Rosie. You can." Sawyer grinned over at him. Rosie loved to talk over food and drink.

"Makes it easier and a little fun, hmm?" he murmured. Not whispered, because then Em would be on fire again.

"Yep," Sawyer agreed. "And I'm hungry anyway. I'll stop at one of the ski area grills. That will have camper parking."

"Cool. We'll grab a snack and have a chat."

"We'll have a snackchat!" Rosie announced.

Em actually chuckled and nodded to Rosie with a smile. "Good one, Rosie."

Rosie stared at her big sister's words, vibrating a bit. "Good one. Yeah. I did a good one."

"You did." Liam chuckled. "Lord help us, she's making up puns now."

He was so proud.

"She's my sister. Of course she is."

He rolled his eyes. This was his life now. Sawyer's low chuckle made him snort too. Asshole.

Sawyer pulled into a hamburger grill, finding a solid place to park the trailer. Then he turned to smile at the girls. "Okay, bathroom first, then we eat, and we talk about some things. Do I need to walk Daisy, baby?"

"She's sound asleep in her crate. I'll walk her before we leave." She was snoring. Little go-baby.

"Cool." They locked up everything, then headed into the

grill. Rosie held his hand, singing happily, and Em walked with Saw, telling him something about a song she liked.

They got settled, the girls deciding about what they wanted to order, and Liam felt a jolt of nerves. Saw caught his gaze, winked at him, as if to say, 'Don't worry.'

He was worried.

"Da?" Emily blinked up at him with a frown. "It's been the best week."

"It has been." He had to chill, or they'd have a meltdown on their hands. "I had a great vacation."

"Okay." She grinned a touch, but uncertainty still lurked around her eyes.

"I—we—me and your daddy, I mean, we want to talk to you guys."

Rosie's eyes went wide. "Are you getting divorced again?"

"No, baby girl. That would be— well, never mind. But we wanted to chat about a decision we did make. See what you think."

Em was getting pink in the cheeks, so he just blurted it out. "I want to move back in with your daddy, and I want to know how you feel about that."

"Are we going to come with you?" Rosie asked.

He blinked at his youngest, stunned. "Well, of course you are."

"Oh good. You said you." Literal child.

"Why? Why do you want to?" Em frowned at him, which was weird, because he thought she wanted this.

"Because we love each other. We miss each other. And we both think we can do this." There. That was as honest as he could be, right?

"Why couldn't you before? You made everyone cry when you left Daddy. Why couldn't you be nice before?"

"Hey." Sawyer grabbed Em's hand. "He didn't leave me.

We got divorced, which means it was a mutual decision. And it was hard on all of us."

"It was." She fastened Sawyer with a glare. "Da cried so much. All the time. He said it hurt just to talk about you."

"I'm sorry about that," Sawyer said. "And that it hurt you and Rosie. And we can't make promises that we'll get back together forever. But we want to try."

Liam nodded. "We want to try and be a family again. To be husbands again."

"Where would we live?" Rosie asked. "At the ranch?"

"Yes. For now. We're going to talk about building another house that I design for us." Liam found Rosie a smile. "Something just ours."

"Okay. Sister, say yes. You want to go home too." Rosie hugged Em tight. "It's what we asked Jesus for."

Oh, sweet babies.

"I need more information." Emily squinted at him, then Sawyer. "What are you going to do different this time?"

"I'm going to talk to your granny and ask her to respect your Da's space," Sawyer started.

"And I'm going to work fewer hours, focus on being more present at home." He wanted to make this work.

Emily put her chin in her hand. "Hmmm."

Sawyer gave Liam a grin before he asked. "What, kiddo?"

"Can we have family meetings?"

Sawyer agreed without a second's hesitation. "Sure."

Liam nodded to her. "Of course."

"With milkshakes!" Rosie crowed. "All meetings with milkshakes!"

"Well, maybe we should say food and drink." Liam winked at her, and she giggled.

"Uh-uh. Milky shaky-shakes." Rosie blew him a kiss. "Do we have to leave our stuff at our other rooms?"

"Nope. If we stay at the condo, we'll all take a bag." Sawyer checked in with him with a glance.

"Yeah, we may stay at the condo if there's a thing in town or something, but it'll be like the RV. We'll have some plates and sheets, but we'll pack to go."

"I can live with that," Emily said. "And Granny will have to knock?" She pursed her lips. "Because it isn't nice, to have her walk in to our house like she owns it. Da's kitchen is the way he likes it. Da folds the towels his own way. Da sometimes has a bad headache and needs the TV off."

Liam stared at his daughter. He didn't get it. He'd never said those sorts of things to her. He would *never* complain about Barb to the kids.

Sawyer nodded. "She won't be able to just walk in, and I promise, no more towel talk."

Rosie raised her hand to talk, blurting out. "And we can have good potty paper?"

Liam fought his urge to crack up at Rosie. Lord, when this child figured out how to barter, she was going to be stunning.

Sawyer blinked. "Uh. Which one is the good one?"

"Da's!"

Em nodded. "Yes. Y. E. S. Yours is scratchy and awful, Daddy."

"It's toilet paper." Sawyer looked at him helplessly. "What does it matter?"

Liam grinned. "Well, it's scratchy. Softer is better."

"I must have saddle butt."

"Daddy!'

Liam cleared his throat. He'd learned a few things about little girls and little girl parts and rough toilet paper, after all. "Saw. Trust me. It's important."

"Okay. I'll let Da pick the poop paper."

"Gross." Emily sighed. "Cowboys."

"Yes." Liam agreed, sharing a smile with her.

"Hooray cowboys!" Rosie's cheer cracked them all up, leaving them rolling.

They got food eventually, and that milkshake, and the girls asked more questions, but he thought overall that had gone really well.

They hadn't told Barb. They hadn't started packing. They hadn't figured anything out, but...they were trying.

Sawyer's booted toes touched his foot under the table. And yeah. They were in this together.

Whatever drama that led to.

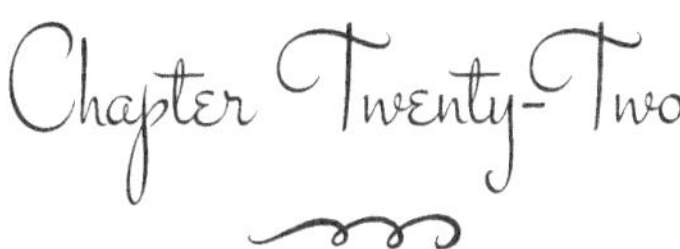

Chapter Twenty-Two

"Hey, Momma. I need to talk to you." Sawyer was going to ease his mom into the discussion with him and Liam. It would happen today. Soon. But he knew it would be better to warn her, and he'd told Liam how he wanted to play it.

Liam was at the main house, getting the girls settled in and all, so he'd driven over to Momma's place to chat.

It was such a sweet little home, and Momma had spent so much time making it exactly how she wanted. The roses were blooming around the front, and there were two white rocking chairs on the covered porch, a table between them waiting to hold a cup of hot coffee or a glass of lemonade. She'd even painted a weird-assed rainbow doily on the top.

"Sure, son. How did the RV do? Did the girls have fun?" He could hear her pottering around in the kitchen as he stepped up to the screen door. "Are you wanting mac and cheese for the girls tomorrow night?"

"Can we sit down with a cup of coffee?" He had to iron this out with her before she showed up tomorrow morning.

There was a pause, then a, "Sure..."

"Thanks, Momma." He smiled when she came to stare at him through the screen, popping the lock. "I'll fire up the Keurig."

"Sounds good. Everything okay?" She was chewing on her bottom lip, worrying it.

"Yes. But I wanted to have a chat." This was hard, because he knew she was going to have hurt feelings. He just knew it. But he needed to do this.

"Okay, what did I do?"

"Momma. Nothing. But Liam and I talked a lot on this trip, and we made a decision."

"You're going to get back together." It wasn't a question, and he was surprised she got it, but he probably shouldn't have been.

Momma wasn't stupid.

"Yeah. Liam is moving back in. So—"

"So you want to talk to me about the house."

"I do." He nodded, because he respected how she was being up front and ready to talk.

"So talk. Don't forget you were making me a cup of coffee."

"Yes, ma'am." He chuckled, filling the Keurig machine with water and grabbing a pod. The big coffee maker up at the main house was a lot less wasteful, but for his momma, this was perfect. She could have a different flavor with every cup. "This feels awkward."

"Well, I reckon it does. But it's part of being an adult."

He glanced at her, a grin curving his mouth. "Okay, Momma. Liam is worried that things will go right back to the way they were before."

"And what does that mean?" Oh, she wasn't going to make this easy...

"Well, some of the particulars are Liam's to tell. But I think we need to set some boundaries, Momma."

"Fine, but Liam has to understand that is a ranch house, not a private house. It's the way things work."

"That's not fair, Momma." He took a deep breath. "Liam works his ass off. He's raising two kids. If he wants to be able to decide where the dishes go, he ought to be able to do that."

She sighed and rolled her eyes. "Fine. I'm sorry. Of course he does."

"Momma." He bit back his urge to snarl at her. "I know how it is with the big ranch house. I do. But Liam wasn't raised on a ranch like we were. And you love your little place here."

"I do. I apologized. What else do you need me to know?"

"That I would like to sit down with Liam and you and talk about all this."

"Maybe in a while. I've got a lot to do over the next little bit."

"Momma..." He blinked at her. "Are you okay?" He got the feeling she wasn't mad so much as distracted.

"I'm fine, son. Just busy. Don't worry, I'll stay out of your hair. Was there anything else?"

Wait. Was this his mother?

"No. No, I guess not." He was totally off-balance. "You want me to bring you supper tomorrow instead?"

"No. No, I'll be fine. No worries."

"Okay. You holler if you need me." Something was wrong. But she wouldn't tell him what it was until she was ready.

"Tell the girls to text me pictures of their trip."

"Sure, Momma." He took his coffee cup with him, not sure what else to say. Shit, he hated this.

She shut the door behind him, and he heard it lock. Damn.

She was really pissed.

He headed back to the big house, checking on a couple of outbuildings on the way to get his head back on straight.

She'd figure it out. She had to. She was just shocked, right? Maybe that was a pipe dream, but Sawyer hoped his mom gave him and Liam a chance.

Hell, she'd liked Liam, hadn't she? That was how it had felt until the divorce. Then she'd been the enemy of my son is my enemy, but that was the way of mommas.

It made sense to him, anyway.

everything ok?

That was Liam.

nope

He sent a sweaty face emoji.

be right there

k. Going to start laundry.

That was his lover. He would simply do what he did. And Sawyer would go find him and talk to him.

He hated feeling at odds with people, especially Momma. She was a special lady, and he adored her so much. But it was important to get Liam comfortable.

Liam was his husband. His lover. His soulmate. He knew it was a balance, but it was important to find it, and not just go with what was easy. That had led to him losing everything.

He could figure it out. It was going to take time and energy and the three of them, but they'd make it work. They were smart dogs.

He got back to the house and unloaded a few more things from the truck.

"Boss?" One of the hands met him in the yard. "Can I borrow you a minute to come look at Halsey?"

Halsey was a riding mare he took out occasionally. "What's wrong?" He texted Liam real quick.

Going to the barn for 5

"She's just acting off. I don't like it."

"Okay, sure." He headed to the barn to put eyes on the mare, not wanting to wait if she was sick somehow.

"Yeah, I haven't found any wounds, and she let me see three of her feet, but you know how she is about that one. It's probably nothing, but—"

"Yeah, but I'm the only one besides Logan she lets touch that foot." Logan was the farrier, and he wasn't a ranch resident, so it fell to him to see what was what.

"Halsey girl, whatcha doing?" Her head lifted as she heard her name.

She nickered at him, limping over to the door of her stall.

"Yep. It's that foot." She'd been born with the tiniest malformation in her hoof—not enough to put her down, but enough that she needed it watched. "Call Logan. Tell him it's Halsey. He'll come."

"Yessir." The hand grinned at him.

"I'm going to be at the house helping the girls unpack. Holler when he gets here."

"Yep."

Sawyer made his way up to the house, letting himself in, finding Liam in the laundry room off the kitchen. "Hey, baby."

Liam searched his eyes, hunting unhappiness. "Hey. Everything okay? Your mom stroke out?"

"No, but she pretty much *kicked* me out."

"You're not serious." Liam went pale, eyes widening. "Oh, Jesus."

"Yeah." But what was he supposed to do? "Do you remember in *Tombstone* when Curly Bill is all, "Well, bye?"

Liam turned back to the washing machine. "Yes. Do you want me to take the girls and go?"

What? "No! God, no. I just thought I would warn you. She was in an odd mood. But she apologized." Sawyer was still a little stunned by that.

"We'll figure it out. If we work together, we'll figure it out."

"We will." He pulled Liam around to face him so he could take a kiss. "We'll get there."

"I'm a little freaked out," Liam whispered against his lips. "I haven't slept in our bed in a long time."

"Well, I'm not sure I want you in the guest room." He grinned down at Liam, hoping to make him smile, and damn if it didn't work.

"I'm not sure that's going to work for me either, cowboy."

"Oh, good." He was relieved by that, dammit. He wanted Liam with him tonight.

"Yeah. We're not roommates, Saw. We've never been that, and I'm not interested." Liam held his gaze, and it was shockingly hot, to see that passion, that hunger in his lover's expression. "I'm interested in something else that needs a locking door."

"Mmmmmm." The bedroom as well as the main house. That way the girls couldn't interrupt. "Did you take your suitcase into the bedroom? Into our bedroom?"

"I was scared to. I didn't know if there was room."

"Baby, there's plenty of room. Half the closet is still empty."

"Yeah?" Oh, were those tears in Liam's eyes?

"Yes. I never could make myself give up hope." Sawyer stroked Liam's cheek, and Liam leaned into his hand. Fuck, his heart was going to crack open.

The kitchen door opened. "Boss, the farrier's coming."

"Daddy, where's my bunny?"

"Da, is Daisy living here? Where is she sleeping?"

"Daddy! My bunny!"

Liam snorted, and Sawyer leaned his head against Liam's for a moment. "The bedroom door does lock. I'll be back. I'll hunt in the RV for your bunny, Rosie."

"Da, Daisy?"

"Put her crate in your room, sweet pea," Liam answered.

"Okay!" Em ran off.

Sawyer followed Jasper out to the barn to meet Logan. Liam was right—as much fun as he'd had on the campground, walking through the metal gate to the pasture, the mountains cradling them, the rye grass under his feet? The horses nickering and stomping as they jockeyed for attention? This was home.

Logan was already in the barn, whistling.

Jasper shot him a wicked smile and cut off before they got to the open door. "I'll stay out here, boss. I know she's grumpy."

"Good man." Sawyer headed into the barn proper, checking the hay bedding in the stables, the habit drilled into him. A horse that stood in filth would end up costing more than paying a hand to clean. "How's she doing?"

"She's got a bit of thrush, and she's a prima donna, so she let you know right off. I'll treat it and come back for the next few days to watch her."

Dammit. She hated being penned up here at the house, but it was the driest area...

"Thanks, man. If she wasn't so picky about that foot..."

"That's okay. I'll check a few of the horses on the rotation sheet while I'm here." Logan grinned up at him. "She's just in love with me, is all, and she needed my hands on her."

"It's probably true. I should sell her to you." He would never, but it was worth the tease.

Logan snorted, just like the critters he loved so much. "Why should I buy her when you can feed her and I can visit any time I want?"

Halsey lifted her head and stared at him as if she understood him, as if her feelings were hurt.

"I'm teasing you, sweet baby." He rubbed her nose, assuring her of her place.

She nickered at him, blowing her lips and nibbling at his shirt. He'd put a bit of apple in there while he was in the kitchen, and she was pretty smart to find it. She nudged him harder, demanding his attention and her goodie.

"You let me know when you're done so she can have her treat."

"I got it." Logan nodded, then stood. "Treat away."

"Cool." He dug out the apple and offered it to Halsey, who lipped it out of his hand.

Logan went to grab the laminated sheet that hung on the wall listing the farrier schedule. "So, you were out camping, huh? How'd that go with the girls?"

"Good. But then I had Liam to help out."

Logan turned his head, one eyebrow lifted, and his lips twisted in shock. "Did he? That's cool."

"Yeah. It was." He grinned, not even trying to hold it back. "He's agreed to move back in."

"No shit." Logan was another friend who got it. Logan understood how his soul had ached.

"Yeah. I'm pretty tickled."

"I bet you are. Congratulations." Logan turned to lean against the wall, grinning at him like a monkey. "You told your mom yet?"

"Yep." He did not roll his eyes. Not notty not not. "She's not so tickled with me, at least."

Logan snorted. "She's a mom. She'll come around. I know it."

"Yeah. I hope so. I mean, if nothing else, she'll love having the kids here full-time again."

"She will. She loves those babies more than anyone but you."

"I know." Sawyer huffed out a huge sigh. "I just hate that look she got on her face. But we got to have boundaries."

"Ah. Yes. Your guy's a city guy at heart. He's used to privacy." Logan gave him a pursed lip, a prissy face, but there was no meanness in it. Logan adored Liam, but it was true. His man wasn't country born and bred.

"He is." Sawyer shrugged. "We're going to build us a house. That way either Mom can move back into the big house or we can use it as a common area."

"Oh, dude. How cool would that be? To have like a ranch space? You could do parties and shit."

"That's kind of what I was thinking. That way we have a place for the kids to have their friends over, and for Momma to have bigger get-togethers."

Logan nodded and brushed his hands off, hanging up the clipboard. "It's a great idea. Well, Halsey's all packed. Keep her in and dry."

"I will." He gave the mare some more apple slices. "You get a little vacation, sweetheart. I bet Em will come out and comb you, and...Peaches."

Oh, Liam was home.

"I want Peaches brought in from the pasture."

"You got it. I'll tell the guys." Logan clapped him on the back. "Congrats."

"Thank you. I'm—" So fucking relieved. "—over the moon."

"I bet. I know it's been a tough time this past year. Well, I better get to work, huh? I'll get Peaches in for you and check her hooves for you, huh? I reckon she'll get some exercise now."

"Yeah." Woo. "I'll send him out to see her in half an hour."

"Got it." Logan gave him a thumbs up.

Sawyer headed back into the house, stopping to get the bunny on the way in.

He could hear the girls laughing and playing, making wild noise inside. He grinned, letting himself in, curious to see what they were up to. He peeked in, and they were playing ball with Daisy in the middle of the kitchen floor.

He loved that. They had always adored the working ranch dogs, but none of them had ever been pets, really. They were hardcore task dogs. Daisy was just a little ball of fluff. An absolutely adorable ball of fluff that was focused on nothing but making them all smile. And he was.

He was beaming from ear to ear.

"Cute, huh?" Liam came to join him, hand slipping into his.

"Yes."

"How's your mare?"

"Thrush. She has a sensitive hoof, and I'm guessing she was in wet for too long. I'm having Peaches brought up and shod."

"Oh, yeah? How's she doing?"

"She misses you."

"Still?"

"Yep. She's a smart girl." Sawyer squeezed Liam's hand.

"I'm glad you think she'll remember me."

"I know she will. There's a reason she hasn't been in with the riding horses."

Liam got a little misty. "She's a good girl. I love her."

He knew. It was why he hadn't sold her, even when seeing her hurt his soul. "Well, she'll have to earn her keep again now." He winked. and Liam laughed.

"I was thinking grilled cheese and salad for supper in a few hours. They won't want much."

"That sounds really good, baby." In fact, he would make it, if Liam just wanted to sit.

"Cool. I'm going to make gazpacho with the leftover veggies. I'm craving."

"Yum." Sawyer had never had gazpacho in his life before Liam, but he loved it now, and he was ready for a summer of cold, spicy soup.

"Yeah. Do you have red wine vinegar?"

"I should?" He had a bunch of stuff to make salad dressing.

"I'll explore." Liam shot him a teasing glance. "It's not like it'll have changed…"

"Nope. I mean, I did have a few mice last month, but then I found an open pack of animal crackers." He gave the girls a stare.

Both girls went wide-eyed. "It wasn't us! It was mac and cheese!"

"Mmm. Those crackers didn't help. Also, they draw bugs." Sawyer didn't roll his eyes. Why else would he have mac and cheese boxes? His mom? The hands? Unlikely.

Liam grimaced, and Sawyer wanted to kiss the expression right off his face. "It doesn't matter. We just need to make sure it doesn't happen again, right? I don't love mice."

"No. Icky." Rosie wrinkled her nose. "They poop all over."

"Yes, and they carry diseases and they smell and they eat things and—"

"Babe. Ease up, hmm?" Sawyer murmured. The last thing they needed was full-scale panic. "But your Da has a point, so we'll all be careful."

"We will. Can we go play in our rooms? Are you going to sleep in Daddy's room?"

"I am." Liam grinned. "It's our room, still, right?"

Sawyer nodded. "It is."

"There you go. I'll be in our room." Liam winked at him. "Go play. I'm going to head to the barns before supper and see Peaches, if you want to come."

"Yeah. I'd like to." Heck, he would settle on being with Liam and breathing. "We can all go. Spend time with the horses."

"Please?" Rosie perked right up.

"Sure." Em kind of shrugged. She was in another phase right now, he guessed. His mom said when she turned twelve the horse fever would come back.

"Halsey's foot is sore, so she's in the stable. She's not real happy."

Em frowned. "What happened to her?"

There was that care. Em loved critters; she just needed to seem cool as a cucumber.

"She got wet, I think. You know how she has that weird hoof?" When Em nodded, he shrugged. "She's got thrush, which is kind of like the white goo you get when you have a sore throat."

Em's eyes went wide. "Oh. Oh, poor baby. I'll brush her for a few minutes. She likes that."

"She does." God, he was proud of his girls. They were ranch kids all over the place, and they could hold their own with the Aspen crowd, too.

"Can I ride Strawberry, Daddy? Just for a little while?" His baby girl was ready to ride, every second of every day.

"We'll see how it goes." He wasn't going to say no, but they might not feel like it once they got out there. "But you can brush her out, for sure."

"Okay, but then tomorrow? It's Sunday. I like riding on Sundays."

"Yep. Tomorrow for sure." He knew it would take them a bit to figure out they were really here full-time.

"Okay. Thank you, Daddy." She kissed his cheek. "I love you!"

"I love you too."

"Okay, everyone grab their muck boots," Liam said. They always had to remind the girls not to go out in their cute flip-flops or sneakers. "Oh. I guess don't have any, love."

"Yours are still next to mine." Where they belonged. Dammit.

Liam stared at him, eyes wide, but he nodded, going to grab his mukluks. Sawyer figured they would end up talking about this shit at some point.

It was going to be one of the good talks, though.

This was his chance. A new start. He took a deep breath, then let it go. Yeah. He could do this. Sawyer turned around and headed back to the barn with his family, making sure not to let Daisy out as they went.

They had some more bonding to do.

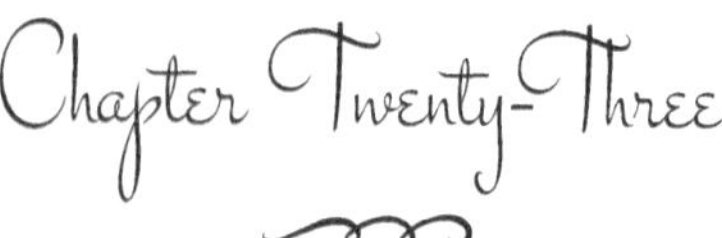

Chapter Twenty-Three

"Why are we doing this again?"

Emily had slammed her door. Rosie was sobbing. Liam wanted to kill someone—he needed a beer, a pizza, and a joint.

Moving was hell. Moving with two girls was like triple hell, especially after Barb had refused to watch them for Saw. She was still pissed they were getting back together, and Liam was sure he was going to have to go apologize. He even got why. As far as she was concerned the ranch was her home. And he was telling her what to do there...

"We're doing it because we want to be together again?" Sawyer grinned at him, coming to rub his back.

"Yeah, yeah." Oh, right there. "Go murder the children?"

"Yep. Kill the beasts." Sawyer's chuckle and goofy Igor impression made him snort.

"Good man." He managed to not crack up for a few seconds.

They did cackle together, which made Rosie come out of the bathroom, wiping tears. "What's so funny?"

"We're happy that we're all going to be in one house again,

Rosie-Posie." He opened his arms to her. "I'm sorry this is hard."

"It is. I love you. I want to go home and play with my Lego."

"We'll go home soon," Sawyer promised. "I know this is so much work."

Rosie sniffled. "But 'portant, yeah? To be a family again."

Liam nodded. God, he hoped so. Was he fucking with his family? Hurting his girls?

"I sure think so, baby girl," Sawyer told her. He bumped hips with Liam, which made him smile.

"Okay. I will pack all my books. My babies are in a box." Rosie wriggled to be let out, and he eased her to the floor.

"Thanks, kiddo. You're doing great."

"I am. Bring the pan for the good rolls, Da."

He chuckled and rolled his eyes. The girls swore the pan decided whether the dough would rise. He knew better. It was barometric pressure. But he would bring the pan. Family legend was important.

"Yes, bring the good roll pan, baby. I still have the good biscuit pan." Saw patted his ass.

"Mmmm. Yay. I want those." With honey butter. And good sausage. "And I want you to make spaghetti sauce."

"I can do that, baby."

"Spa-sketti!" Rosie sang, shaking her little butt.

"Do you like Daddy's spaghetti?" he teased, and Em's head popped out of her door.

"Daddy's making spaghetti?"

"I will totally make spaghetti. I have all the stuff at the house. If all of my people want that as y'all's first meal after moving back in, so be it."

"Seems like all of your people want that, cowboy. I'll make salad and garlic bread."

Em actually came out of her room. "Brownies?"

Liam nodded. "If we get done in time, absolutely."

"Woo!" Sawyer hooted for him, twirling him around.

"If we get done loading the trailer, Saw." Liam winked at him.

"Right. Okay, troops. I am taking boxes down. Keep packing!" Sawyer marched off.

"Okay, lovelies. Do you need me to help in there or should I keep doing the kitchen?"

"I'm good, Da!" Rosie cheered, and Em just disappeared back in her room, but the door was open, so he'd take it as a win.

Liam finished up the kitchen as quick as he could, because Rosie would pack one doll in a box and consider it full. Saw was trekking in and out with a couple of hands, though, carrying boxes in and out of the condo.

"Da, what are we doing to do with this house?" Em asked, and he had to admit he didn't know.

"Your daddy and I will discuss that together. We haven't had a chance to yet." He guessed that was one of the amazing parts about being a couple. That he didn't have to make every decision by himself.

"Okay. I mean, I kinda like it, and it's right above your office..." She chewed her lower lip.

"What?" *Talk to me, baby girl.*

"You're not going to sell it, right?"

"I bet not, since it is right over the office. But we'll see what happens, huh? Did you have any thoughts?" Ask leading questions, he told himself.

"I think we should keep it. It's a...vestment?"

"Investment. It absolutely is."

"Those are good, Da. People talk about them."

"Do they?" Who talked to a kid her age about investments?

"Uh-huh. Kylie's dad talks about it *all* the time. About how we might be poor without investments."

"Ah. Well, I guess I can see that." He bit back a grin. Kylie's dad was a dead bore.

"She says he cares about money a lot. It makes her mom crazy. Did you and Daddy fight about money?"

"No." No, they fought about...nothing. Everything. Money was the one thing they'd been together on the whole way, though sometimes he'd felt as though he wasn't pulling his weight. "The important part is that we never—not once—fought about you two."

Emily watched him, her eyes shadowed, but she nodded. "I know, Da. Ginny Marks at school? Her parents got divorced this year. They had a big fight at the school. It was really ugly."

"Oh, that must have been scary." He opened his arms to give her a hug.

"It was. They called the police."

He frowned. "I didn't get an email about that." Usually all the parents got a notice of an incident.

"I don't know, but they both went away in the police cars and Coach Ayers took her home with her to her house."

"Holy crap." He blinked, reminding himself to talk to Saw about this.

"Right? O. M. G. I was freaked."

"Why didn't you tell me?"

She shrugged, pinked. "I didn't want you to say I couldn't go to her house anymore."

"Well..." He tilted his head. "Whose house do you stay at when you go?" He wracked his brain. Ginny Marks...

"I haven't gone since the fight. I—It's a little scary, so..." She shook her head. "I need to finish, Da."

"Sure. Okay." He kissed the top of her head.

"I brought reinforcements." Sawyer came back in with

two ranch hands and a cowboy he didn't know. "Okay, guys. Haul boxes." Sawyer pointed.

"Aye-aye," one of the hands said, saluting like a smart ass.

Saw glanced at him. "You good, baby?"

"Nothing serious. We'll talk later. Not about us."

"Okay. Hey, Morgan brought us a coffee."

"Morgan?" Would that be Morgan who'd gone with Sawyer to the cowboy ball? The Morgan of the Goony Golf?

"Hey." Morgan waved over, the guy dressed to work. "Sorry to show up when you're all in a flurry of moving, but I figured I could help."

Sawyer handed Liam a coffee in a to-go cup. It smelled like his favorite latte.

"Thank you, and it's great to see you." Liam held out his hand to shake. "Thank you for the coffee. You got my favorite. You either have an amazing memory, or my husband texted and asked you to grab it for me. Either way, you're amazing, and I appreciate it."

Morgan gave him a firm handshake and a cheerful grin. "I so am, man. I owed Sawyer congratulations. He got you back. He did good." He grabbed a box and headed down the stairs.

"So?" Sawyer shot him a glance. "Everything okay?"

"I think so?" No, not really. "Did you hear about a fight between two parents at school?"

"Huh?" Sawyer blinked at him like an owl. "No."

"Weird. I—it's no big, but I don't like it." He didn't love feeling out of touch with his girls. It was going to happen. He knew that, but he wasn't ready.

"Do we need to call someone?"

"We will when they start school again, yeah." Liam lowered his voice. "Em says there was a fight between two of... Ginny Marks? Yes, that girl with the neat rainbow glasses that plays piano, you remember her?" At Saw's nod, he continued. "It was bad enough the police came and a coach took Ginny home. That's messed up on its own, but Em's worried about going to spend the night over there, and now I'm thinking I don't even know where over there *is*."

Okay, maybe he was more worried than he'd thought.

Sawyer came and kissed him. "Hey. Hey, that's totally reasonable for us to discuss and make a plan about. We need her to be safe. Want to talk it over tonight?"

"Yeah." Every night. Every one, from now on.

"Good deal." Sawyer nodded like that was that, and they all got back to work.

The guys moved boxes like machines, the girls finished packing, and to his shock, they were out of the condo by midday.

"We did it!" Rosie danced around. "Sghettis!"

"*And* brownies!" Em hugged him.

"And brownies. I need to stop at the store."

"Okay. You want me to come with or give you my list and head for the house?" Saw asked. They'd brought both vehicles.

"Can I go with Daddy?" Em asked.

"I'll go shopping with Da! I need juice boxes!" Rosie grabbed his hand. "Daughter and Da date!"

"That answers that. Daughter and Daddies Dates it is." Liam winked at Saw, tickled they could do this again.

"Cool." Sawyer nudged Em. "But you have to talk to me."

"Okay. We can do that. Talk." Em nodded, taking a deep breath.

Sawyer looked over her head at him, mouthing, "uh-oh."

He waggled his eyebrows, going for dramatic.

That got him a wink and a kiss. "Okay, see you back at the house, you two. Be careful, please."

"We will. Text me your list. Love you."

"Love you." Sawyer took Emily down to the truck and headed out not too much later, leaving him and Rosie to lock up.

"Bye-bye little house. We'll visit!" Rosie patted the door on her way out.

He patted it too. "We will. Maybe we'll put in one of those game tables with all the different games."

"Like what?" Rosie blinked at him.

"Like, uh, pool and we can do puzzles and stuff?" He didn't know. He just knew that folks had game rooms.

"Oh. Boy games. I like puzzles, though."

"You like air hockey too." Boy games. Jesus.

"Uh-huh."

He could tell she had lost interest, so he changed topics once he'd gotten her in her car seat and they got on the road. "What do you think is best about going back to the ranch, Rosie-Posie?"

"I like it there. I like horses and Granny and my bedroom, 'cause it's super big." She gave him a worried stare. "You okay?"

"I am. I'm a little nervous, because I want this to be good with my whole heart. I'm scared I'll mess up." He was going for honest, but not worrisome.

She smiled at him through the rear-view mirror. "We'll help you, Da. Me and Em. We'll have fambly meetings."

He had to grin at her old mispronunciation of family. She hadn't done that for months. "We will. Just to check in with everyone."

"Uh-huh. Make sure we're all okay. That we're all still loving each other."

They pulled into the City Market parking lot and parked, and he grabbed his phone.

Rosie waved and worked her car seat open. "Don't forget the baby in the back seat!"

"There's a baby?" he teased as he opened her door.

"Your baby, Da. Your best baby."

"That's absolutely right." He ruffled her hair, which made her groan.

"Da."

"I know. No touching the hair." He shook his head, took her hand, and headed into the City Market. "So, we need something yummy for breakfast tomorrow. Sausage biscuits?"

He could make those easily.

"Yummo. Can I have some of those teeny pancakes?"

Yummo. Lord. "Or maybe Eggos?"

Both girls would eat those.

"Pancakes," she stated.

"All right. Teeny pancakes it is. Anything else?"

"Hmmm. Sister wants those weird little pies."

"Ah. Okay." Hostess fruit pies for the win. "Apple or cherry?"

"Cherry." She wrinkled her nose.

"I know. You like the Swiss cake rolls."

"Uh-huh. And Daddy likes oatmeal ones."

"Right on." He was an Eggo guy, really, so he'd default to those.

She hummed, happy to be going to the store, and Liam was suddenly so grateful that his kids were amazing. "Thank you, baby girl."

Rosie blinked up at him. "What for, Da?"

"Being you, Rosie."

"Oh." She beamed at him. "I am super-duper good at that, huh?"

"You are. I adore you." He grinned at her as they chose a cart. "You're my Rosie-Posie."

"I am! Yours and Daddy's, and now we're not going to be divorced no more!"

"Any more," he corrected, not even thinking about it.

"Any more. We're going to just be us again."

Yes, but better, please God. Just us, but better.

"Right on, baby girl. Now, it's time for spaghetti-supplying."

"With brownies!"

"All the good stuff." And as he and Rosie sang along to the music in the store, her little voice soaring, he could really believe that, too.

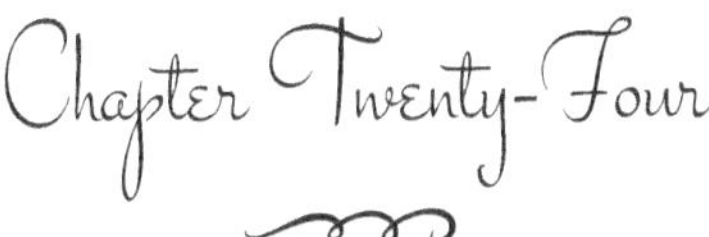

Chapter Twenty-Four

"You think we can make potato salad, baby?" Sawyer was getting all the meat ready to go on the grill. The smoker had been going since last night, and that was all good, but Momma usually made the salad and the deviled eggs, and he wasn't sure she was going to even show up to the annual July Fourth do this year.

She was still pretty... peeved.

"Sure. Potato salad, eggs, coleslaw. Beans are already on." Liam was so pretty in that cobalt T-shirt that matched his eyes, the raven's wing hair just long enough to curl around his ears.

"Okay, cool. I know Mara Tallent is bringing banana pudding and Lena is bringing chocolate pie and a big icebox cake." He counted hot dogs.

"Terry is bringing drinks, ice, plates, and cups."

"Morgan is bringing buns, chips, some kind of cookies, and beer." He grinned. Cowboys. "I have no idea what Koby and Tom will bring."

Liam shrugged. "I've only ever spoken to them on the phone. I can't say that we know each other that well."

"I think you'll really like them, baby." He knew Liam was

a little embarrassed about hiring someone from Cowboy Wanted, but those guys were solid citizens.

"Yeah, well…" Liam blushed and shrugged. "I guess it worked."

"It did. I was insanely jealous." He grinned, because he thought they owed a lot to the stroke of genius that Liam had come up with, hiring Terry for that ball.

"Yeah? You wanted to dance with me?" Liam offered him a kiss.

"I wanted to be the only one you even looked at." Sawyer grinned, going to wash his hands so he could grab Liam and pull him close. "I'm not one to share, baby. And you're *so* mine."

"Am I now?" Those warm hands wrapped around his hips. "I love you, you know? I love being home with you."

"Yeah? I think it's just because I let you rearrange the cabinets." He laughed for sheer joy, though, and kissed Liam hard.

"Oh, God. The satisfaction, lover." The whisper was mostly tease, but there was a hint of pleasure there too.

"I know. I saw." The knock on the kitchen door had him sighing and letting Liam go. He grinned when he saw Morgan waiting there, laden with bags. "Hey, man. Let me get the screen door."

"Thanks. How's it going? I brought stuff for the beer fridge."

"It's good. And beer is yay." He grinned at Liam, who rolled his eyes.

"Liam. Good to see you," Morgan said.

"Nice to see you again. I'd better make some food for all you hooligans." Liam nodded and headed to check the potatoes.

"What can I do?" Morgan asked.

"I need to go check the smokers. I got all the burgers and dogs ready to go, but they can go back in the fridge until everyone gets here." He waved Morgan outside with him where two hands sat in the shade, starting with Dr Pepper instead of beer for now.

"So, how's it going? You seem happy." Morgan just wasn't one to beat around the bush.

"I am. This is a damn good thing, Morgan, this being home together."

"How are the girls? Handling it?"

"Off and on." He checked the brisket. Yeah, that was the stuff. "They're still trying to roll with it."

"Yeah, Adults are a mystery to those of us that are still kids."

"Hey, now." He chuckled. "You're adulting these days, man."

"Not like you." Morgan snorted and waved one hand toward the barns. "You're an overachiever."

"Well, I'm a dad."

"Daddy! Watch me!" Rosie cannon-balled into the pool.

He grinned and waved, making sure he kept it up until she popped back up to see him. "That's my girl."

"She's fearless, huh?"

Sawyer glanced over his sunglasses at Morgan. "You have no idea."

"What about the older one, Em?"

"She's got two little friends over for the night. She is in her room. She'll be in the pool later; I have no doubt." How had he become the father of a little girl who had sleepovers?

"They're wild. They make me think I might want kids."

"You think?" Okay. Damn. That was unexpected. "I always knew I wanted them, and so did Liam, so it was easy. We were sure."

"Are you done?"

He nodded. "We have gymnastics, dance, robotics, riding, swimming — there's not enough time for another little one."

"Yeah. Well, you'll have grandkids eventually, huh?"

"I will." That was the crazy thought. It really was. "Jesus. Shut up."

Morgan chuckled, and the sound grew to real laughter. "Uh-huh. Grampa."

"Shut up."

"Am I allowed to take the food into the kitchen?"

He sighed without letting any real sound out, his back muscles tightening. "Hey, Momma. Of course you are. What all did you bring?"

"Macaroni and cheese and green salad."

"Yum." Look at her, not bringing potato salad and deviled eggs and letting Liam do it. "Rosie's swimming, and Em's having a slumber party and is in her room."

"I'll just pop this inside and then go sit by the pool, then." She gave him a glinting smile and headed into the house.

"That was chilly," Morgan said.

"Yeah, I had the boundary talk with her when we got back from camping. This is the first time she's spoken to me directly since."

"Dayum. I mean, I guess that's her house, huh?"

And that was the basis of the issue, wasn't it? It was her house. Not Liam's, not the girls', and not even his.

"It is. We're going to build a new one. This house will be for stuff like this. And she can move back in if she wants."

"No shit? You moving far?"

"No, we're just going to keep moving on the far side of the pool. Basically, use the old house as an office and all if Momma wants to stay in her little place."

They needed four bedrooms, three and a half baths, a big basement and main area. Something that would blend.

"That makes sense." Morgan nodded. "Well, if you need help..."

They both turned as a big pickup pulled up at the parking

area at the end of the driveway, a cowboy hopping out and grabbing a cooler out of the back. Ah. Liam's fake date.

"You going to let him come to your party?" Morgan teased. "You ain't worried about your man?"

"Not one bit." Liam and him, they were solid as a rock. He would never question that again. He might poke Liam to talk to him, or they might squabble, but he would never, ever question Liam's fidelity.

"I'm just giving you shit, man. That man wouldn't have moved back here if he wasn't sure."

"Exactly."

"Hey." Terry stopped at the porch. "Where should I unload?"

"Drinks can stay out here. Food inside. Terry, right?" Sawyer asked.

"Yep. Nice to see you."

"I'll help you," Morgan said, popping up like a jack-in-the-box.

"Thanks. I brought a ton of ice and Cokes and paper stuff. Liam said it was the best idea."

"I'm grateful." Sawyer grinned, waving them off as he moved on to the pork loin.

"We've been watching the smokers, boss." That was Jack, his hat tilted down low to shade his face.

"Good deal. Did y'all get fireworks for us?" They did the little ones—cones and sparklers and all.

"Yessir. Nothing the girls can't handle. Told the guys if they wanted to do anything more energetic, they'd have to go somewhere else."

"Good man." The dogs didn't love anything big or booming, and a couple of the hands were veterans who had issues as well.

"Yes, sir. You need anything brought from the Walmart? I want to grab some of them folding chairs for us."

"Daddy! Come swimming!" Rosie called.

"Would you ask Liam if he needs anything? I'm being summoned." He had his suit on with his T-shirt and flip-flops, so he might as well.

"Sure, man." Terry waved and headed inside.

Rosie squealed and waved at him. "Daddy!"

"Hey, baby girl." He pulled off his shirt when he reached the pool, then kicked off his shoes. "You and Miss Elaine having a good swim?" Elaine was Jack's wife, and she and Rosie were besties, really. Elaine was trying IVF, but they weren't sure it was going to take, so she tended to care for the ranch kids a lot to get her fix, he thought. Or hell, maybe to practice for when it did happen. What the hell did he know about it?

"Yes! But I needed you too. Come and play." Someone was so jealous that her sister had company, but she was trying.

He hopped down into the pool, then waded over to his baby girl. "What are we playing?"

"Marco Polo?"

"Mmm." He grinned. He was pretty good at that one. "Maybe let's see who can do a handstand?"

"Ooh…I can! Daddy, I can do it! Watch!" And up and over she went, little feet kicking wildly.

Elaine winked at him. "You just made her day."

"Yep." He waited until she surfaced, then applauded. "That was amazing, kiddo."

"Now you!"

He made a great show of splashing and not doing much hand-standing.

Her baby hands grabbed his legs, trying to help steady him. God, she was strong for five. Sawyer would be damn lucky if she didn't drown him.

"Careful, Rosie. Don't make Daddy stay under too long." Liam brought out some bottled water and more sunscreen.

He shook off water as he stood. "Terry and Morgan head off again?"

"Chairs and more buns and dogs. Laurel and Harlan are coming too."

"Ah." Those two were former hands who now had five kids. They could all eat. "I thought Jack was going."

"Your mom needed him to help her grab something out of storage. She doesn't seem great, honey. She's awful pale."

"Yeah?" He blinked. He hadn't noticed, but then, he'd been trying not to get snarky with her. "I'll go make sure she sits down. Maybe the heat is getting to her." Had she walked over? Somehow with all the food he figured she'd at least hop in the golf cart he'd gotten her to zoom around in.

"Well, she's headed to the shed, but she's agreed to come eat this afternoon."

"Da! Come swimming!" Rosie bounced and waved.

"I'm cooking, baby girl. I'll swim later, though. I promise."

"Okay." Rosie evinced disappointment so well.

"I'm going to go get Granny, okay? I'll be right back." He hauled his ass out of the pool and put on his flip-flops to go find his momma.

"Okay. Tell her I'm waiting for her!" She paddled in a big circle.

"All right, baby girl. I will." He walked back toward the house with Liam.

"Did I do something wrong with your mom, honey?" Liam asked.

"No. No, I know I pissed her off, but if she's all pale and stuff, then she's not feeling well. If it was a case of the mad, she'd be all flushed and tense." He was a touch worried, in fact. His momma wasn't prone to summer colds or allergies or anything.

"Well, if she needs something, holler. I'll help."

"I will." He let his hand trail over Liam's back as he went by. He found Momma standing in the kitchen, just a bit lost.

"Hey, Momma. Can I get you a drink?" He studied her, trying to decide if she was sick.

"I don't want to touch anything…" She sighed softly. "I should just go home."

"Nonsense." That was Liam. "Barb, we can't do this. Be all tense together. Did Saw tell you we're going to build a new house and turn this into a common area? A place for meetings, parties, guests?"

"I know he talked about making plans for something." She shook her head, her lips twisting in a wry smile. "I got to admit, I wasn't listening by that point."

"Well, we thought that might be the best answer. We need the space for meetings, and obviously your grand-daughter is into sleepovers." Liam rolled his eyes as the girls squealed.

"She is." Momma chuckled. "I like that idea. I could have the ladies over to play cards."

"Absolutely. And I promise to let you keep the kitchen organized as you want." Liam winked, and Sawyer held his breath.

"You little shit," she muttered, but grinned.

"You want to come out and sit by the pool?" She did seem kind of pale and sweaty, but not feverish.

"I think I'll get a glass of iced tea and sit in here in the air conditioning." She waved toward the dining area right off the kitchen.

"Sure." He glanced at Liam, who frowned a little.

"Doctor?" Liam mouthed.

Sawyer nodded. Not today unless she started acting worse, because Momma wouldn't want a fuss on a holiday, but he was going to get her in for a checkup this week. He would call first thing in the morning.

His momma had to be feeling like shit if she wasn't soldiering through.

Yeah, he'd get her to get a checkup.

"I'm going to finish up the potato salad, Saw. You'd better put an eye on your mermaid daughter."

"Will do." He poured Momma a glass of tea, then went to check on Rosie.

She was playing with her water blocks, singing to herself, so happy.

"Time for sunscreen, cowgirl," he called.

"Okay, Daddy!" She climbed out of the pool. "Spray me down!"

"You got it." He toweled her off, then sprayed her, and when she waded back in, he checked to make sure adults were there before going to meet Koby and Tom as they drove up, their big Dodge super truck making him grin. Koby had won the who-drives war, or there would be an Escalade.

"Hey, guys! How goes it?" He and Koby were good friends now, and Tom was going to get along with Liam like a house afire.

"Good. Great weather for a to do." Koby grinned, his eyes shaded by his hat. "Where do we put all the goodies?"

"Food in the kitchen. Drinks in the coolers in the back porch. The pool is open." He got a hard, one-handed hug from Tom.

"Is Liam in there? I have to meet him in person."

"He is. He's cooking away, and there's some snacks out, too." He jerked his chin toward the screen door.

"I'll go say hi." Tom hauled a load of Tupperware and sacks with him.

Koby snorted. "I'm ready for a Coke. I'll switch to beer in a bit."

"Come on over. Did you bring your swim trunks?" They wandered to the back.

"We did. You said pool and hot tub and Tom made plans to make sure someone else did the feeding so we could stay and make asses of ourselves."

"Excellent. Em's having a slumber party, and Rosie will have kids more her age coming soon."

"I'm not worried about the kids, man. And Tom loves being around them, so he'll be out there swimming with Rosie in no time." Koby was in laid-back mode, which was nice. "Morgan about?"

"He and Terry went to the Wal-Mart."

"Really? I hear that you met him at the Ball..." Oh, butter wouldn't melt in his mouth.

"Terry? I did, yes. Thanks for the head up, asshole."

Koby's look was bland as longhorn cheese. "Hmmm? About what?"

"Man...you set me up."

"Nope. Tom was doing business. You weren't supposed to go all Nolan Ryan on him!" Koby just barely kept his shit together.

"Nolan... Nah. I was more John Wayne, you know? Swagger up and hit him once really hard." Sawyer snorted. "Of course, he just rocked on his heels and then told me I hit like a giant butterfly."

"Well, buddy. You don't go waling on a guy willing to make a living as a roughstock rider. That's dumb as all get-out."

"No shit. I'm used to delicate damn roping horses." He winked, and Koby roared with laughter, drawing a few glances and smiles.

"Cowboy Koby! Hi! I'm swimming!" Rosie called.

Koby chuckled and nodded. "I see that! Hey, little chick!"

"Hey!" She bounced and splashed. "Gonna have brisket!"

"I know. That's my favorite."

"Yep. All the meats!" She giggled and splashed off, so tickled at all this attention.

"Out of the mouths of babes," Koby murmured.

"You're a shit." He did have to laugh, though.

They heard the murmur of voices and laughter in the kitchen too, and they grinned at each other. Yep. Liam and Tom were already buddies.

"So what's the plan—y'all just starting back where you left off?"

"More like we're starting over in a lot of ways. We're going to build a new house. We've made some new ground rules, too."

"Good on you, man. You need to be able to make your own way, huh?"

Sawyer nodded. "That's the plan. We need to feel equal, and Liam can't in this house." And he got it. He did. He'd felt that way whenever he'd had to go to a work thing with Liam. He'd felt... uneducated. Rough around the edges.

Erik had pushed that agenda for some reason. The thing was, he wasn't uneducated, literally or in practice, and Liam had never so much as suggested it, but— Well, that son of a bitch knew how to poke at people.

So now he was going to talk to Liam, and vice versa, whenever someone else interfered with their shit. They were a united front instead of a divided one.

As if Liam could hear him, the guys came out together and each grabbed a beer before going to see Rosie.

"Now we have our permission to switch." Koby grabbed a beer as well.

"Right?" Sawyer would wait until after he played with fire.

One of them had to be completely clearheaded with all these folks here. Liam would never get drunk or anything, but he deserved to be able to let loose and enjoy himself.

"I like your set-up here." Tom looked around, then squinted at Koby. "Are you taking notes?"

"Do I need to be, babe?"

"You do. Chop-chop." Tom winked and stripped down to his trunks. "Give me the lifestyle I wish to become accustomed to."

Liam laughed. "I like him, babe."

"I knew you would." Sawyer gave himself a dramatic pause. "Even if he did set us up."

Tom snorted. "I filled the request as it was given."

"He so did. I told him I wanted to make you blind with jealousy."

"Yeah, yeah." Sawyer flexed his right hand. "I went all cave-cowboy."

"Well, it was a catalyst," Koby said.

"What's a catty-twist, Daddy?" Rosie asked.

Sawyer forced himself not to crack up. "It's something that makes something else happen."

"Like when you eat a pan of fudge you have the poopies?"

That was more than any father could take, and Sawyer hooted. "Something like that, yeah."

"Not fun." She shook her head, then paddled off to see Em, who had emerged with her friends, all of them in their bathing suits.

They piled into the pool, and Liam passed out the diving toys, sliding into the water to keep an eye on things.

He loved that. Liam was always willing to do his share or more, especially when it came to the parenting. More folks arrived, and he winked at Koby. "Time to go char meat."

"Make me a burger, honey? Yours are the best." Liam's words made his spine stretch. "I think Terry's here."

"Good deal. I was worried they'd just go hit a rodeo or something." He hadn't been worried about that, but he'd been surprised that Terry and Morgan had taken on the Walmart run.

"We got the chairs, the extra buns, and some cool pool toys for the kids," Morgan told him, coming to join him and Koby. "Hey, Liam."

"Hey, there!" Liam waved, then went back to throwing things for the girls to dive for.

Terry came through wearing swim trunks. "Time to swim!" He jumped into the deep end where he wouldn't hit the kids.

"Da! Who's that?" Em asked, and Liam chuckled.

"My good friend Terry."

"Oh! Hi, Terry." Em waved, then went back to her friends right away. She was a focused girl. But at least no one was being mean to Rosie.

In fact, it wasn't long until people started coming, and the pool was filled with little ones, and Rosie was having a ball, diving and laughing and playing hard. She would sleep like a rock tonight.

Sawyer put dogs and burgers on the grill like a machine, and Kody and Morgan passed them out. Jack worked the smokers, pulling out brisket and pork loin and slicing it like a pit master.

Momma finally came out in time to eat, and he thought she seemed better, more like herself.

Before he knew it, he was sitting at the edge of the pool, Liam floating between his legs, and the sun was about to go down.

This was like a fantasy, a dream, and he wasn't even drunk.

"You happy, babe?" Liam asked.

"You have no idea, baby." He was... He had no words. "I never want to move again, I'm so happy."

He felt more than heard Liam's chuckle. "Me either."

"You think the kids will even want to do sparklers?" Rosie

was dozing on a deck chair, and Em had disappeared with her guests.

"I think Rosie is going to crash hard. Maybe she should do them now. Or we can do them tomorrow for a second special night."

"We could. We'll just play it by ear. The hands will want to set off a few, but anyone who wants the big stuff went into town."

"Yeah." There were only the six of them left — Koby and Tom, Terry and Morgan, and him and Liam. They were all a little sun-soaked, lazy. The beer had flowed well enough that the guys might all end up spending the night, but that was okay. They had the space, and driving at night on the Fourth was a hazard.

"Thinking about pie," Terry said.

"There's banana pudding, too," Liam said, hand sliding over his calf.

"Mmmhmm." Terry didn't seem too inclined to move, though. He pretty much sat, holding his beer. Sawyer got it. It was damn pleasant out.

They floated, the music playing, Rosie snoring softly, the older girls giggling and raiding the kitchen.

He was home. Really home.

Happy damn Independence Day.

Chapter Twenty-Five

"Liam! Liam, I need you to look over these plans. I want to add another bathroom here, but I don't want to have to do another set of surveys and shit."

Hank Bell was going to be the death of him. Complete and utter death. Thank God the man had a secondary office in Vail village. Otherwise, he'd been spending his time in coffee shops sucking Wi-Fi.

"Show me what you need, and I'll see what I can do." The nice thing was that Hank wasn't unreasonable. He simply didn't understand how plumbing worked. Or local laws. Or environmental impact.

"I want this here." Hank made some scribble on a mock-up of the elevation Liam had been working on.

"Hrm. Well, we can do that, but it's going to cost you. Are you willing to put another bathroom here?" He tapped the plans. "It'll save you big money, you can keep that glass wall, and you won't have to do another impact survey."

Hank tilted his head, lips pursed as he considered what he wanted versus what he wanted in his pocket. "Yeah. Yeah, okay. We could work with that."

"Good deal. I'll update the plans and talk to Mark."

"I could do it for free."

Fuck, he hated that voice. "Erik. Funny seeing you here."

"I'm sorry, Mr. Bell! He just walked right in." Helen shot him an apologetic look.

The *asshole* was implied.

"I just happened to be in the neighborhood, thought I'd stop by. Hank, good to see you."

"Mathers." Hank seemed surprised, which was good, at least. He hadn't pitted them against each other on purpose. "What are you up to? Did you need something?"

In Vail. Two and a half hours away from Aspen.

He crossed his arms, waiting for the answer.

"I was over here about that condo unit over by the highway. I thought I would stop in, see how you two were getting along." Erik glanced at him, and that son of a bitch winked.

God, Erik was so full of shit.

His eyebrow lifted. "Mr. Bell is a dream to work with, thank you. Honest, fair, straightforward—I couldn't ask for better."

"Sure, sure. Liam isn't cheap, though, is he, Hank?" Erik's eyes darted back and forth between them.

"If I'd wanted cheap, I'd have hired you when you low-balled him." Hank rolled his eyes. "I'm happy to save a buck, but I need quality work. You have a reputation."

Erik's eyebrows rose and red stained his cheeks. "Don't listen to Liam here."

Hank blew out a breath. "I don't have to. It's not a secret, Mathers. Everyone in Pitkin County knows."

"Erik, I'm trying to work here. Please. Just leave me alone." He wasn't going to scream. He wasn't.

"I'm just in town to have lunch and thought I'd give Hank a better offer." Erik shrugged, but he moved along when Hank glared.

"I'm sorry, sir. That's embarrassing." And he hated this shit.

"Bah. He's a dick. *He* should be embarrassed, not you." Hank waved a hand. "Now, if I have to move this bitch, it needs to be impressive."

"Okay, bring it on. You want me to get Mark in here?"

"I do." Hank grinned. "Let's talk turkey."

"Gobble-gobble." He headed for the little makeshift office they'd created for Mark, who was currently screaming at some subcontractor on the phone.

He sat in the chair across the desk, winked at Mark, and texted Saw.

Erik came. Tried to take the Bell job.

Like he wasn't under contract. Like he hadn't already billed a huge chunk of his hours.

WTF?

He had to grin as that shot back super-fast.

Do I need to kick his ass?

Has a nice long fantasy about that…

God, yes. The son of a bitch had ruined his marriage. Or at least he'd tried.

I'm available

He could literally see Sawyer's grin.

Nope. Taken. All. The. Way.

Asshole.

> I meant for your ass kicking jobs, baby. You
> staying in Vail or coming home

He wasn't sure. It depended on what Mark said and whether they needed him.

Oh, who was he kidding? He was more interested in seeing whether Erik was going to bother Hank or not.

> I'll get back to you on that in half an hour?

> Cool. Love you

Mark and Hank were talking bathrooms, so all he had to do was wait for the decisions to be made. He made notes about adding the bathroom in, get the plans updated, move plumbing around. He'd update everything in Aspen and get them printed here in Vail for Mark to pick up.

"You headed back to Aspen?" Mark asked when all was said and done about forty-five minutes later.

"Do you need me here?" Has that asshole been sniffing around? And why? Why be such a dick, long-distance?

"Nope. I would watch your back, though. Make sure Erik doesn't run you off the road or something on your way back." Mark jerked his chin at where Erik was sitting at the bar in view of the office, having wings and a beer.

When Erik noticed them watching, he raised his beer. The urge to flip the asshole off was huge, but he avoided it.

"I think I'll stick around. Something's up, and I don't know what it is. I know he's losing business. Constantly. Hell, he even used me as a reference for a job."

"No shit? Why?"

"I have no idea. None." But he didn't like it at all. "Want

to walk across the street, share a beer, and see if he sends a photo to my husband?"

"Sure." Mark grinned. "Always happy to be part of a sting operation."

"I knew I worked with you for a reason."

"You know it. Only a douche tries to screw with a guy's livelihood."

"Yeah. This guy has gone after my bottom line more than once." They settled in, and he texted Saw.

> Having a celebratory beer with Mark. want to see what Erik is up to

> Be safe. Love you

> Wait for the pic. ;-D

They sat together at the bar, far enough that Erik couldn't hear their conversation, because he was interested in the new bathroom fixtures.

Sure enough, twenty minutes later, he got a picture of him and Mark, heads together over the table, the angle done so the plans weren't visible.

"Score."

> Did u send back a dick pic?

"No shit? Did you seduce his wife?"

"Accused him of cheating his clients and being a twat publicly."

"Well, he clearly is that." Mark rolled his eyes.

> No dick pic, but I was in the barn so I sent one of the donkeys

> Oh, nicely played. *applause*

"So, we're going to build a new house outside Aspen. I don't suppose you're interested in the general contractor job."

"No shit? I am totally interested if it's your house."

"Yep. On the ranch. And it'll be at least four bedrooms and three baths."

"Now you're singing my sexy song. I bet your hubby gets more pics of my lusty face."

He had to laugh at that. "I bet he would if he didn't just send Erik a picture of a donkey and then block his number."

"Oooh...nicely played. I can't wait to meet him. Let's talk floors, baths, everything."

"Yep. I mean, Saw will want a say, and aside from sealed granite in the kitchen, he hasn't said much. I know he likes hardwood, and I want some cool shit in the master bath. Like, really luxurious so Sawyer feels pampered."

"And you want full baths? No halves?"

"Maybe one powder room. I want the girls to have their own baths." He didn't want them to fight.

"I can see that. A powder room out by the front room and kitchen for guests. It's a smart move." Mark made some notes.

"Right? I think it's the easiest thing to do, too. Maybe off the laundry room?"

"I can see that."

"I want the kitchen to be a doozie, too. The girls will use that as much as a family room as anything if we have a good eating and sitting area."

He wanted a place for homework and projects, Christmas cookies and art.

Liam wanted memories. Years and years of memories.

He knew Sawyer had that in the old house, and that would stand for generations. Who knew? Their Rosie might move back into it one day and make it her own.

But he wanted something theirs. Something that he'd designed, with his family in his heart.

"Kitchens are my great love, man. They're the heart of a home." Mark grinned wide.

"No shit on that. They are the center of everything." Mark got it. "So, we need to start planning."

"Sure. You give me the kind of plan you want, and I can start working up estimates."

"You have a deal." He shook Mark's hand, making sure Erik saw the action, saw the friendship. *Take a picture of this, you prick.*

"You good to drive back? You want me to distract him so you can get on the road?"

"You think we're good on Hank's end?" At Mark's nod, he grinned. "Then I'm heading home."

"Cool deal. I'll call you as soon as you send me plans. Or if I have any questions about this job." Mark winked.

"Thanks. Lord have mercy. I'll holler, but I appreciate the visit." He stood up to leave, his back popping.

"You know it." Mark waved him off, and he fought the urge to stop and give Erik a piece of his mind.

Really, though, what did he have to say? He'd told the truth. He meant what he'd said. He didn't give a shit about Erik's butthurt.

Erik met him at the door of the club.

"Excuse me." Liam brushed past him, because really, he had dick-all to say to the asshole.

"You and I are going to talk."

He shook his head. Nope. He wasn't interested, full stop. He had nothing to say to the man.

Erik followed him, too damn close for comfort. "Dammit, Liam, I need to talk to you."

"What about?" Jesus, he was tired of this shit. Erik could send a Photoshopped photo of him fucking another man and Saw would know it was fake. He and Saw were figuring shit out. They were working together. "You and I have nothing to say to one another. You did not ruin my marriage, you did not ruin my reputation, and you did not ruin my life. I win. Leave me the fuck alone."

"You owe me."

He whirled around. "I owe you dick! You set out to make my life a living hell."

"You are the little upstart that dragged my reputation through the mud!"

"No." No, he hadn't had to do that. "I am the person that fought back. That was it."

"You made everyone believe—"

"Nope. No way. I didn't lie or convince anyone of anything. You cheated and lied your way into a bad reputation." He was not about to take the fucking blame for anything. Erik had cut corners and broken rules and regulations. If Liam had pointed it out to people, it was Erik's own damn fault.

"I ought to kick your shiny queer ass."

"'Shiny'? Honestly? That's the adjective you came up with?" That was dumb as fuck.

Erik almost smiled, but then his expression tightened again. "I need this job."

"That's not my problem. It's mine." He had a contract. It was a done deal. Hell, Hank was crazy-making, but what client wasn't? And he paid well. Really well.

"Hank was my client."

"Well, you fucked that up, Erik."

"Damn you, Liam, you're so fucking smug."

"No. Honest. The word you're searching for is honest. I don't cheat on my husband, I don't cheat the laws, and I never cheat my clients!"

"Fuck you." Erik roared, and before Liam could even blink hard, Erik stepped forward and popped him right in the nose with a clenched fist.

Ow.

His head tilted, and a smile began to bloom on his face. "I think that was assault."

Erik's eyes went wide, his mouth falling open. "No."

"I think it was too, man." Mark hooted, sounding tickled as hell. "Good thing I was recording."

Erik's mouth worked. "You wouldn't—"

"I've called the police," the hostess of the club said, sticking her head out of the door. "Do you need a napkin for your nose?"

"Am I bleeding?" It was still numb.

"A trickle."

Erik started to slip away, but Mark moved around to block him. "Nope. You can wait. The cops are coming."

"You can't make me stay."

"You want me to post this on Insta, man? How about TikTok?"

Liam swore, if he wasn't in love with Sawyer, he'd fall for Mark. Right now.

"I say go viral and post it on all the reels."

"No!" Erik held up his hands as if to ward them off. "I'll stay. But you can't mean to press charges."

"I can't? You hit me, man. You just hit me, for no reason."

"You provoked me."

Liam rolled his eyes, then pulled out his phone to text Saw.

> Gonna be even later. Need to talk to cops.
> Erik hit me

> WHAT

> Got it on camera.

> Holy shit. Do I need to come

> No. I got it. I didn't want you to worry

He didn't know how long this would take.

Hopefully not long.

Call me when you're on your way home

He grinned, loving that Saw seemed to trust him to handle this shit. It was a good feeling. He was ready to be used to it.

Mark nodded at his phone and raised an eyebrow. "All good?"

"Yep. Just letting my husband know I'm going to be late getting home."

"Good deal." Mark texted someone too. "Thanks for reminding me. The wife would kill me if I didn't let her know I was waiting on the cops."

"She's going to be waiting by the TV to see if you're on the news." And it was funny as hell.

"What kind of worthless bitch calls the cops when a senior citizen accidentally touches him?"

"It was a hit. There was blood." He shot back, because he wasn't going to let it go. Senior citizen. The man was fifty-two for fuck's sake. Sure, that qualified for AARP but not a senior discount at Denny's.

"You assaulted him, and that was after stalking him, man." Mark crossed his arms and stared. Hard.

"Stalking?"

"Totally. You asked for that table so you could watch them," the hostess said.

"Who the fuck asked you, you little bitch."

Her lips firmed up into a hard line. "You can bet the cops will ask." Her head tilted then, and she smiled. "Bitch."

The sound of a siren made Erik flinch. "I can't believe you're doing this."

Liam showed Erik the bloody napkin. "You did this, man. Not me." And it gave him a deep, savage sense of satisfaction, he had to admit. "Don't worry, Erik. I'm sure the cops will understand. We'll just explain you were trying to steal a job from me, stalking me, and then you attacked me."

The first of two police cars pulled up, a stout man in a uniform stepping out. "Someone called in an assault?"

The hostess stepped up, phone in hand. "I called it in. My manager is also a witness, but she had to stay inside due to us being shorthanded today."

"What happened?"

"I have it all on video," Mark said, and that was the easy part.

He hadn't had to do a damn thing.

Chapter Twenty-Six

"Dammit, Jack get a hold of her head. I need to give her this shot." Sawyer was about done. He'd dosed about a dozen horses today, and every damn one of them had fought him like a tiger. He was tired, sweaty, and grumpy. And he still had to deliver a mare to another spread about thirty miles down the road.

Maybe he could get someone else to do that.

Hell, he was the fucking boss. He'd make someone do it.

His phone rang, Momma's face popping up. Oh, dammit. That couldn't be good. She had the girls at her house today, since Liam had to drive out to Vail for the groundbreaking of that project he was heading.

"Hey, Momma. What's up?" He jabbed the injector where it needed to go, and grunted when Whirlwind smacked him into the damn gate.

"Rosie bit her sister, and Em smacked her. I sent one to the sunroom, the other to the guest room, but Rosie ran out. You know she's headed to you."

"I do. I'll meet her halfway." Shit. "Sorry, Momma."

"They're just hyped up. If Em wants, I'll let her stay and watch a movie or something."

"Oh, that's fine, but Rosie will be coming back to apologize."

"Sure, but I think she needs her daddy for a second. She's grumpy."

He understood that, bone-deep. Little Rosie was his girl, to the core. His sparkly baby cowgirl had some crazy mood swings sometimes, but she was constantly growing right now, right? That was a hormonal mess. And the move had been draining on all of them, from Momma to him and Liam to the girls.

"I'll spend some time. Love you." He hung up with Momma.

Jack gave him a grin. "Trouble in paradise?"

"Rosie bit Em."

"Ouch. I'll get this finished. Want Trace to deliver that mare?"

"I do. Thanks." He took off his thick leather gloves and shoved them into his back pocket.

Rosie could run, but her legs were only wee, and it was hot, so she was probably going to make it to the dirt road between their houses.

"Come on, guys." He whistled up the dogs. "Find Rosie."

They set up to barking, more than willing to find their favorite girl, the one who was always willing to sneak them cookies.

He followed them on foot. He'd grabbed a couple of bottles of water from the cooler before he set out, and the walk would give him time to get an attitude adjustment. He didn't need to be all loaded for bear when he found Rosie.

If they were both on fire, they just caused an explosion, and he didn't need that. Shit, neither did she.

He caught sight of her, kicking rocks and yelling her five-year-old soul out until she saw the dogs. Then she just plopped her butt on the dirt and opened her arms to the pack, sobbing like her heart was broken.

He hung back, letting them slobber all over her and try to comfort her while the storm raged. When she was down to sniffles, her face buried in Kodiak's fur, he walked up to her, his heart hurting for her little self. "Hey, baby girl."

"Hey, Daddy. I'm running away from home. You wanna come?"

"Sure." He nodded easy as pie, holding his hands down to help her to her feet. "Are we walking?"

"I was gonna go get Pancake." Pancake was an old buckskin gelding who was the color of a slightly underdone breakfast dish. He was also docile enough to ride bareback and with nothing but his halter anywhere someone wanted to go.

"I can see you put some thought into this. Are you just really mad at Em?"

She threw her baby hands up in the air. "Oh, Daddy. She's so...She's always so right. She's always better. She's always bigger than me!"

"That's true." Sometimes the fact he was an only child worked against him as far as sibling advice. "And I know how frustrating that is once in a while."

"All the whiles! I'm never going to catch up with her, Daddy! Never!"

"Sure you are. You remember my cousin David? Momma's sister's son in Texas? I always thought I would be behind him, but we're about even these days." He should call that side of the family, in fact, see if they wanted to come see Momma.

"I'm so tired, Daddy." The words cut him deep, sliced his soul like razor, because she was five, and those words? They came from him and from Liam. They had taught that to her already.

"I'm sorry, baby girl. How about we have a nap instead of running away?" Apologies were important, but they could wait. Em would get her movie and granny time, and he and Rosie could hang out on the couch and be together.

"Okay. Can I have a hug? My heart needs one." Those big eyes stared at him as if he held the secrets to the universe.

"Yes, ma'am. I could use one too." He lifted her up and gave her a big old hug, letting their hearts meet, as she would say. He held on tight, ignoring the dogs, who saw hugs as a touch worrisome.

She took a deep breath and relaxed, the tears coming again, but easier this time, and fast. "Love you, Daddy. Let's go home."

He nodded, shifting her to one arm so he could pull out his phone and awkwardly one hand text Momma.

> Nap time. I'll get Em in a bit

> Em's watching soaps with me. She's got a headache. Bet they're getting sick.

> Yay

He grimaced. They probably were. They were worn down, and at their ages, everything on earth turned into a sniffle. Good thing they hadn't gone into town to the pool today. He would be sure to take his vitamin C stuff today once Rosie was asleep.

"Can I have a drink, Daddy?"

"Yep. I brought waters."

"You always have waters. Cowboys carry waters and love aminals. Are the horses okay?"

"They are. I got the last shot done before I came to get you, and Jack is doing the last of the worming. Killeen is going home today. She's all trained up for her mom."

"She's very high-stringed," Rosie said seriously.

"She is, but her momma wants to race her, and that can be a good thing in a barrel horse if you handle it all the right way."

She frowned at him. "Okay. Why? I need to know so I can do it."

So serious about her goal to have permission to ride solo. She'd never believe him if he told her she had a lot of her sister in her.

"Well, because it's kind of related to speed. Like, think of Pancake. He's old now, but he was never fast. He was always gentle and slow. But then there's Windflower, right?"

"She bites," Rosie said.

"So do you," he shot back. "Why did you do that?"

"I was so mad in my heart. I wanted to run and play and no one else did!"

"What did Em want to do?"

Rosie sighed. "She and Granny were making cards. That's so boring!"

"Ah." Crafts were hard with Rosie and Em because they were at such different skill levels physically. Rosie was still learning scissor and paintbrush skills, while Em was light years ahead. "Well, love, did you ask Granny to do something different?"

She shrugged. "Kinda."

He chuckled. "So that's like Windflower. She wants to go and run, she hates to be caught up in the stables, and she gets mad. She doesn't want to be quiet."

"No, Daddy. Me too." Rosie nodded like he was speaking her language. "Me too. I don't want to be a lady."

"I know. You want to be a wild cowgirl." He swung her in a circle, waltzing her toward the house. "But that doesn't mean you have to bite, huh? And you'll have to tell Em you're sorry. Hurting someone is never the way." God knew, he knew that. He was still smarting over punching Terry.

"I know. I will. Daddy, will I get to run someday? Will I run?"

"Oh, baby, you are a cowgirl, hat to boots. I swear to God, one day, you'll race the wind and leave it behind you." He had no doubt. His Rosie would ride.

She leaned her head against his shoulder. "Promise?"

"I do." It was a solemn vow. "You're my girl, huh?"

"Yes, sir, Daddy. I am all yours. I am a cowboy."

He chuckled, kissing the top of her head. He loved his girls so much, and each of them for different reasons. He was a damn lucky man.

"Is Da a cowboy?" Somehow the question seemed important to Rosie, like his answer in this mattered.

"Heck, yes." Liam might not seem like a ranch hand, but the man could cowboy up and be tough. He lived by the code, dammit. "In his own way, your Da is very much a cowboy."

"So you like him a lot? You're going to let him stay?"

"Oh, baby girl, I love your da so much. I wanted him to stay before, but it was just really hard sometimes. We both got real mad, and we got our feelings hurt, and we didn't talk like we should have. We're going to try again, though."

"Good. I didn't like being 'vorced. I like this better."

God, she was killing him. "Me too." They got back to the house and he put her down, going to wash up. "Should we have a little snack before our nap?"

She nodded for him, and her baby eyes were damn near bruised, they were so dark. "Apples and peanut butter?"

"Perfect." He started getting things together. He needed to text Liam, let them know the girls most likely had a bug, dammit. He got Rosie some juice, then cut up apples, chopping up a couple of extra to put in a baggie in the fridge for the horses. Always multitasking.

By the time Rosie had finished adding peanut butter to their plates, she was drooping, and he wasn't surprised when she only ate about half her food before crashing, snuggling heavy against his chest.

He turned on a movie real low, one that wouldn't bother Rosie, then texted Liam one-handed.

I think the girls are getting sick

Faboo. Just what we need. This client is a nightmare. Wants Le Bernadin for McD's budget

ugh. you at least get wined and dined?

fuck burgers and beer. Need me to come home?

when you can. momma has em right now and Rosie is napping

k. If I get out of here at 5, I'll be home by 730. Text with what you need. Will bring supper

Thx baby

He hated that Liam had to drive so much, but he also wanted them to do this together.

Anytime. Love you

Love you too

He put his phone down after that and just held poor Rosie while she snored. She was definitely not feeling great, but he would watch over her. That was his job.

Good thing he was pretty solid at it.

He watched the movie until he dozed off, but his phone

woke him up, ringing insistently. When he looked, it was *Momma* that popped up. Shit.

"Hello?"

"Daddy? Daddy, I need help." Em's voice was high. Panicked.

"What? What's wrong?"

"Granny fell down, and I can't wake her up! Daddy, you have to come right now! Daddy, *please*!"

"What?" He sat up, making Rosie almost tumble to the floor. "I'm coming. I'll bring the truck, so just give me a minute and a half, okay? I'm on my way, so stay on the phone with me. Tell me what happened." He tucked Rosie under his arm like she was still a toddler and raced to the back door to step into his boots.

"She was making a Sprite, and she made this noise and fell down! Granny! Granny, you can't die! You hafta wake up! Daddy! Daddy, hurry! Call 911! Somebody call 911!"

"I'm halfway to you." That was mostly true. He was in the truck now with a very confused Rosie in her car seat, and that meant he would be there in literally two minutes. He did need to call 911 if his momma was unconscious, but he needed to get to Em first and see what the hell was going on.

He pulled up, gravel flying, and she threw the door open, and it was like hearing her screams in stereo.

"Emily! Emily McMartin Canton, you stop it!" He knew he was being short, but he needed her to stop. She was going to make herself sick. "Go sit in the truck with your sister. Now."

He would hug and comfort after he checked on Momma. He needed her to get it together.

She ran to the truck, hanging up on him.

He passed her in a rush, charging into the house. "Momma! Momma, can you hear me?"

She was breathing, but she wasn't conscious; she was pale and sweaty. Fuck.

He dialed the phone, the world swaying on its axis for a second.

"911, do you need police, fire, or ambulance?"

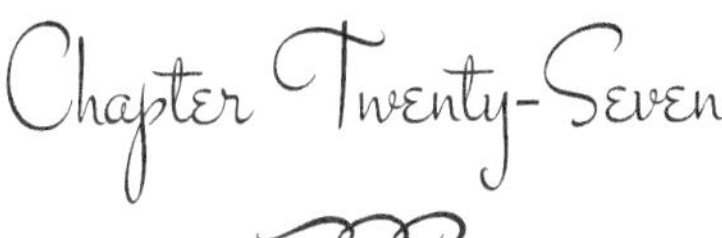

Chapter Twenty-Seven

Liam had never driven so fast in his entire life.

He had to get to his babies. He'd heard the utter panic in his oldest girl's voice and he had run out of Hank Bell's offices and had dared anyone to stop him.

The calls kept coming in. Saw. Em and Rosie on Barb's phone. Over and over.

"Da! I want to go home!"

"Da, please! I want to stay. I don't want to go!"

"It was a massive heart attack, babe. She's in surgery. I don't know what to do."

Then the community started to call and text with offers of help and food, care and babysitting.

He had never been so happy to get into Aspen. He circled the lot at the hospital, trying to find a spot. It wasn't quite time for the day office workers to head home, so he had to work to grab one as someone pulled out, but he slid into an opening and rushed into the hospital to find where the surgery waiting room was.

He ran right to Sawyer, kneeling before him. "Hey. Heard anything?"

The girls were with Em's gymnastics coach and her wife, and he'd go get them, but not yet. They were safe. Sawyer needed him first.

"Hey. Nothing yet." Sawyer was exhausted already. "Jesus, baby. She was down and out when I got there. Clammy and pale. I was sure she was a goner."

"That sucks. Have they said anything else?" *How's Em?* "Are you okay?"

"I am trying to cowboy up." Sawyer sighed. "They're saying she doesn't need a bypass, but they're putting in a stent and doing a few exploratory things, whatever that means." Saw paused again. "I think you might need to go get the girls. Em is having a rough time."

"I will. I totally will, but I can give you a few minutes here." His heart was still racing as if he'd run a marathon. "I'm so sorry. Did the doctor not check her heart when she went after the Fourth?"

"I'm not absolutely sure she even went. I let her give me the 'I'm-fine' speech."

"Dammit." He wasn't mad at Sawyer. Or Barbara. Just— This sucked, and Em was going to be freaked for a long while.

"Yeah. I feel like a fuck-up, for sure."

"Hey. You have a life, and she is a fucking adult. She owns her own health, just like we do." No guilt. None of them had time for that shit. "Do you need food or a drink or anything?"

"I could use a cup of coffee. I have her number for the board, but I didn't want to leave and go all the way to the cafeteria."

"No. No, I get that. Let me get you a Snickers bar and a coffee, and I'll bring it back to you." He kissed Saw's cheek and headed toward the elevator, checking his phone. Em had called another ten times. He dialed Barb's phone and pushed the button on the elevator.

"Da? Are you coming to get me?" Em's voice trembled

when she answered, but she knew it was him, at least, and she wasn't actually crying.

"I am. I'm getting your daddy a cup of coffee, then I'm going to come get you, and we're going to run home and pack some bags, grab supper, eat with Daddy, then come to spend a couple days at the condo so we're right here in town with Daddy and Gran, okay?"

"Okay. Rosie is asleep again. I think she's hiding."

"Mmm." He would bet that was the truth. He stopped as he stepped out of the elevator to read signs, then he turned left.

"Is Gran going to be okay?"

"She's in surgery. She'll probably be in the hospital a few days, and then she'll need a ton of help for a while. She had a heart attack."

"Was it because me and Rosie fought today?"

Oh, Christ. He shook his head and grabbed a Butterfinger and a Snickers. "No, baby. It just happened. It wasn't about you at all."

"I have a headache," she whispered.

"I bet you do. Gran said she thought you two were trying to get sick." Which meant maybe they shouldn't have supper here with Saw... And Sawyer needed some of those amazing facemasks, too.

Jesus.

"I didn't mean to, Da. Neither did Rosie. I think Lila Morgan was sick when we saw her at the pool."

"We'll worry about that later. I'm fixin' to get your daddy a cup of coffee and then I'll be heading up to you."

"Okay. I love you." She sniffled, but she was holding it together.

"I love you. You did good, baby. You called Daddy. You saved her life. You did good."

"Thank you, Da." She hung up, and his damn heart broke for her. She should never have had to deal with that.

But she had, and she'd managed, so he would simply be proud of her.

He grabbed a coffee at the 24/7 machine and headed back to the waiting room. He wanted to stay with Saw, but the girls were in a bad way...

He called Tom, who had given him his personal number at the Fourth of July.

"Hello?"

"Tom? Hey, it's Liam. I'm sorry to bother you."

"Hey, Liam. What's wrong? I can tell."

"Sawyer's mom had a heart attack. She's here at the hospital in town, at least for now. I have to go get the girls. I was wondering if Koby knew how to get a hold of Morgan. I thought maybe he could come sit with Saw."

"I know he has Morgan's number. They rope together. Where are the girls?"

"With Kimberly. Their coach for gymnastics. She and her wife are here in town. I'll take them to the condo."

"Sure. Okay, you leave it to me. Sawyer won't be alone. Is he at the surgery waiting room?"

"For now he is, yes."

"Got it. I'm on it. And I'm so sorry. I'm sure she'll be okay."

"Yeah. Thanks, Tom."

"You're welcome. Tell Sawyer to hang in."

"I will." He hung up right about the time the elevator got to the main floor, and he headed to the waiting room, trying to get his brain to work.

"Here, baby. I grabbed a face mask in case you need it, and I got a soda and some candy bars. Em is straight up losing it, so I need to go soon. Go take a potty break, and I'll wait here."

"Yeah. She's afraid this is her fault." Saw was shaking hard, and Liam felt horrible for his lover, but he was doing every-thing he could.

"I know. It's not hers, and it's not yours. Or your mom's, come to that. It just is what it is." He waved Sawyer off. "Give me the number thing."

He waited until Saw came back. "My plan is to get the girls, go home, get Daisy and some clothes, then I'll bring you supper. The girls and I will be at the condo, so you can just come over once you hear about your mom and be close."

"Thanks, baby." Sawyer took a hug, just holding onto him for a long moment. It felt as if Saw was soaking up whatever strength he could give.

"It's going to work out, babe. I swear. She's in amazing hands." And she was, really, in pretty good shape.

"I know. Okay. Go see the girls and get them settled at the condo. I love you." Saw stepped back to let him go.

"I'll bring food, but if they're feverish, they can't come in. So, I'll just call, cool?"

"Yeah. Yeah, just keep me posted and I'll do vice versa," Sawyer said.

"Okay." Liam sighed. "I have to go."

"I know." That got him a little smile. "Thanks for getting here so fast, baby."

"I've got your back. The condo is less than ten minutes away, so you're close." He kissed Saw, then headed out. He needed to get his girls.

When he got to Kimberly's, Em rushed to meet him at the door, throwing herself at him and sobbing. "Da! I'm sorry!"

"For what, baby girl? You did great." He held her in one arm, scooping up Rosie with the other. "You're both my brave, good girls."

Kimberly shook her head. "She's worked herself into puking."

Yay. "Thanks, lady. I owe you."

"You're welcome. Do you need anything? I can go get food and bring it to the condo."

"I'll see what I need. But thank you so much." He gave her a smile, a nod. "Trust me, I'll call and ask for help."

"Okay. Just let me know. I know how hard this kind of thing is. We went through cancer a few years back with Olivia's mom."

"I appreciate it. I'm going to need help in a day or two, but the girls and I are going to get clothes and Daisy, grab some food, and stay at the condo so Sawyer doesn't have to drive so far."

"A sound idea. Okay. Well, you get going. Here's Rosie's backpack."

"Thanks. Come on, girls. Let's go to the condo, huh?"

"After we get Daisy?" Rosie asked.

"Yep. After we get Daisy and clothes and some stuff, hmm?"

"Okay." Em nodded, and she was clearly trying to put on a brave face.

"We'll have a slumber party at the condo so we're close to Daddy, right?"

"That's right, baby girl. We'll do that. We can have pizza, even."

"Okay." Rosie yawned. "Or maybe eggs."

Oh, eggs were her stress food.

"Or both. Eggs and pizza!" he teased.

"Da. Ew." Em chuckled though.

"Do they put eggs on pizza?" Rosie asked in all seriousness.

"They put anything on pizza, baby girl. Anything."

"Wow. Like shrimp?"

"Yep. I've even seen squid."

"Ewwww!" That was a chorus from both girls.

"I know!" He had to laugh. He had to. "But it's true."

"No squid, Da. Or eggs on pizza." Em sounded very definite.

"Maybe we should wait on the pizza for your daddy, since he loves to share with y'all. We can grab tacos." The girls loved those.

"Daddy wants steak ones with red sauce." Em almost grinned. "And you want chicken with green."

"He does and I do. What kind do you want?"

"Squid," Rosie teased, and he was actually able to laugh.

"Tentacles!" Em yelled, and that helped. His girl was going to be okay.

And so were his husband and Barb. Dammit.

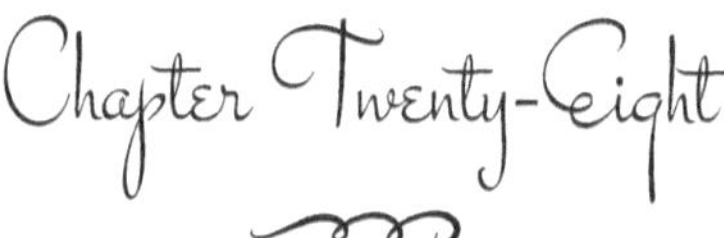

Chapter Twenty-Eight

Sawyer let himself into the loft, waving Koby and Tom off with a tired smile. They'd been really good to him, coming to sit with him, making sure he had coffee and a ride.

His momma was out of surgery and resting, and he'd been able to see her for a bit. But now he wanted to get his boots off and sit on a padded couch and eat something that wasn't a candy bar or chips.

The condo was dim, but the television was on, and the table was set with candles.

Candles.

So sweet.

He locked the door, then leaned down to pat Daisy as she trotted up. "Have you been out, little bit?"

She jumped on his leg, begging to be held, even as Liam walked out of the hallway.

"She's just gone, and the girls are dosed and asleep. I have our tacos on warm in the oven."

"You rock, baby." He picked up Daisy for a snuggle, then put her down so he could kiss Liam.

Liam kissed him long and slow, just letting him be there, hold on.

"Mmm." He hugged it out, wanting to lean on Liam forever.

"How's she doing? Did you talk to her?"

"I did, yeah. She was super groggy and has no idea what happened. I just told her I loved her and that we would see her tomorrow."

"We so will, but tonight, we'll have tacos and orgasms."

"Now, that's a combo I can really dig." He reached down to squeeze Liam's ass. "You know the way to my heart."

"Hey, it's my job. Em picked your tacos out for you."

"Did she? She knows what I like." Sawyer grinned. Em paid attention. Rosie would get him tempeh or something.

At least if she did that, Liam would eat them.

"That's better." Liam traced his smile with careful fingers. "Come on, babe. Let's eat and then you can grab a shower and we can go to bed."

"Yes, please." He let Liam lead him to the table where he grabbed a chair. "I love the candles."

"It was Rosie's idea."

"That was so sweet." He sank into the chair and took the beer Liam handed him, grateful as fuck for that.

"She's a doll. I've made sure that the feeding is arranged, that I can keep the girls here with me for a few days."

"Thanks, baby. Koby and Tom are going to check in, too. Morgan says he closed up Momma's house."

"Yeah. There are a lot of moving pieces, but we can juggle." Thank God Liam was here. Sawyer would let him juggle for them any day.

"You're okay with work?" Sawyer asked.

"I'll be working from up here, but at least I'm in the office, right?"

"Yeah. I'm—"

"Don't you dare apologize. We're in this together." Liam gave him a mock glare, then kissed him. "Everything is good. She's in the best place, we're home, and there are tacos."

"Mmm. Yep. Tacos." Sawyer's eyes had crossed at that kiss. It was inspiring.

"Beer? Margarita? Tea?" Each word was sealed with a kiss.

"I'll go with the beer for now, baby. I still love the candles."

"Rosie is a romantic. Em rolled her eyes, asked me to buy her an audiobook, and went to bed."

"Of course she did." The tacos smelled amazing when Liam opened the oven. "Man, I didn't even know I was that hungry."

"I thought you'd be. Worrying is hungry work." Liam passed over a plate and a beer, before bringing his own food over and sitting close.

"Yeah, I guess it is, come to that." He sprinkled salsa on the inside of the tacos. "You sure made good time from Vail."

"I drove like my ass was on fire. You needed me. So did the kids."

He paused. "Thank you, love. That means a lot, but you also need to be careful for me, huh?"

"You know I'm a way better driver than you, yeah?" Liam squeezed his thigh, though.

"I do. You always have been." Sawyer knew it. Hell, he drove everywhere like he was on the ranch and had no traffic to worry about. Liam was a technical driver and had grown up in city traffic.

Both of them were wicked careful behind the wheel when their girls were in the vehicle.

Liam chuckled. "You're not even gonna argue, huh?"

"Too tired."

"Well, just eat and we'll go to bed and snuggle."

Oh, now...Liam had promised orgasms. "I'm saving energy for the part between eating and snuggling, baby."

"Oh? You mean the part with rubbing and tongues?"

"And hands and cocks." He kept his voice low just in case, but he did love to tease, and it was the best kind of distraction.

"Nice. I like the 'and cocks' part. I could totally ride you into next week."

"Yes, please." He grinned, taking a bite of taco. He would need his energy for the pre-snuggle hotness.

Liam finished eating quick enough that he stood and started rubbing Sawyer's back, thumbs digging into his shoulders.

"Oh." He dropped his head forward on his neck. "Baby. That's good. Thank you."

"Breathe through it. In and out. I'll make you feel good."

"I know you will. You always do." Liam was so damn good to him. And so fine.

"I love you. I've always loved you." Liam's lips brushed his ear.

"Good. I love you too. So much." He reached up to grab Liam's hands.

"Yeah. She's going to be okay. Don't worry. She's going to be fine."

"I know it." Hand to God, she had to be. She was his momma. "But she sure gave me a scare. And Em too."

"Yeah. Em and I had a talk about how smart she was, about what bravery meant."

"Good." Sawyer stood, taking the dishes to the sink. "Because I was a little frantic. But she was fucking amazing."

"She was. She did it— She called you and saved your momma's life."

"Yeah. We'll have to have a daddy and daughter date to talk about that, huh?"

"And you have to make it a good one," Liam agreed. "Something she doesn't get all the time."

"Maybe we'll go to the hot springs in Glenwood..." he teased, knowing that Liam and Rosie both adored that huge hot spring pool.

"Rosie's feelings would be hurt."

"Not yours?" He turned, pressing his face against Liam's chest as they both moved to the side of the chair, kinda.

"Maybe a little. That's a treat for when Barb feels better, hmm?"

"Yeah. The water would do her some good, huh?" Hot springs were supposed to be very healing. "You ready to head to bed?"

"Totally. You want to meet me there? I'll toss the trash."

"I'm on it." Sawyer got up, his back protesting. Damn, those hospital chairs were uncomfortable.

"If you need a shower, take one. I'll be up in a sec."

"Hey, I'm not going to get started on anything without you." Unless he smelled like hospital and antiseptic...

He chuckled as he heard Liam hurrying with the trash, then following him right behind.

Sawyer slowed down, and they met at the bathroom door. He'd only just gotten his shirt untucked.

"Come on, cowboy. I need to get slick and soapy with you."

"Damn. You know how to sing my song."

"I know all your tunes, honey." Liam's fingers slid up under his shirt. "Every one."

"You do. I'm hoping we learn more together." He grabbed Liam's hips. The soft pajama pants slipped under his fingers, and Liam shivered for him.

"Mmm. Kiss me, babe."

"Yes." Sawyer bent to take Liam's mouth because he had to. He needed this.

Liam pushed right into the connection, tongue parting his lips. They struggled for control of the kiss, hips rocking together, hot as hell right off the bat.

Such a gorgeous mouth, so fucking hungry.

He moaned, backing Liam up against the doorframe of the bathroom.

One thigh climbed up his leg, and his lover moaned for him. They wandered into the bathroom, staggering a bit.

"Want you." Liam worked his belt open, popping his fly.

"Yes. So much." They got the clothes wrangled, got the water on, all the while kissing and touching and squirming to get closer.

Liam bent over to get the water started, and he couldn't resist that sweet, tight ass. His hands just reached for it, his palms burning. He needed to feel Liam's skin. He needed them to be on fire together.

"Mmm...love your calluses."

"My hands love your skin, baby."

That earned him a wiggle and a moan, a low sound that made him smile like the Cheshire Cat. He did adore the feel of Liam in his grasp, and he squeezed, then shifted them both under the spray of the water.

Liam soaped him up, teasing him and dragging those fingers over his skin, catching his short hairs. His breath caught, his cock rising hard and proud, his body ready for Liam. So ready.

"I want to ride you, cowboy. I want to be sore tomorrow."

"Mmm. I can't wait to watch you on top of me."

Liam rinsed him off, then washed himself with quick, efficient motions. He watched, but he kept his hands to himself, recognizing Liam's impatience. It was time to move this to bed.

He wanted to feel his lover all around him, and he needed to see him stretched up tall above him. Saw shivered as they turned off the water and stepped out of the shower, his cock so hard it ached.

"Cold, babe?" Liam wrapped him in a towel.

"Nope. Hot as fire."

"It's going to get hotter. We just need our bed. Our bed away from bed."

"That's it." Sawyer dried Liam off. "Lead the way, baby."

"Follow the bouncing butt." Liam made him so damn happy, the way he remembered how to play again.

Sawyer wolf whistled, and Liam laughed, wiggling. They fell on the bed together after Sawyer closed the bedroom door, though he wouldn't lock it. Not after the day the girls had experienced.

They would stay covered up as best as they could, just in case, and they'd be quiet. They were used to this part.

But they were together, and that was what mattered to him tonight. He had a terrible need.

And God, wasn't he grateful he was here now. Being loved. Not alone and scared and worrying. He kissed Liam with everything that was in his heart, his whole self leaning into it.

Liam opened up, thighs sprawled over his hip. So damn hot, the way Liam trusted him, let him in. Amazing.

"Get me ready, cowboy. I need to feel you all the way."

"Yeah. I can do that, baby." He found lube in the bedside table, glad to note that it was brand new. Liam scooted up, shifting to make it easier to reach.

He stroked Liam's belly, fingers lingering just above the curls crowning Liam's cock.

"Love that visual, your fingers on my skin."

"Me too, baby. Trust me. I can't get enough of watching you." But all the looking in the world wasn't going to beat touching, feeling. He popped the lube open and got his fingers wet. He wanted to get Liam slick and open so he could take that sweet ass.

Liam nodded and knelt up tall, begging for attention, for touch.

Far be it from him to not give what was asked. Sawyer slid his fingers against Liam's hole, rubbing in lube.

"Uhn." Liam swallowed hard, those ass cheeks tensing.

"So tight. I love how you hold me, baby. You make me feel humble." He kept touching, stroking Liam deep, pushing into that tight ring of muscles.

"Love when you're in me." Liam watched him like a hawk, the intensity there hardcore enough he forgot to breathe.

Liam began to rock for him, body tight and hard, riding on his fingers like a dream. He could do this forever if his balls would let him, but they wouldn't. He was going to explode soon.

"I'm ready. I need you to make love to me now." Oh, thank God.

He nodded, blowing out a breath so he could get a little control.

Liam sat up tall and grabbed his cock, rubbing it against his hole. He moaned, his body on fire, his skin too damn tight. He needed to move inside, but he waited for Liam to do it.

Slowly—impossibly slowly—Liam sank down on his prick, easing himself lower and lower.

Sawyer watched him, licking his lips, letting Liam take him in. Then he gripped Sawyer's hips and started to move, rocking upward.

"Hey, now. I'm doing the riding," Liam told him.

"Uh-huh." He grinned and punched up again, and Liam's eyes crossed.

"Babe. That's no fair."

"All's fair in love and orgasms," Sawyer countered.

"Uhn. Uh-huh..." Liam stared at him, lips parted, hungry.

He grinned wider and eased Liam down harder, even as he pressed his hips up. Liam ground against him, body rolling in circles.

They rocked together, both of them moaning as they hit sensitive spots.

Liam's belly was jerking, damn near vibrating with his need, and Sawyer felt like he was a thousand feet tall. He had done that. He had made Liam's body dance with pleasure. Damn, it was fine.

"I love you." Liam rested one hand on his chest. "I love you, cowboy."

"Damn. Damn. Yeah. I love you too." He pulled Liam down for a kiss, his lips taking Liam's mouth by storm.

That stopped the lovey-dovey shit, because he just wanted to feel it—the burn of his muscles, the way Liam's ass gripped his prick, the way the world spun. His balls drew up, and he knew his grip would probably leave bruises on Liam's ass, but Sawyer couldn't let go.

His toes curled and he bent his knees, bracing himself on the mattress so he could take Liam, fill him up.

"Gonna, babe." Liam sat up, gasping as their position changed.

"Then come on, baby. I'm ready."

"Uh-huh." That sweet ass gripped his cock, holding him tight. He could barely move, but he could reach for Liam's dick, stroking it good and hard. His thumb worked Liam's slit, digging in enough to make his eyes cross.

"Fuck. Liam. Come on, baby. Come on. I'm with you."

"Always." Liam bucked and shot, his eyes rolling back in his head.

Sawyer's moan tore out of him, his body strung like a taut fence wire. Then he snapped, filling Liam with liquid heat.

Liam whimpered, his long throat working as they shivered

together. He held Liam as they slumped down to the bed, both of them gasping for air.

"Damn, baby."

"Yeah. Whoa. We should do that more often." Liam's heart beat hard enough Sawyer could feel it against his ribs.

He hugged Liam to him, needing to hold on. This connection was the perfect medicine for his shitty day.

"I have you, lover. I have you. It's all going to be okay."

"I believe you." He had to believe it. He had no choice. Liam didn't lie to him.

"Good. Sleep. Rest. I'll be right here." Liam kissed his chin.

"Promise?" Was that pathetic? He hoped not.

"I swear to God. I have you."

"Thank you, baby." He pulled the covers up over them, blocking out the world, and when he closed his eyes, he knew he would dream about Liam and not some possible family tragedy.

Liam has him.

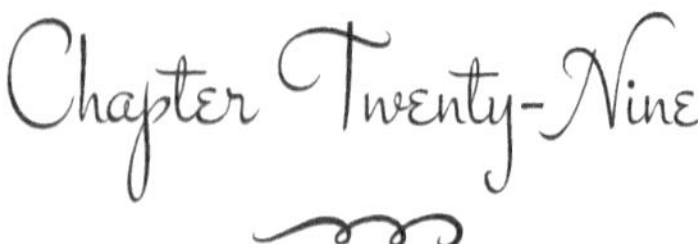

Chapter Twenty-Nine

"Da? Where's Daddy?"

"Da, when do we go see Granny?"

"Da, I want to go home."

"Da, can we go to the bookstore?"

"Da, what's for supper?"

Four days into Barb's heart attack, and she was beginning to heal. Sawyer was taking care of her at the hospital.

And Liam was going to hang his children up by their toenails. God love the little monsters, they were bored. Worried. Used to running around like hooligans.

They were feeling cooped up and he was going to lock them in a room and see who was still alive at the end of the day.

His money was on...

Hrm.

This was hard.

Em was smarter, but Rosie was brutal and fearless...

He grinned a little, taking a deep breath. Okay, yeah. Yeah, he could do this.

"We just need to be patient. We'll go the library when Daddy gets here, okay?"

"But wheeeen."

"Don't whine, Rosie. My head hurts, huh?" He made himself another cup of coffee.

"Are you going to have an attack?" Her eyes went huge. "Do I have to call one-one-one?"

"Nope. I just need to be quiet for a few minutes and sit with my best girls." That might make them simmer down. He hoped. "And it's nine-one-one. That's the number for police, ambulance, or fire. If you have an emergency—and that means something super real like Granny's heart attack, not something like fighting with your sister—you call nine-one-one."

"We learned that in school." Em bit her lip. "But I knew Daddy was on the ranch, so I just called him. Is that okay?"

"Perfect. Absolutely perfect." He sat with them, letting them all just be still. "You girls were—are—both brave and smart. You did the right things, and you know what? It's okay that you were scared. *We* were scared. The important thing is that you stayed and called for help, but it's fine that you were frightened or cried."

"It was so scary, Da." Em got up to come hug him hard, sitting on his lap like she used to, and he was so glad she was opening up about it.

"I bet it was." He held her gently, letting her have room between them for words.

"She just fell down. She was mad at us for acting out. She was talking, and I wasn't listening because my head hurt, and I was laying down. Then she went into the kitchen, and I heard her fall down."

"And you helped her. I'm so proud of you." He hugged her hard.

"I love her. I was so glad to see Daddy."

"I bet. I drove really fast to get back here to you." And he was going to have to hope they didn't need him in Vail again. It should be fine. Mike was one hell of a general contractor.

"You did." Rosie grinned across the coffee table at him. "Daddy says you musta flew."

"I was careful, but I was worried. I'm serious. I needed to be here for my girls and for my husband."

"He's not your husband anymore, though, right?"

Well, shit. "No. You're right. I need to fix that."

Em pulled back, eyes wide. "Would you and Daddy get married again, Da?"

"Yes. Yes, we would. It was a mistake to not work out our problems. It was wrong, but we can fix it." He believed that, and he thought Sawyer did too.

No, he *knew* Sawyer did. They'd talked about it. And dammit, he was taking Sawyer at his word.

Now they just needed time to breathe to decide how to go about it all.

Em nodded firmly. "We should have a party. A wedding with—"

"Dresses and flowers! Da! We got to have dresses!"

"We'll have a party for sure." They'd had a sizeable wedding the first time, so this time maybe they could have a few friends and a bouncy house for the girls.

"Can we wear purple?" Em asked. "Rosie and me, we both look good in purple."

"Purple sounds great to me. We all love purple, don't we? Let's ask Daddy."

"No, Da!" Rosie's eyes were wide. "You got to popose to him. On your knees. With a video!"

"Hmmm." He grinned at the thought of that. So Sawyer had proposed the first time, in a public place, with lots of people around. It had been a grand gesture. He could totally return the favor, only this time with their kids there at their favorite pizza or taco place. Casual but hilarious.

"Okay. Should I get him a new ring?"

Em shook her head. "No. I know where the old one is. I will get it for you."

"Okay." He sort of wanted to know how she knew, and he sort of didn't. But Sawyer had kept his, like Liam had. So.

Yay.

"And I can take the video." Rosie boogied in her chair.

"No, you have to be in it. I'll have my friend Terry take the video."

"Wait, isn't Daddy jealous of him?" Em asked.

"Is he?" He went wide-eyed, hoping for innocent. "I hope not, because he's at the ranch right now helping."

"Oh." Em blinked. "Okay, then he got over it." She shrugged.

"It happens. He's kind of reasonable, your daddy." Sort of. Most days. And at least it had worked. Sawyer had been incredibly jealous...

He bit back an evil kind of a grin. "So, should I ask him over pizza?"

Rosie nodded, and Em thought it over, then nodded. "After we make our pizzas, but before they come."

"That's fair." God, he loved these kids.

"Do you need shirt flowers?" Rosie beamed. "I can draw some."

"I would love that, baby girl. I think you draw such pretty flowers."

"Oh, I do. Thank you. I drawl pretty things." Rosie plopped down on her back. "A wedding!"

Em grinned. "And we get to go! Woo. Can I ask my friends to come?"

"How about to the party after? The wedding can just be for a few close folks."

"Okay. Is there going to be dancing?" she countered. "Maybe...a bouncy castle?"

"I was just thinking a bouncy house would be fun, huh? And I bet we could set up a slumber party." Some of the hands' wives would help...

"Oh, cool. We can watch movies and—what about your honeymoon? You have to have a honeymoon!"

He grinned at his Em. They were too busy for a trip right now. "We had one a long time ago."

"But, Da..."

"Nope. We're going to build a new house, remember? That will be our honeymoon."

"Oh. Oh, right. A new house and more bathrooms!" Em wiggled, so excited. "Daddy says we can paint our rooms and our bathrooms!"

Oh, did he? "Yeah?"

"I know! I want hearts and kitties."

"Hearts and kitties in your room?" Wallpaper. The answer was wallpaper.

"Uh-huh. You know, the white one from the Claire's store."

"Hello Kitty," Em said, sotto voce.

"Oh, thanks, Em. What about you? What are you thinking?" Hello Kitty...it could be worse, right?

"I want cottage core, Da."

"Uh..." Okay, he'd seen that in some architecture and design magazines, but for a girl her age that seemed pretty intense. "Sure. You have a Pinterest board?"

"Of course."

"Of course," he repeated. "We'll hit some of the antique stores down in Glenwood. They'll be way cheaper than up here."

"Oh yeah? That would be cool, Da. Thank you. I'd love that." She kissed his cheek. "Love you."

"I love you too."

"I can shop too?" Rosie asked.

"Most thrift stores have hearts, kiddo." He winked at her. "And we can search online too, when we get closer to the decoration phase."

"I like that."

The door opened, Sawyer coming in. Daisy leaped to her feet, wagging madly. She was kind of in love with Sawyer these days.

"Go on and welcome your daddy. He's had a long day."

Daisy ran to Sawyer, who picked her up, then hugged the girls, who also mobbed him.

"Daddy! We love you! We love you and purple and kitties!"

All Liam could do was roll his eyes.

"Wow. As much as purple and kitties, or less?" Sawyer grinned over Rosie's head at him.

"As much, of course," Em drawled. "Purple and kitties can't drive to the library."

"Ah. Good to know. Is there food?"

"We have pasta salad and tuna salad and bread. Does that work?" It was enough to hold off for a nice supper later.

"Sounds fab." Sawyer grimaced. "I couldn't face that caff line at the hospital. It was some kind of Salisbury steak."

"Yay." Gag. He was not a fan of the meat of mystery.

"You know it. I like my steak to look like beef." Sawyer hung his hat once everyone let go. "So, library, huh?"

"Library! You can eat first."

"Thank you, Rosie," Saw murmured.

"Welcome." That little girl was so pleased with himself.

"How's Granny?" Em almost managed not to wince, but Saw still drew her in close.

"She's way better today. She's awake and yelling about how she wants coffee and to go home." Sawyer just hugged Em and kissed the top of her head.

"Can we see her, then?"

"Oh, babies. Y'all'd need to be twelve to visit, but we can Facetime. Does that work?"

"Okay." Rosie nodded, so serious. "I need to see her face."

That sounded so much like Saw it hurt.

"Me too. I need her to tell me she's not mad."

"Okay, let me call her. She should still be awake. She was watching the TV." Sawyer pulled out his phone.

"I'll make you a plate."

She didn't need to talk to him.

"Thanks, baby." Sawyer hit the call button, and thank goodness, Barbara answered.

"Hey, Momma. You up to talking to the girls?" Saw asked.

"I am. Where are my babies?" She sounded like hammered shit, but she was talking.

"I'm so sorry…" Em started sobbing, and he took a deep breath.

Don't be short to her. Please, Barb. She's so worried.

"Whatever for? Your daddy told me how amazing you were. You saved my life. You are my hero, baby girl."

Liam's knees actually buckled. That was what Em needed to hear, but he also knew Barb well enough to know she meant it. That was her hand-to-God voice.

Thank goodness.

He got a plate of stuff together for Sawyer, handing it over while the girls cried and Barb talked until she was a little hoarse.

Liam was the one to shut it down. "Granny needs to rest, girls."

"You come home soon, Granny? We'll babysit you." Rosie smiled through her tears.

Yeah, that would help…

"Yes, ma'am. They say it will be no time." He caught a glimpse of Barb as he moved around behind Saw, and she was downright gray. Damn.

"Feel better, lady," Liam told her. "We all want you home."

"Lord, me too, Liam."

"I bet, Mom. Get some rest. I love you."

"I love you, all. Going to sleep."

"Sleep good, Granny! Love you!"

They hung up, and Em sniffled. "She looks sick."

"She'll get better, honey," Saw told her. "It's like when you have the flu, huh? Those first couple of days are bad."

He squeezed Sawyer's shoulder. Barb had seemed pretty tough. Still, she was alive, sitting up, talking. That was better than it could be.

Sawyer gave him a smile over that same shoulder, then tucked into the food. "So why the library?" he asked.

"We need more books," Em said, like that was the perfect answer. Which it was.

"Ah. Well, then. I get that. I could use a few more to take when I go sit with Granny, huh?"

"Do you want Da to go sit? He would, and you could nap with us?"

"Oh, no one needs to go back today. Granny said she was so tired she wanted to just be alone." Sawyer mouthed a name at him, and he thought it was Ruth, who was one of Barb's best friends. So someone was giving Sawyer a break today. Hooray.

"Eat your food, love, and we'll head to the library in a bit."

"Gotcha." Sawyer grinned at the girls. "I will totally nap when we get back. We can all read and doze together."

"Yay!" Em kissed his cheek. "I'm going to go get my stuff." She liked to be ready. Rosie would still be hunting for her shoes ten minutes after they left.

"I'll go get my bag," Rosie said.

"I better hurry, huh?" Sawyer wolfed down food.

"You don't have to. The girls will putter." He sat across

from Saw. "Terry's at the ranch. He says everything is going well."

"I do have a foreman, you know."

"I know, but I have this friend who needs work that I trust." He winked over, teasing. "I may see if the boss can't hire him, full-time."

"Mmm. Do you think so? I mean, does he really need work that bad?" Sawyer winked. "You know if he needs a place, he has it. We can always use a good hand, and he's worked his ass off since Momma went down."

"He's a good man, and we'll need help once the house is started." He met Saw's eyes, holding out his hand. "Do you still want to build the house? I know this is...I know we don't want to push her."

"I do, actually. She'll need to be in her little house more now than ever, but it will be way less stress if the big house is a common space where she can have people over and do barbecues and such. It will just smooth things down." Sawyer shrugged. "I mean, it was a blockage. Not stress from us. But it will be good for all of us. And we can do whatever we want with the new place. Have boundaries."

"Sure." He never knew what to say when Sawyer waxed long these days. Sawyer had never been one to open up like he was now, and Liam didn't want to misstep and upset him.

But he also felt as if he needed to make sure Sawyer knew how much he appreciated what was going on.

"Is that okay?" Sawyer asked, studying him like a hawk.

"It so is. I know the girls are super excited about new rooms and about getting to pick the decor."

"Good deal." Sawyer rolled his head on his neck. "Man, the chairs at the damn hospital are freaking uncomfortable."

"You should take you a pillow tomorrow. Are they going to put her in a rehab facility?"

"They don't think so. The surgery went real well, so they'll send her home with an order for home health until she heals up from it, and then PT and a nutritionist and all."

Oh, he could just see how Barb would take to someone telling her how to eat. God love whoever took on that job.

"I see that look in your eye," Sawyer told him. "I agree."

He chuckled. "Your momma is a Texan."

"She is. She likes her beige food."

"You done yet, Daddy?" Rosie asked, dragging a heavily loaded backpack to the front room.

Sawyer stared down at his plate, appearing surprised that it was empty. "I think I am. Let me brush my tuna teeth, and I'll be ready to head out."

"I'll get Em. Come on, Rosie-posie. Shoes."

"Okay, Da." Rosie trotted back to her bedroom, and Liam started gathering the books they'd read, wondering what was in Rosie's pack. Probably all of her damn shoes.

That was okay. He was feeling much better than he had an hour ago anyway.

Chapter Thirty

"You guys want to go get a pizza?" Sawyer felt as if a huge weight had lifted off him. His momma was settled at her own house. His cousin Bethany was up from Texas, just out of nursing school and tickled to death to have a patient to practice on, since she wanted to do home health. Well, and maybe hospice, but he wasn't telling Momma that, and neither was Bethany, since that wasn't the case here at all.

"Sure, honey, we can—"

"NO!" Rosie glared at Liam, shaking her head violently. "We. Can. Not."

"Why not?" Sawyer blinked at her vehemence. She loved pizza, so he was confused.

"I—" She stared at her sister, obviously frozen.

"Tacos," Em offered. "We want tacos."

Rosie frowned some.

"Oh." Sawyer blinked at Liam, who shrugged. "But I thought y'all loved pizza, and I'm craving."

"I—Da! Da, you can't. You aren't ready?" Rosie was damn near in tears.

"For pizza?" He didn't follow, and he didn't understand the amusement in Liam's eyes.

"How about burgers and milkshakes?" Liam offered.

"Burgies! I hate pizza. Uh. Today." Had Rosie gotten into the Froot Loops?

"Okay. I could go for one." He mouthed "what the fuck" over at Liam.

Liam was flushed, but that grin was the definition of shit-eating. "Sounds great to me. I could murder a chicken sandwich."

"Sure." Huh. He was feeling like he'd missed a punchline. "Does that work for you, Rosie?"

"Yes, sir! Sounds amazing." She grabbed her sister's hand, whispering, sotto voce, "That was close."

Em nodded, and he shook his head. "Y'all go get your shoes, huh?" The endless cry of summer. The girls were always hunting something, whether it was shoes in the summer or coats and hats in the winter.

Liam chuckled as the girls ran off, and Sawyer raised an eyebrow. "What was all that about?"

"Oh, lord. It's—"

"We're here, Daddy! Let's go! Hurry!" Rosie started pulling Sawyer out of the door.

"Okay." He followed her, Em pushing him from behind. They locked Daisy in, locked the other dogs out so they wouldn't torment her, and headed to the SUV.

"You want to drive?" Liam offered him the keys to the car, swinging them on one finger.

"Uh-huh." He did love to drive this big beast. They got the girls into the vehicle and headed for the diner in Basalt instead of going into Aspen.

"So, Daddy, do you like purple?" Em asked.

"Uh... Purple what?" He liked purple on principle, but he would draw the line at socks or shirts.

"Em!" Rosie sounded like she was going to cry.

"I like purple just fine. Don't worry, Rosie." They were losing their minds.

Liam was just grinning, though, so clearly he wasn't worried. So what gave? He would figure this shit out.

"I was just asking," Em said in a long-suffering tone. "It wasn't like I mentioned a bouncy castle."

Curiouser and curiouser. Was he missing a birthday?

"Still! We have a secret! A SECRET!" Rosie was losing her shit.

"Easy, girls." Liam gave them both a smile. "Breathe."

"Hey, you know I can keep secrets. Or I can hang out until you're ready to share. No need to get upset." Whatever it was, Rosie was really worried, so he would try to be as gentle as Liam was managing to be right now.

"Okay. Okay, it's a good surprise, Daddy. A great surprise. The bestest surprise ever!"

"Good. Those are my favorite kind." They coasted into the parking lot at the diner several songs later on the radio, and Rosie seemed to be in a much better humor.

They walked in and heard, "Dude! Liam! Sawyer!"

He glanced around and found Morgan and Terry sitting there, eating. "Hey, guys!"

Rosie gasped. "Oh no!"

Em blinked at them, then at Liam. "Did you invite them?"

"Invite who? The guys? I didn't even know we were coming here. It was supposed to be pizza."

"But Granny's not here, Da!" Rosie started to cry.

"No. And I won't do anything without her, baby girl. I promise."

Sawyer stared at Rosie, lips pursing.

Liam shook his head, grasping his hand and squeezing.

"Em, go take your sister to the bathroom to wash up, huh?

I promise. Everything is okay." Liam winked at Em, who sighed dramatically, but nodded.

"Are you going to sit with them?"

"Maybe. It's all right."

"Okay." She grabbed Rosie. "Come on. We can trust Da."

Sawyer waited until they left. "Okay, what the hell?"

"Shit." Liam rolled his eyes and lowered his voice. "I told them I was going to ask you to marry me, and we'd have a little family wedding and then a little party for them. It's going to happen at the pizza place once your momma feels better."

"Oh," His cheeks heated, pleasure rushing through him. "Seriously?"

"Yes. They want purple dresses. I told them that was fine. They're very excited, so you'll need to say yes when it happens."

"Well, hell, baby. I'll say yes now and save some worry. I'll try not to ruin their surprise." But he wanted to shout it to the fucking rooftops.

"Oh, good. I'm glad to know." Liam kissed his cheek. "They're just so nervous. They want to know we're serious, and this is how they can parse it. Come on. Let's go say hi to the guys and sit."

"Sure." He took Liam's hand, and they went to greet Morgan and Terry. "Look at you two, all out together."

"I know. Terry invited me out. Y'all want to join us?" Morgan grinned and nodded to the table. "There's room, and I'll get to sit next to Miss Rosie-Posie. She okay?"

"She's having a wee meltdown, but she'll be all right." He assumed. Who knew? At her age, all sorts of things were crazy emergencies. And this whole thing came with a bouncy house and a purple dress.

Who could compete with that?

He slid into the chair next to Liam as the girls came out of the bathroom, Em leading Rosie over.

"There they are. What do you two want to drink?"

"Coke?" Em asked, and Liam rolled his eyes.

"Sprite?"

"Sprite." Rosie bounced. She was much calmer.

"I'll take a Coke, though," Sawyer told the server, who came right at that moment.

"I'd like a glass of water," Liam said. "Because I'm going to have a coffee milkshake for dessert."

"Mmmm. Milkshakes." Well, if Liam was going to have dessert, he might have to rethink his plan about spoiling the surprise. Dessert seemed like a hell of a time to propose in his own right.

"Right?"

Rosie frowned. "If I have milk, can I have ice cream?"

"Yes. That sounds nice to me," Liam agreed, and Morgan and Terry shared a tickled glance.

Em snorted. "I want Sprite." And she would negotiate for dessert anyway, and they all knew it.

"Fine with me." Liam bumped shoulders with Rosie. "Are you going to have a burger or a cheeseburger?"

"A chicken sammich like you!"

"Oh, branching out."

"Bock bock," Morgan said, which made Rosie giggle. "So, how's your mom, Saw?"

"She's doing well. It's a bit of a road, but we're lucky it was caught when it was. She's with my cousin at her house, and Bethany wants to spend the winter."

"Hey, that works all the way around, huh?"

"You know it." He would love that. And the girls already adored Bethany.

"And in the springtime, we're going to build our new house! Did you know? It's going to be so cool!" Rosie was back to being all sunshine.

"Your dads have asked us both to help," Terry said.

They ordered, and settled in, and the more Sawyer thought about it, the more he knew he was going to have to freak Rosie out. The urge to ask Liam now was riding him.

"Are you okay, Daddy?" Em whispered. "You didn't answer Da about the French fries."

"I want to ask him before he can ask me. Do you think Rosie will forgive me? He can ask me again when Granny is with us."

"We just want you to be married again, Daddy. We just want to know it's over. We can have a bouncy castle any time." She was so serious, so grown-up. "We just want our dads together forever."

"I love you so much, baby girl. You know that right?"

"Uh-huh." He thought she seemed a little teary, so he decided not to wait until dessert.

"Don't be mad at me, Rosie." He slid out of his seat, going down to one knee. "Liam? I need this to be official."

"Saw?" Liam's eyes were big as saucers. "What are you up to?"

"I'm asking you to marry me again, baby. I've been carrying our rings around in my damn shirt pocket for weeks. I want us to be an us again, officially. We got witnesses here, so I thought I would ask."

"That's why I couldn't find them!" Em gasped. "Sneaky Daddy!"

"You couldn't find them because you don't snoop in your dads' room." He pulled out Liam's ring. "Will you, baby?"

"With all my heart, Saw. I love you." Liam's eyes gleamed at him, bright and blue.

"I love you too."

"Daddy! What about Granny!" Rosie wailed.

"I just recorded it for her, Rosie." That was Morgan. "And he can ask again when you see her next."

"Promise? Can we still have dresses?"

"Of course you can, Rosie. You and Em will have dresses and a party." Liam encouraged Sawyer to stand.

"Yay!" She bounced. "Chickenmurmurs and a party."

Liam nodded, tears on his cheeks. "Yes. Yay. A happy ending and a party."

"That's the best way to go, huh, baby?""

"Yes." Liam pulled him to his feet and took a kiss to a smattering of applause. "I love you, cowboy. So much."

"Love you too. Let's get married and stay that way."

"You've got a deal." Liam laughed. "And I'll build you a house."

"Sounds like the best plan. Right, girls?"

Em nodded, beaming. "The best."

Rosie hugged his leg, tight-tight. "So long as there's a bouncy house."

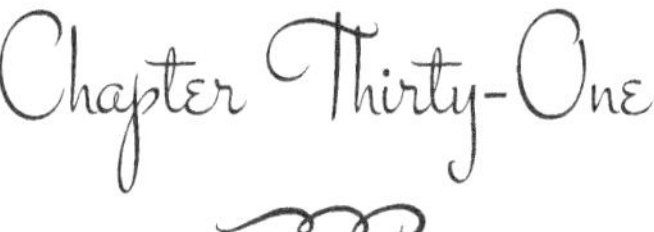

Chapter Thirty-One

"They do know how to throw a party at this ranch," Koby said, watching a passel of kids jumping in a bouncy castle that was bigger than his master bedroom.

"They have a lot to celebrate. New house. New wedding party. New contract for Liam in town. Things are going well." Tom beamed over at the happy couple, as if they both didn't know that Liam and Sawyer hadn't gotten married at the courthouse without any fanfare, just to keep everything legal and easy.

This party was for the girls, for Sawyer's mom, and for the ability to show off their new house Liam had managed to design in a way that fit in exactly with the rest of the ranch, and having the old ranch house as an entertainment/meeting space was brilliant.

"I like it. A lot." The outdoor entertaining space had always been great out here, but this was next level. "I have outdoor kitchen envy."

"Me too." Sawyer's mom wandered by with a smile. "Good thing I get to claim it too."

Her laughter was soft, happy.

"They count on you to make country ribs, Barb."

"That's because Sawyer doesn't cook them enough." She grabbed a Sprite out of a cooler. "Thank you for recommending Terry—he works his butt off." She stopped, then grinned nice and slow. "And he brought my family back to me."

Koby grinned back. "We aim for one hundred percent satisfaction with Cowboy Wanted, lady."

"It's a good goal." Barb glanced over at Liam and Sawyer who were talking to Terry and Morgan. She nodded once, like a bull rider, and grinned. "It's a good deal, all the way around."

Koby winked at Tom as she headed back out to sit in the shade and watch the kids, and he followed Tom's gaze to the group of cowboys who were pretty pleased with themselves. "That does seem like Liam's plan worked, huh?"

"I told him I'd make sure to make his dream come true, lover. Thank God, I could make it happen."

"You're magical, lover." Koby clinked his beer bottle against Tim's glass. "Now, what do you say we head home soon and do some celebrating of our own?"

"Talk about dreams coming true." Tom leaned in, kissed him softly. "Let's go tell the happy couple congratulations. I'm ready."

Koby took Tom's hand to tug him down to Liam and Sawyer to say goodbye. He was ready to kick off his boots and relax.

Their work on this job was done.

Interested in learning more about BA's cowboys? Want free fiction and news? Join my newsletter or follow me on Ream!

About BA

Texan to the bone and an unrepentant Daddy's Girl, BA Tortuga spends her days with her basset hounds, getting tattooed, texting her grandbabies, and eating Mexican food. When she's not doing that, she's writing. She spends her days off watching rodeo, knitting and surfing Pinterest in the name of research. BA's personal saviors include her wife, Julia Talbot, her best friends, and coffee. Lots of coffee. Really good coffee.

Having written everything from fist-fighting rednecks to hard-core cowboys to werewolves, BA does her damnedest to tell the stories of her heart, which was raised in Northeast Texas, but has heard the call of the high desert and lives in the Sandias. With books ranging from hard-hitting romance, to fiery ménages, to the most traditional of love stories, BA refuses to be pigeon-holed by anyone but the voices in her head, insisting her cowboys get their happily ever afters.

Welcome to the Pack

Tails and Whiskers

Above the Fold

Brownie's Sway

Thack's Angel

Here, Kitty Kitty

The Recovery Series

Refired

Slip

The Release Series

The Terms of Release

The Articles of Release

Catch and Release

The Road Trip Series

Racing the Moon • Steam and Sunshine

Under Pressure • Walking on the Sun

Roughstock Series

Blind Ride

And a Smile

File Gumbo

Back to Back

Pulled from All Sides

Coke's Clown

Leading the Blind

The Sanctuary Series

Just Like Cats and Dogs

What the Cat Dragged In

The Spirit Quest Series

Crossing the River

Chasing the Moon

Breaking the Ice

The Stormy Weather Series

Rain and Whiskey

Tropical Depression

Hurricane

Two is Never Enough Series

Claiming Their Mate

Needing to Breathe

Contemporary Standalones

Adding to the Collection

Back Forty

Best New Artist

Boys in the Band

Broken In

Elite Connections *(April 2024)*

Fighting Addiction

Latigo

Living in Fast Forward

Mud, Movies, Bullets, and Bulls

Needing To

Old Town New

Rainbow Rodeo

Rough in Wranglers

Say Something

Seashores of Old Mexico

Soft Place to Fall

Stetsons and Stakeouts

Truth or Consequences

Wicked in Wranglers

Historical Standalones

Cabin Fever

Hammer and Tongs

Oranges and Peppermints

Paranormal Standalones

Baker's Dozen

Calling His Bluff

Forged in Magic

Long Black Cadillac

Luck of the Draw

Redemption's Ride

Roman and Cage

Setting His Sights

Things that Go Bump in the Night

Unearthed

Wolf Run

Lesbian Romance

Summit Springs Series

Christmas Bizarre w/ Jodi Payne

Honeymoon in the Cards w/ Jodi Payne

Tipping the Barrel

Contemporary Standalones

Bright Lights and Boobjobs

Games Girls Play

Historical Standalones

Bustles and Doeskins

With Jodi Payne

The Collaborations Series

Refraction

Syncopation

The Cowboy and the Dom Series

First Rodeo

Razor's Edge

No Ghosts

The Soldier and the Angel

The East Meets Westerns Universe

Temptation Ranch

Les's Bar Series

Just Dex

Hide Bound

Wholly Trinity

Lone Star Series

Tending Tyler

Roped In

Merry Everything Series

Window Dressing

Cowboy Protection

Cowboy and Cupcakes

Wrecked Series

Wrecked

Flying Blind

Special Delivery

Seeds and Sunshine

Pick Up Man

The Higher Elevation Series

Land of Enchantment

Keeping Promises

Bigger than Us

Heart of a Cowboy

Home Free

The Sin Deep Series

Sin Deep

The Trouble with Cowboys